Buffy the Vampire Slayer™

Uninvited Guests

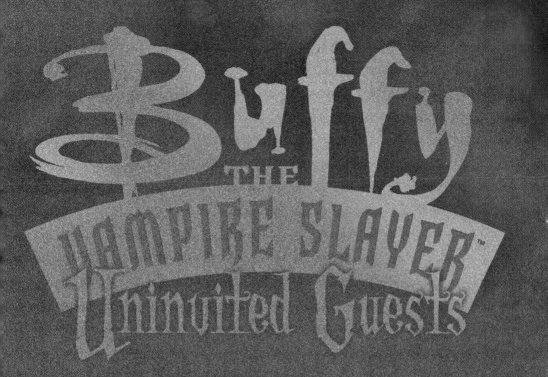

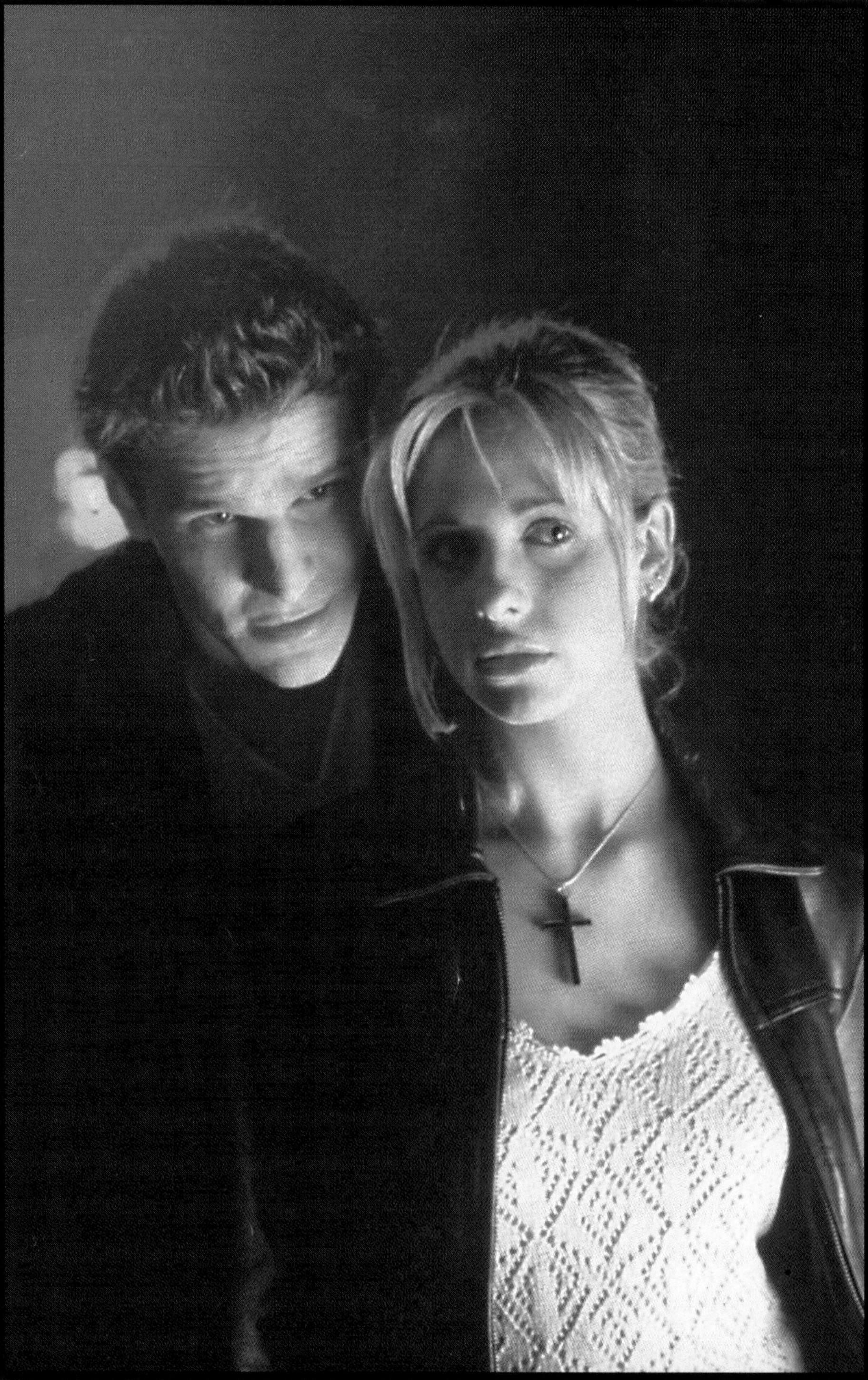

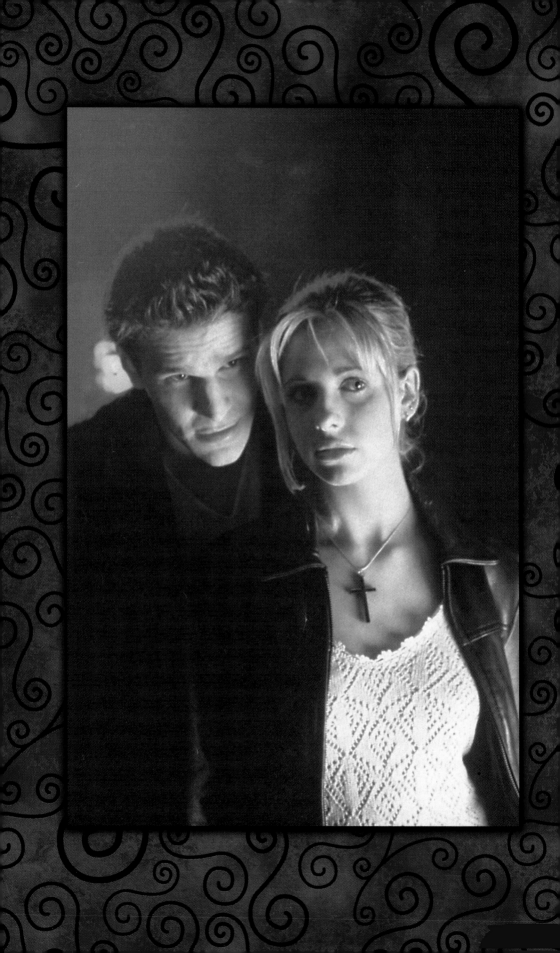

Buffy the Vampire Slayer™
Uninvited Guests

based on the television series created by
JOSS WHEDON

writer **ANDI WATSON**

"New Kid on the Block" co-written with
DAN BRERETON

penciller **HECTOR GOMEZ**

inker **SANDU FLOREA**

colorist **GUY MAJOR**

letterer **JANICE CHIANG**

These stories take place during Buffy the Vampire Slayer's second season.

Dark Horse Comics®

publisher
MIKE RICHARDSON

editor
SCOTT ALLIE
with ADAM GALLARDO *and* BEN ABERNATHY

designer
KRISTEN BURDA

art director
MARK COX

special thanks to
DEBBIE OLSHAN AT FOX LICENSING,
CAROLINE KALLAS AND GEORGE SNYDER AT *BUFFY THE VAMPIRE SLAYER*,
AND DAVID CAMPITI AT GLASS HOUSE GRAPHICS.

PUBLISHED BY
DARK HORSE COMICS, INC.
10956 SE MAIN STREET
MILWAUKIE, OR 97222

SEPTEMBER 1999
FIRST EDITION
ISBN: 1 - 56971 - 436 - 3

1 3 5 7 9 10 8 6 4 2

printed in canada

introduction
by andi watson

Vampires. They're everywhere. Look around and you'll see vampire books, games, trading cards, Popsicles, mouse pads, TV shows and comics. Just when you think every vampire angle has been covered— you're right—it's been done to death! Pop culture is full of images of half (un-)dressed actresses chowing down on some loser's neck. Or another angsty guy in a frilly shirt following a similar po-faced routine. Unless he's a Vampire Cop, which calls for a change of uniform.

I can't deny the appeal of the genre; I'm not entirely innocent myself. I had Chinese-hopping-hockey-vampires in my own book, *Skeleton Key*, a while back. I guess I can't help but inject a little humor into the proceedings. Which may explain why Jamie S. Rich (the first editor on the series) gave me a call many moons ago to ask if I'd be interested in writing this *Buffy* book that Dark Horse was bringing out.

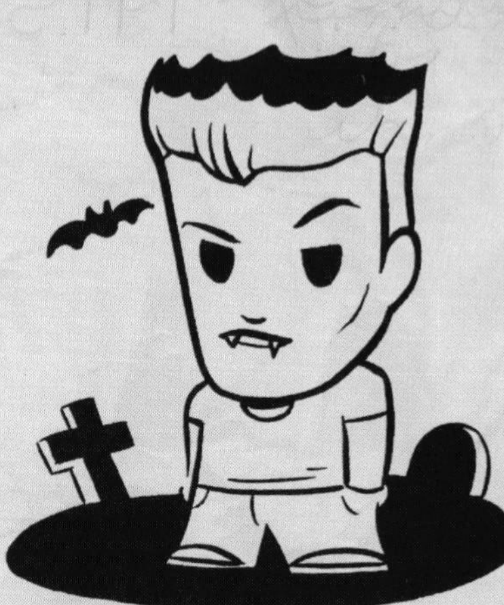

At that time the show hadn't reached Jolly Ol' England, but I had seen the movie. I'd warmed to the concept—*Heathers* meets *Dracula*—neato! And any movie with Luke Perry, a guy willing to play Krusty the Clown's despised half-brother, is okay by me. Horror has never been my thing, in fact the only horror I've experienced is the searing back pain felt by trying to lift one of the genre's best sellers off the shelf. I'd misspent my youth watching trashy teen movies, not trashy slasher flicks. And while I lacked an encyclopedic knowledge of horror shower scenes, I did know my Molly Ringwalds from my Ally Sheedys. All of which has held me in good stead since, to my surprise, I got the job. *Buffy* is all about being a teen. It's funny and ironic and has a very healthy amount of self-deprecation.

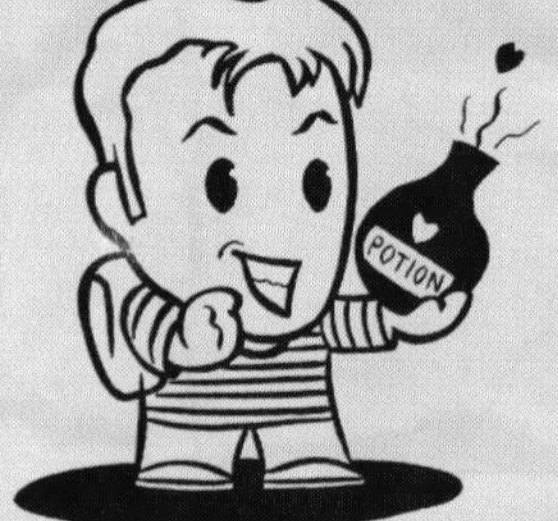
POTION

After all if you can't find humor in frilly shirts then you're missing out on life.

Andi
June '99

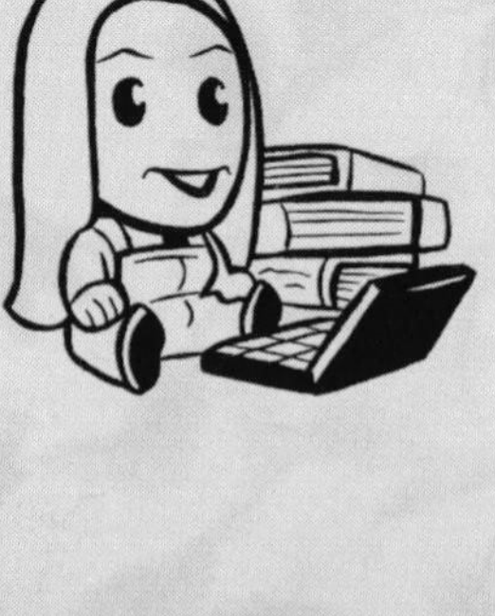

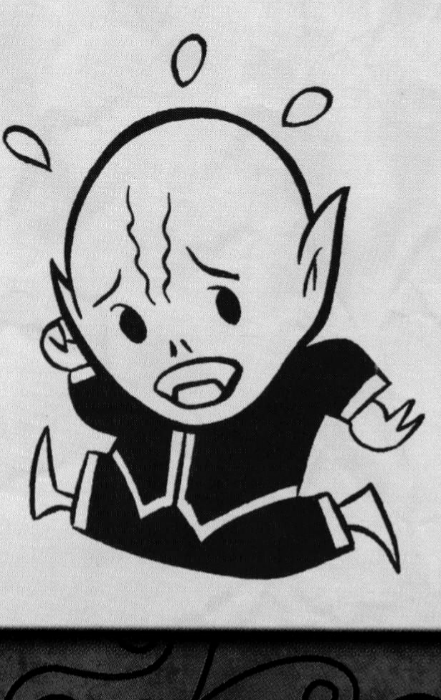

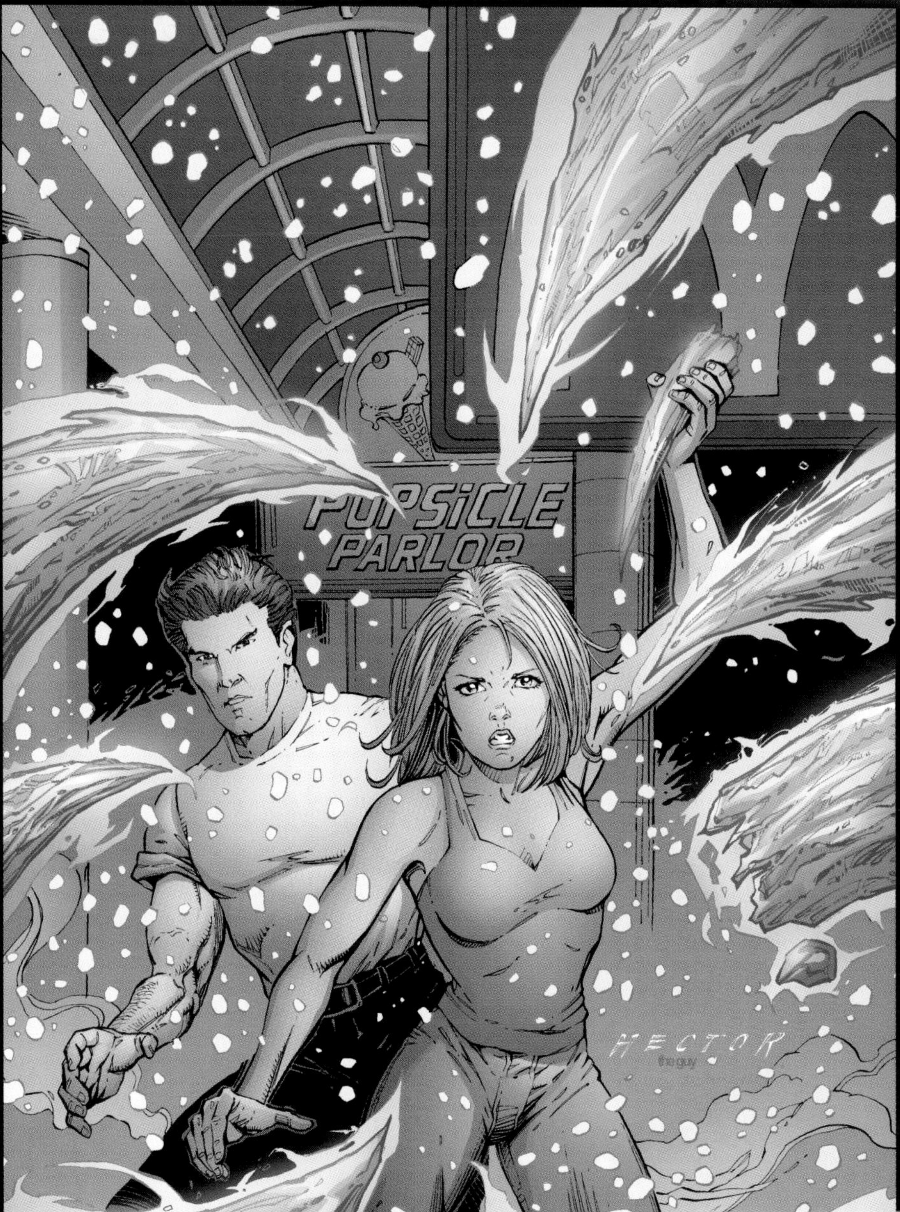
POPSICLE PARLOR
HECTOR the guy

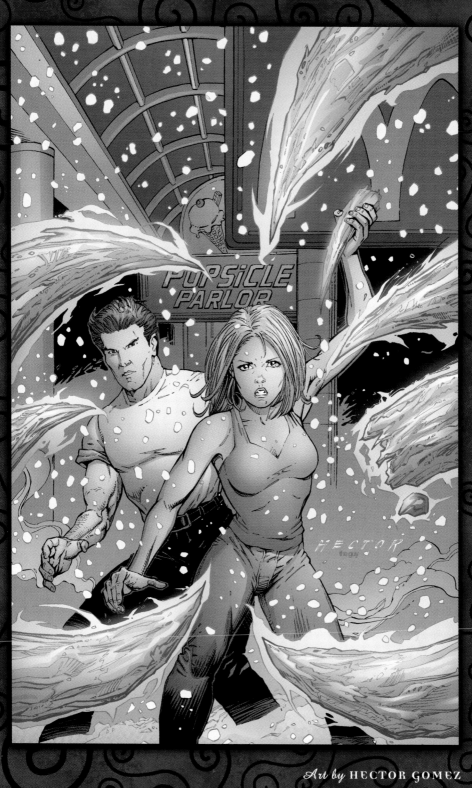

Art by HECTOR GOMEZ

White
Christmas

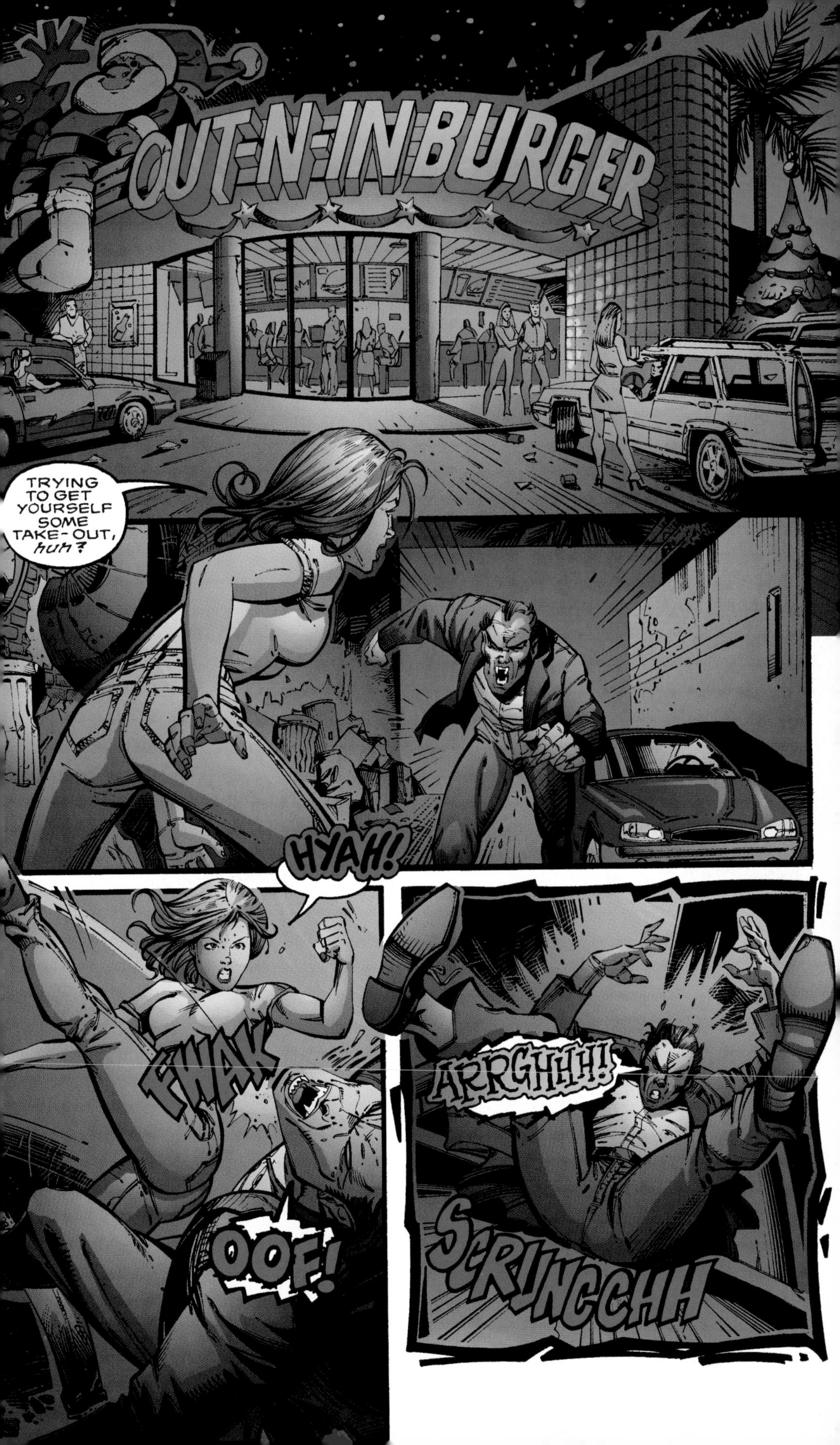
OUT-N-IN BURGER
TRYING TO GET YOURSELF SOME TAKE-OUT, *hum?*
HYAH!
FWAK
OOF!
ARRGHHH!
SCRINCCHH

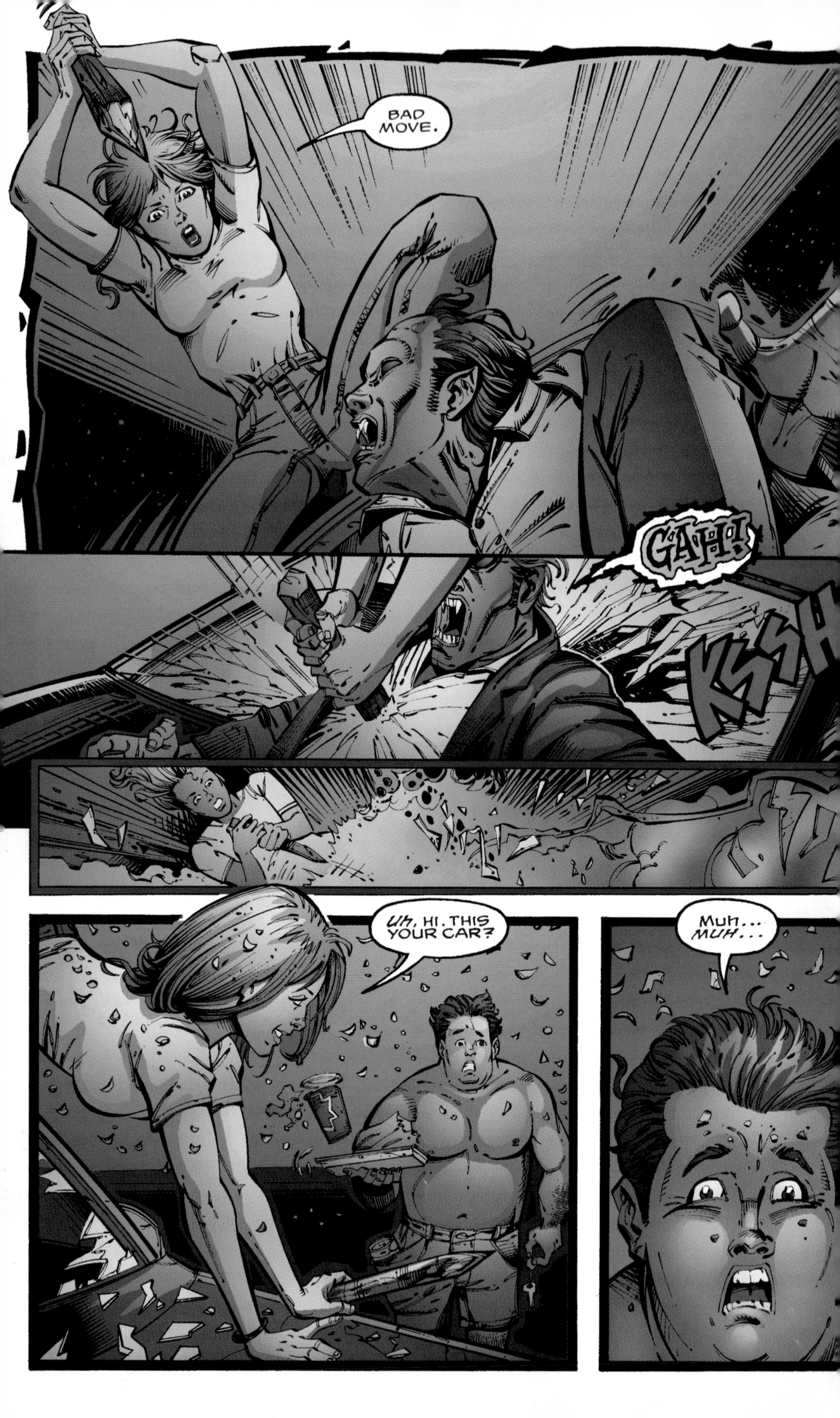
BAD MOVE.
GAH!
KSSH
UH, HI. THIS YOUR CAR?
MUH... MUH...

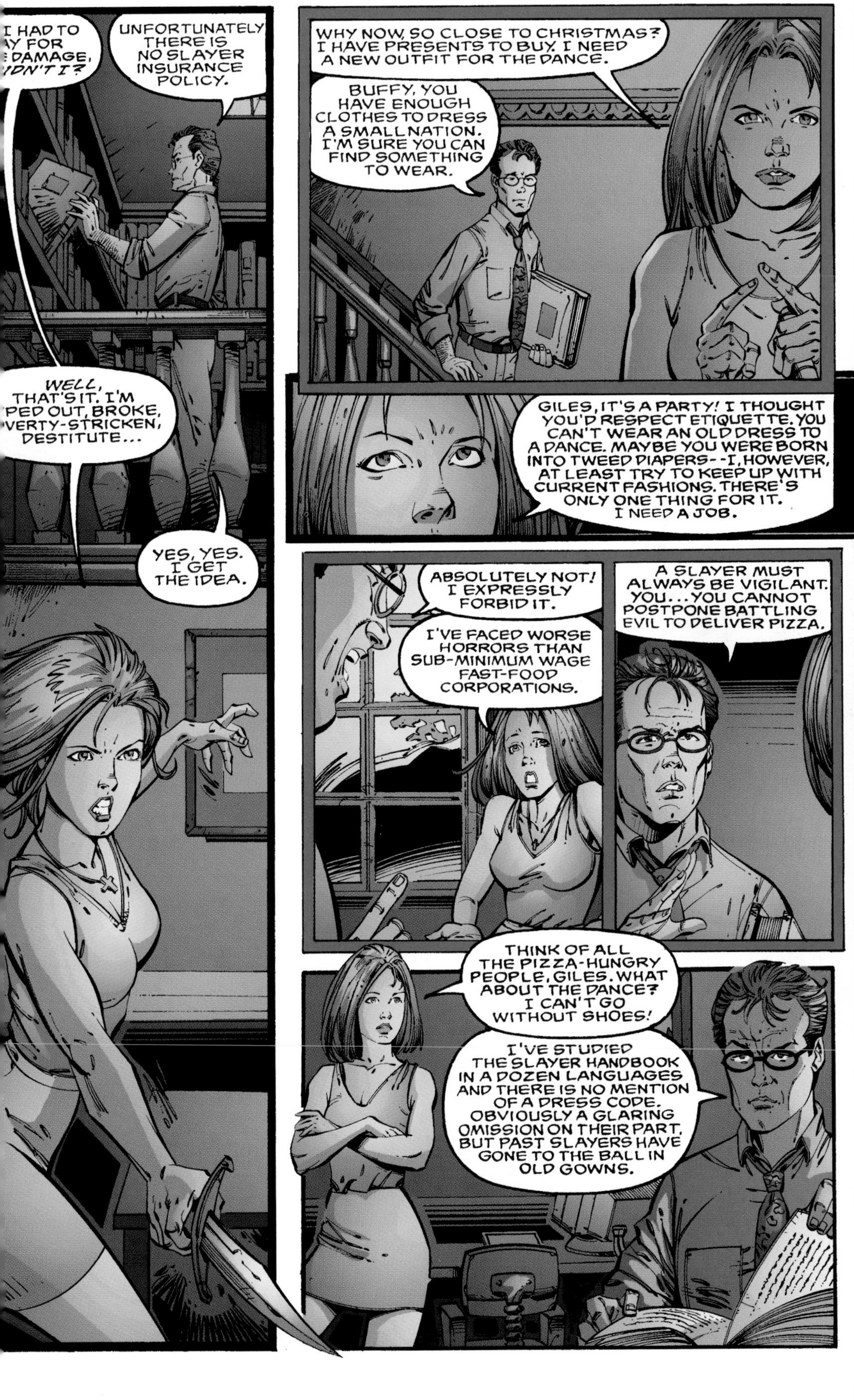
I HAD TO AY FOR E DAMAGE, IDN'T I?
UNFORTUNATELY THERE IS NO SLAYER INSURANCE POLICY.
WELL, THAT'S IT. I'M PED OUT, BROKE, VERTY-STRICKEN, DESTITUTE...
YES, YES. I GET THE IDEA.
WHY NOW, SO CLOSE TO CHRISTMAS? I HAVE PRESENTS TO BUY. I NEED A NEW OUTFIT FOR THE DANCE.
BUFFY, YOU HAVE ENOUGH CLOTHES TO DRESS A SMALL NATION. I'M SURE YOU CAN FIND SOMETHING TO WEAR.
GILES, IT'S A PARTY! I THOUGHT YOU'D RESPECT ETIQUETTE. YOU CAN'T WEAR AN OLD DRESS TO A DANCE. MAYBE YOU WERE BORN INTO TWEED DIAPERS--I, HOWEVER, AT LEAST TRY TO KEEP UP WITH CURRENT FASHIONS. THERE'S ONLY ONE THING FOR IT. I NEED A JOB.
ABSOLUTELY NOT! I EXPRESSLY FORBID IT.
I'VE FACED WORSE HORRORS THAN SUB-MINIMUM WAGE FAST-FOOD CORPORATIONS.
A SLAYER MUST ALWAYS BE VIGILANT. YOU...YOU CANNOT POSTPONE BATTLING EVIL TO DELIVER PIZZA.
THINK OF ALL THE PIZZA-HUNGRY PEOPLE, GILES. WHAT ABOUT THE DANCE? I CAN'T GO WITHOUT SHOES!
I'VE STUDIED THE SLAYER HANDBOOK IN A DOZEN LANGUAGES AND THERE IS NO MENTION OF A DRESS CODE. OBVIOUSLY A GLARING OMISSION ON THEIR PART, BUT PAST SLAYERS HAVE GONE TO THE BALL IN OLD GOWNS.

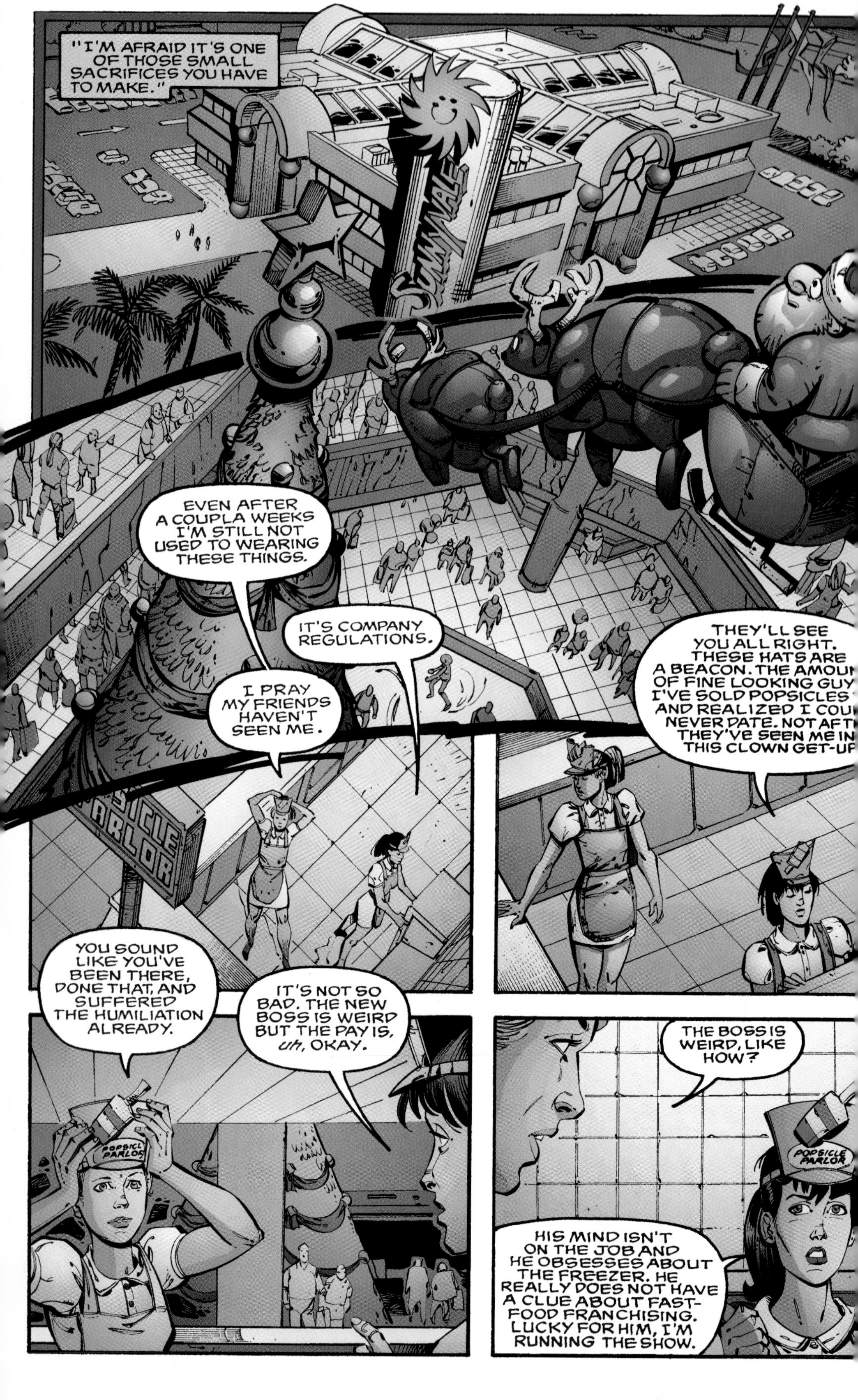
"I'M AFRAID IT'S ONE OF THOSE SMALL SACRIFICES YOU HAVE TO MAKE."
SUNNYDALE
EVEN AFTER A COUPLA WEEKS I'M STILL NOT USED TO WEARING THESE THINGS.
IT'S COMPANY REGULATIONS.
I PRAY MY FRIENDS HAVEN'T SEEN ME.
THEY'LL SEE YOU ALL RIGHT. THESE HATS ARE A BEACON. THE AMOU OF FINE LOOKING GUY I'VE SOLD POPSICLES AND REALIZED I COU NEVER DATE. NOT AFT THEY'VE SEEN ME IN THIS CLOWN GET-UP
SICLE PARLOR
YOU SOUND LIKE YOU'VE BEEN THERE, DONE THAT, AND SUFFERED THE HUMILIATION ALREADY.
IT'S NOT SO BAD. THE NEW BOSS IS WEIRD BUT THE PAY IS, *uh*, OKAY.
THE BOSS IS WEIRD, LIKE HOW?
POPSICLE PARLOR
HIS MIND ISN'T ON THE JOB AND HE OBSESSES ABOUT THE FREEZER. HE REALLY DOES NOT HAVE A CLUE ABOUT FAST-FOOD FRANCHISING. LUCKY FOR HIM, I'M RUNNING THE SHOW.

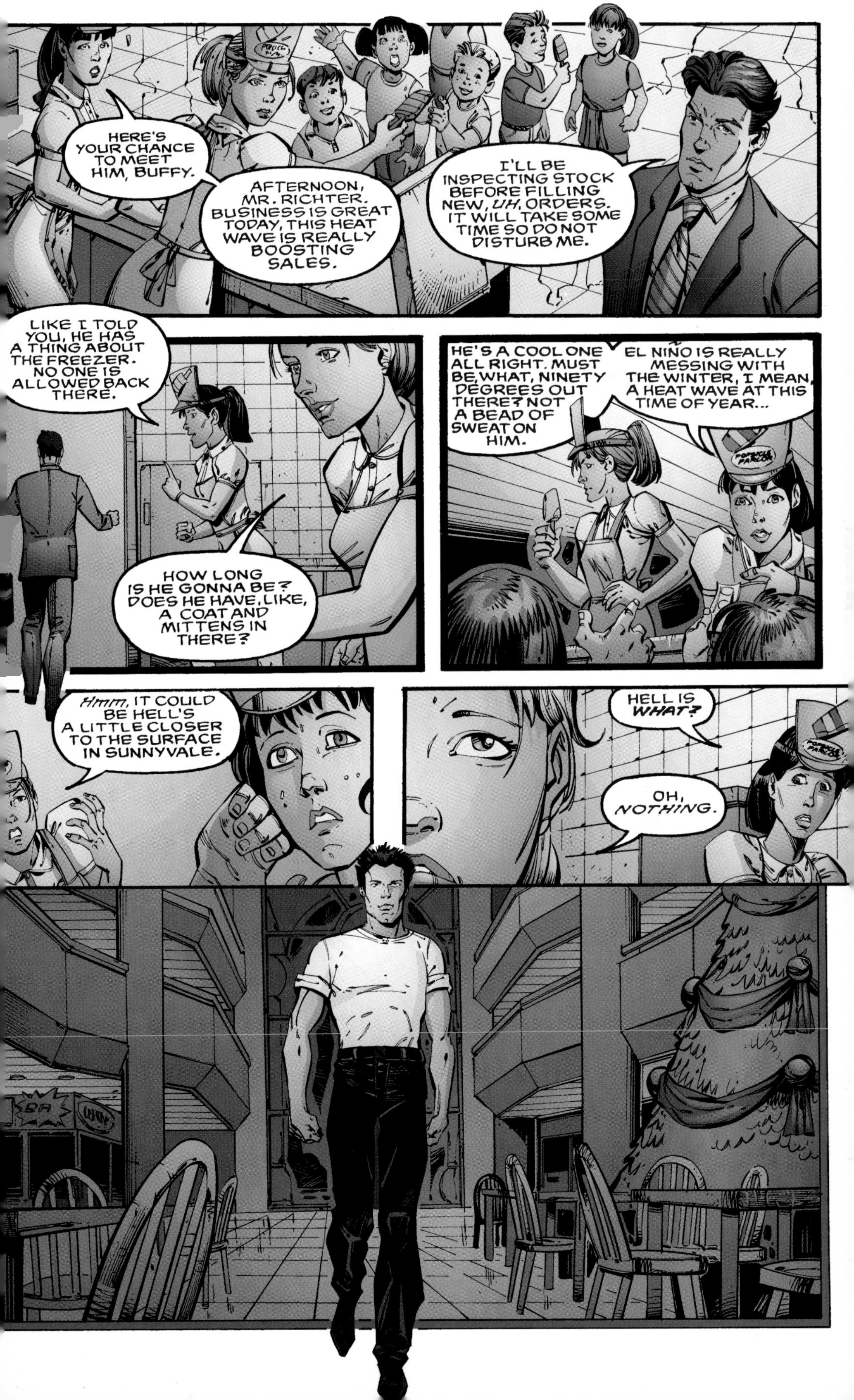
HERE'S YOUR CHANCE TO MEET HIM, BUFFY.
AFTERNOON, MR. RICHTER. BUSINESS IS GREAT TODAY, THIS HEAT WAVE IS REALLY BOOSTING SALES.
I'LL BE INSPECTING STOCK BEFORE FILLING NEW, *UH*, ORDERS. IT WILL TAKE SOME TIME SO DO NOT DISTURB ME.
LIKE I TOLD YOU, HE HAS A THING ABOUT THE FREEZER. NO ONE IS ALLOWED BACK THERE.
HOW LONG IS HE GONNA BE? DOES HE HAVE, LIKE, A COAT AND MITTENS IN THERE?
HE'S A COOL ONE ALL RIGHT. MUST BE, WHAT, NINETY DEGREES OUT THERE? NOT A BEAD OF SWEAT ON HIM.
EL NIÑO IS REALLY MESSING WITH THE WINTER, I MEAN, A HEAT WAVE AT THIS TIME OF YEAR...
HMM, IT COULD BE HELL'S A LITTLE CLOSER TO THE SURFACE IN SUNNYVALE.
HELL IS *WHAT?*
OH, *NOTHING*.

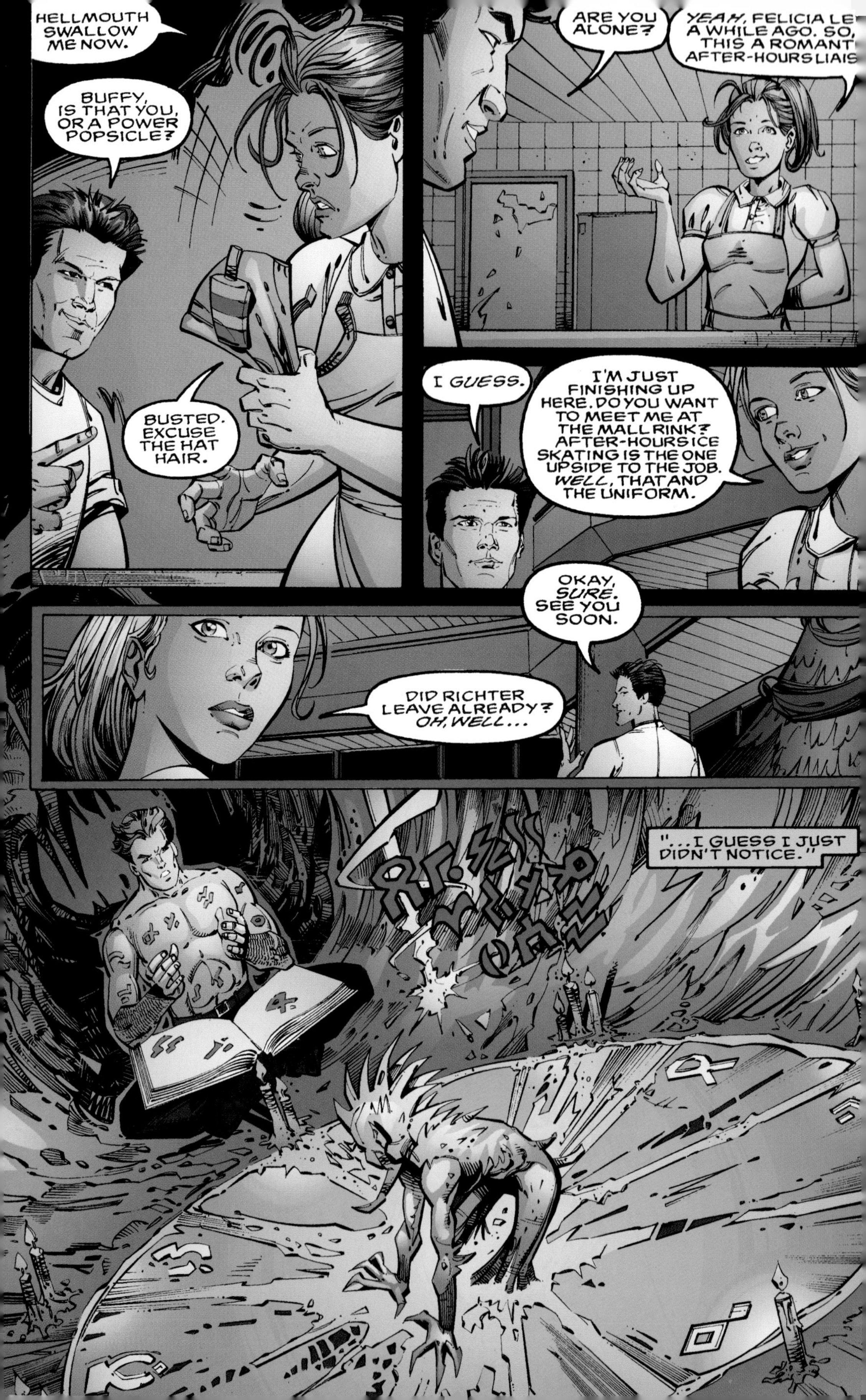
HELLMOUTH SWALLOW ME NOW.
BUFFY, IS THAT YOU, OR A POWER POPSICLE?
BUSTED. EXCUSE THE HAT HAIR.
ARE YOU ALONE?
YEAH, FELICIA LE A WHILE AGO. SO, THIS A ROMANT AFTER-HOURS LIAIS
I GUESS.
I'M JUST FINISHING UP HERE. DO YOU WANT TO MEET ME AT THE MALL RINK? AFTER-HOURS ICE SKATING IS THE ONE UPSIDE TO THE JOB. WELL, THAT AND THE UNIFORM.
OKAY, SURE. SEE YOU SOON.
DID RICHTER LEAVE ALREADY? OH, WELL...
"...I GUESS I JUST DIDN'T NOTICE."

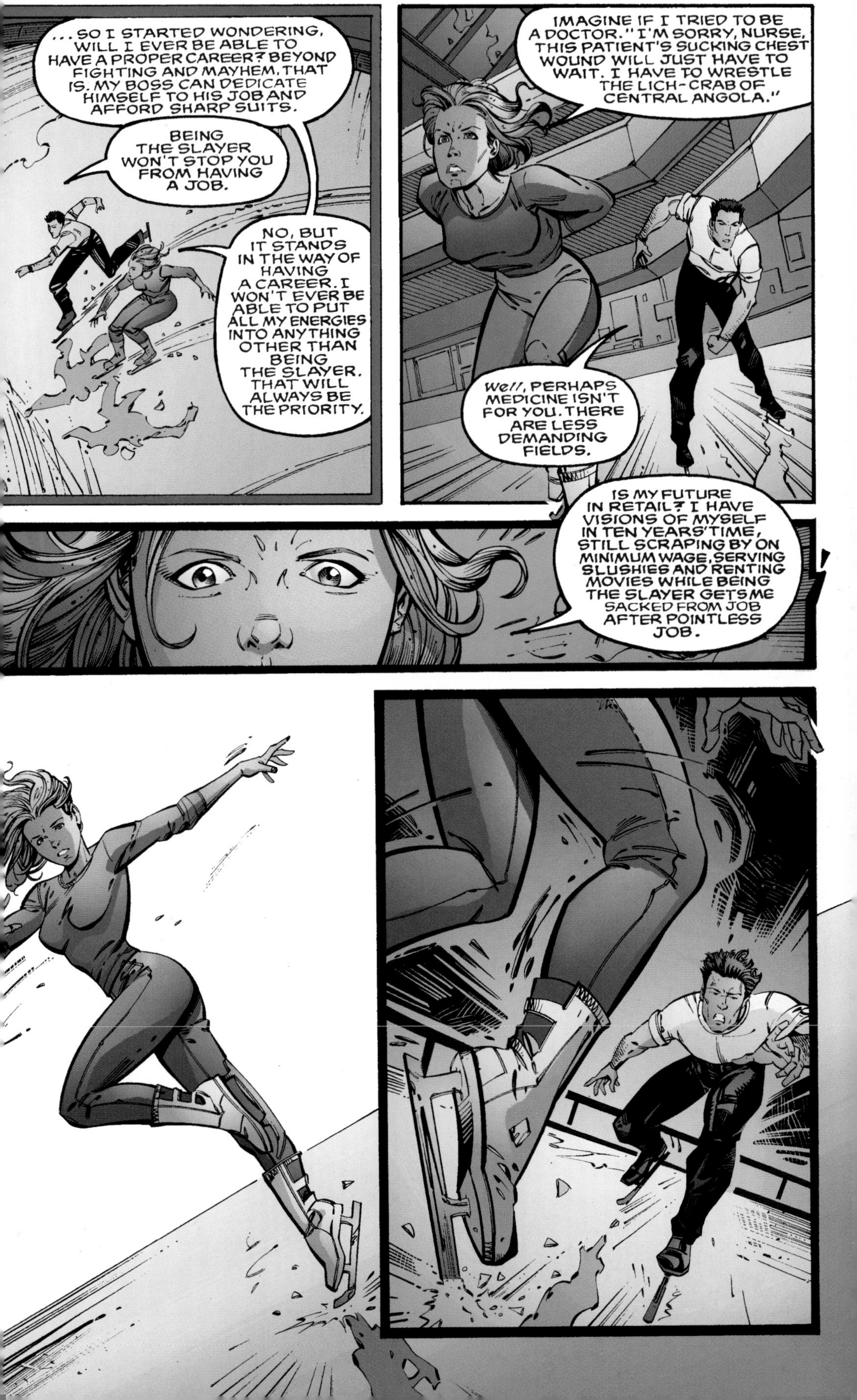
...SO I STARTED WONDERING, WILL I EVER BE ABLE TO HAVE A PROPER CAREER? BEYOND FIGHTING AND MAYHEM, THAT IS. MY BOSS CAN DEDICATE HIMSELF TO HIS JOB AND AFFORD SHARP SUITS.
BEING THE SLAYER WON'T STOP YOU FROM HAVING A JOB.
NO, BUT IT STANDS IN THE WAY OF HAVING A CAREER. I WON'T EVER BE ABLE TO PUT ALL MY ENERGIES INTO ANYTHING OTHER THAN BEING THE SLAYER. THAT WILL ALWAYS BE THE PRIORITY.
IMAGINE IF I TRIED TO BE A DOCTOR. "I'M SORRY, NURSE, THIS PATIENT'S SUCKING CHEST WOUND WILL JUST HAVE TO WAIT. I HAVE TO WRESTLE THE LICH-CRAB OF CENTRAL ANGOLA."
Well, PERHAPS MEDICINE ISN'T FOR YOU. THERE ARE LESS DEMANDING FIELDS.
IS MY FUTURE IN RETAIL? I HAVE VISIONS OF MYSELF IN TEN YEARS' TIME, STILL SCRAPING BY ON MINIMUM WAGE, SERVING SLUSHIES AND RENTING MOVIES WHILE BEING THE SLAYER GETS ME SACKED FROM JOB AFTER POINTLESS JOB.

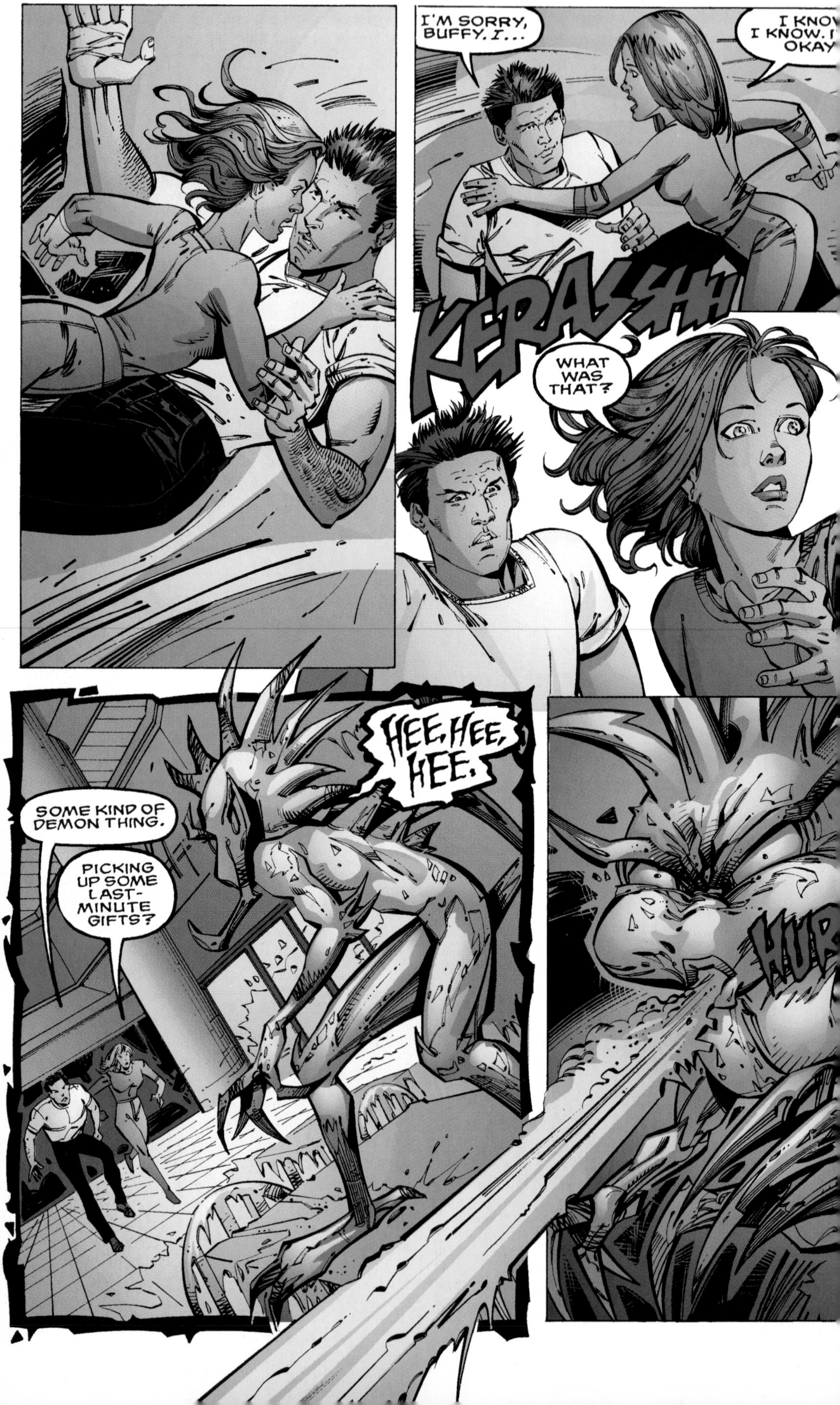

I'M SORRY, BUFFY. I...
I KNOW I KNOW. I' OKAY
KERASSHH
WHAT WAS THAT?
HEE, HEE, HEE.
SOME KIND OF DEMON THING.
PICKING UP SOME LAST-MINUTE GIFTS?
HUR

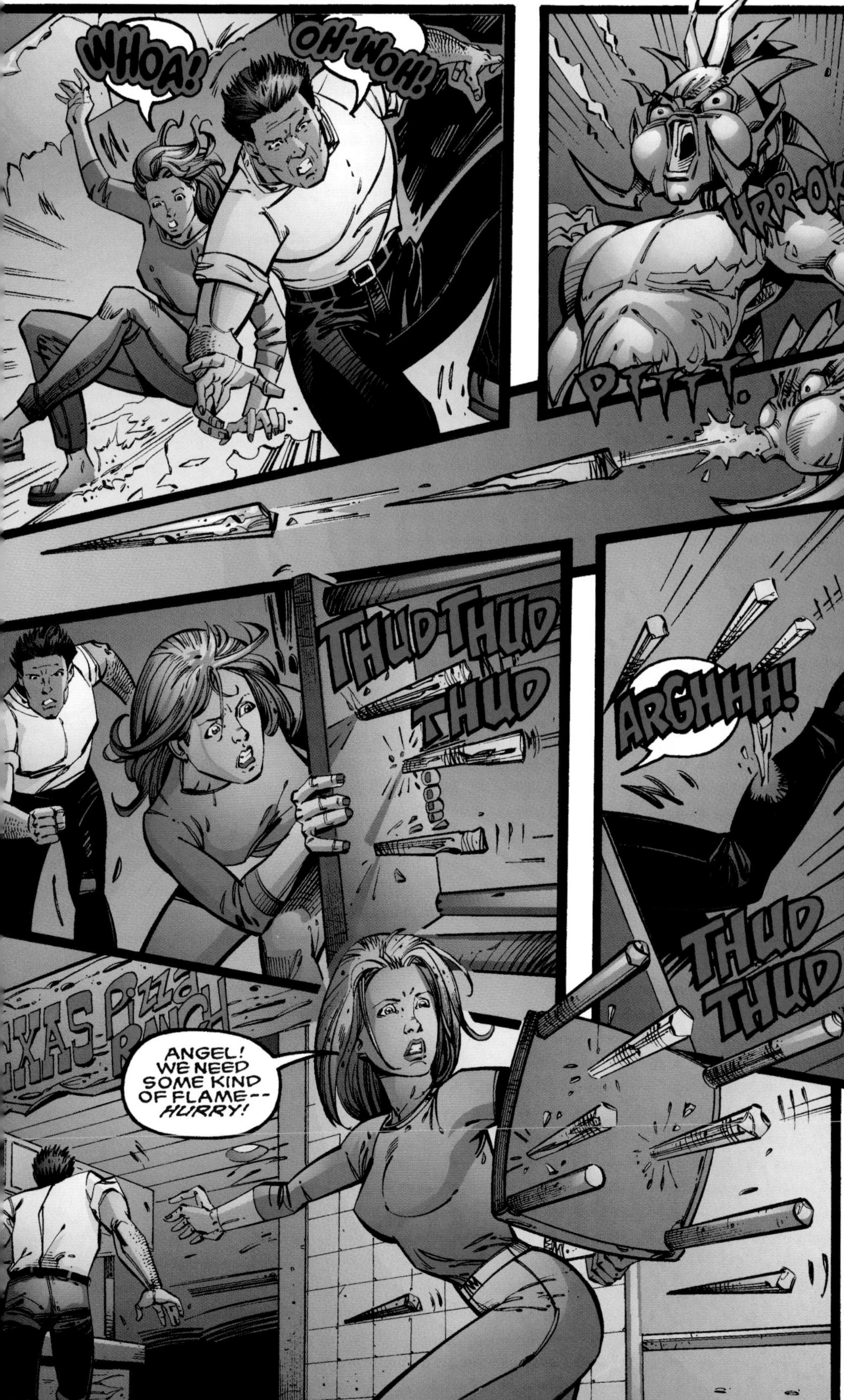
WHOA!
OH-WOH!
HRR-OKK..
PTTTT.
THUD THUD THUD
ARGHHH!
THUD THUD
ANGEL! WE NEED SOME KIND OF FLAME-- HURRY!

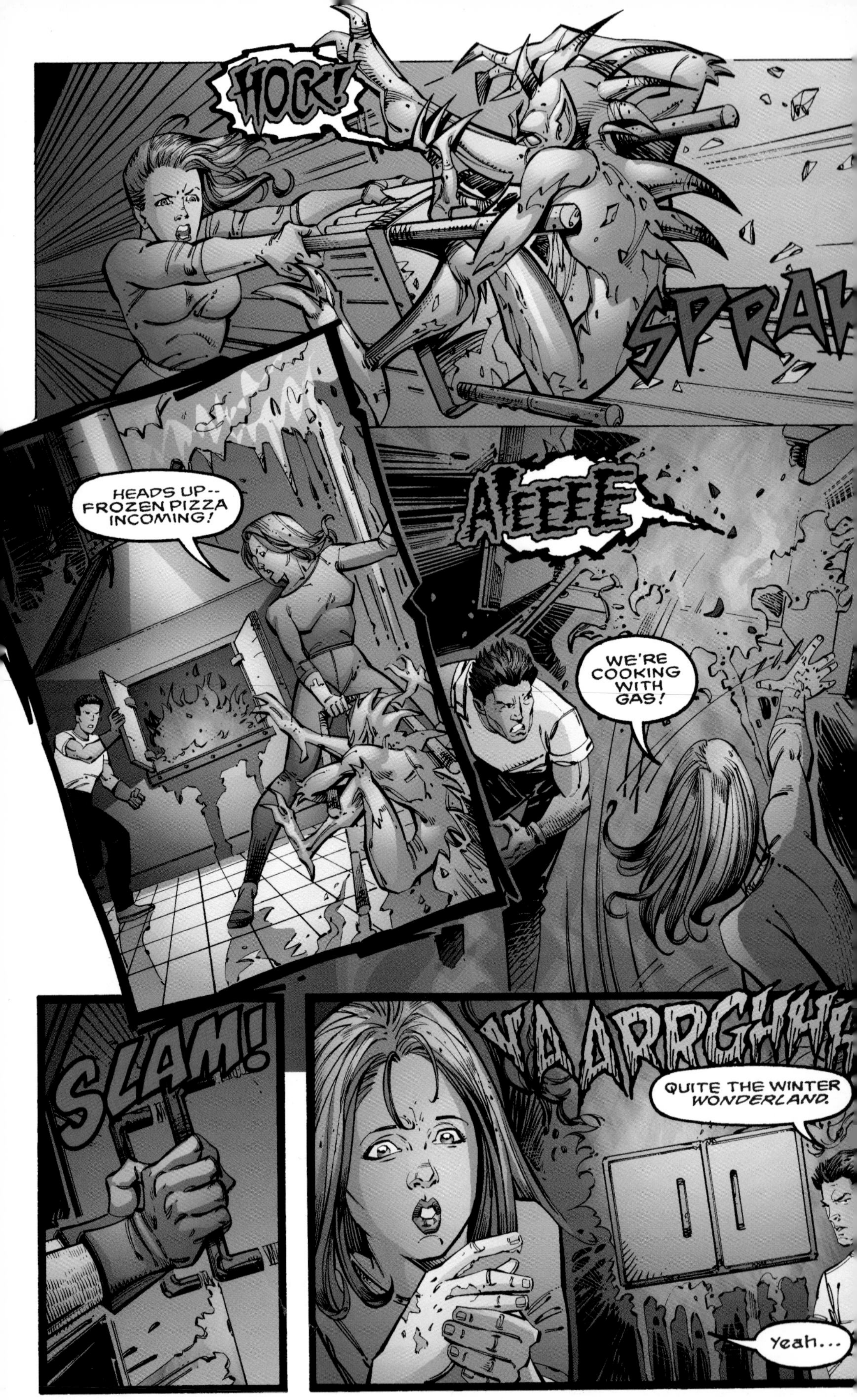
HOCK!
SPRAK
HEADS UP-- FROZEN PIZZA INCOMING!
AIEEEE
WE'RE COOKING WITH GAS!
SLAM!
QUITE THE WINTER WONDERLAND.
Yeah...

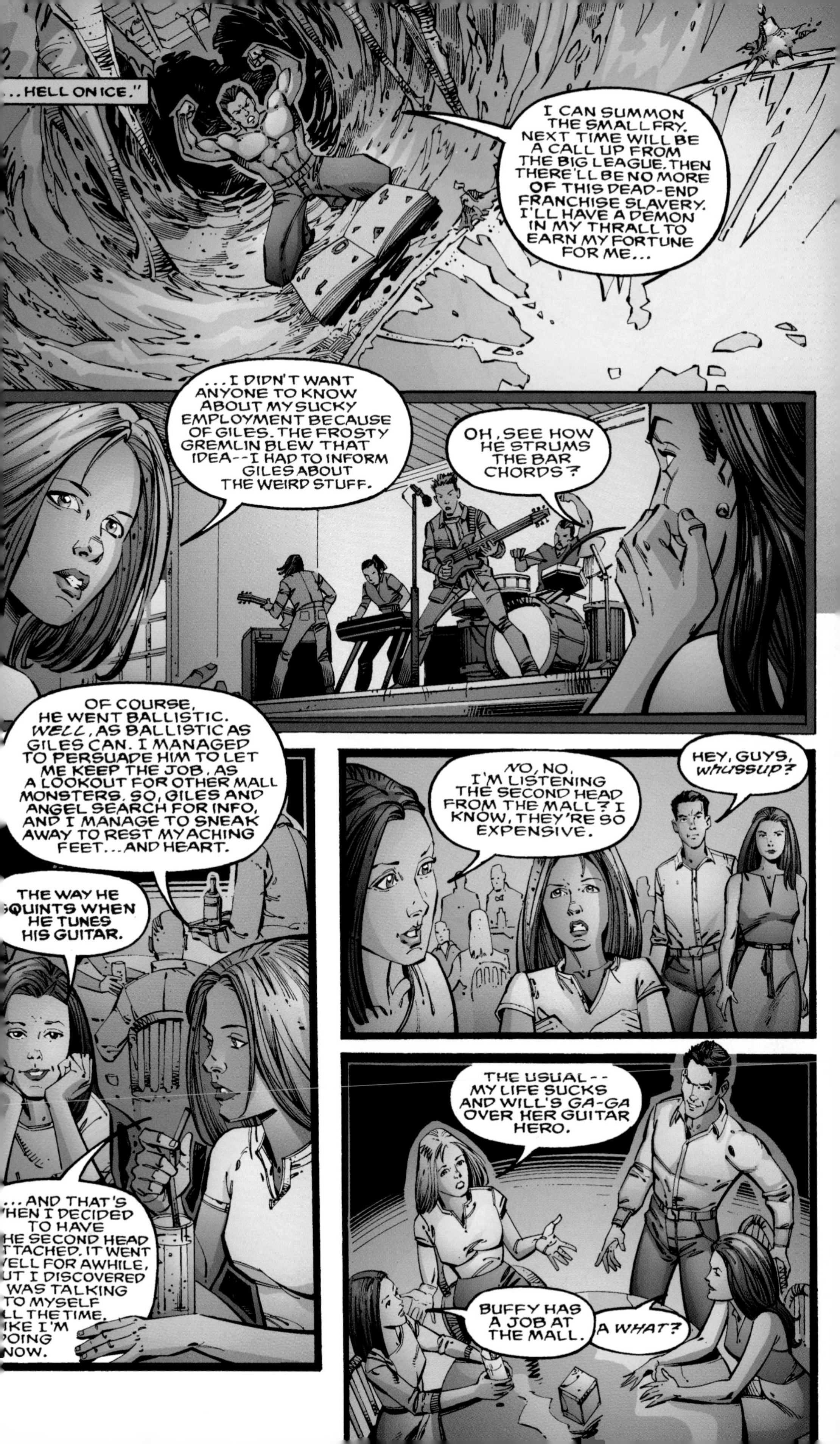

...HELL ON ICE."
I CAN SUMMON THE SMALL FRY. NEXT TIME WILL BE A CALL UP FROM THE BIG LEAGUE. THEN THERE'LL BE NO MORE OF THIS DEAD-END FRANCHISE SLAVERY. I'LL HAVE A DEMON IN MY THRALL TO EARN MY FORTUNE FOR ME...
...I DIDN'T WANT ANYONE TO KNOW ABOUT MY SUCKY EMPLOYMENT BECAUSE OF GILES. THE FROSTY GREMLIN BLEW THAT IDEA--I HAD TO INFORM GILES ABOUT THE WEIRD STUFF.
OH, SEE HOW HE STRUMS THE BAR CHORDS?
OF COURSE, HE WENT BALLISTIC. *WELL*, AS BALLISTIC AS GILES CAN. I MANAGED TO PERSUADE HIM TO LET ME KEEP THE JOB, AS A LOOKOUT FOR OTHER MALL MONSTERS. SO, GILES AND ANGEL SEARCH FOR INFO, AND I MANAGE TO SNEAK AWAY TO REST MY ACHING FEET... AND HEART.
THE WAY HE SQUINTS WHEN HE TUNES HIS GUITAR.
...AND THAT'S WHEN I DECIDED TO HAVE THE SECOND HEAD ATTACHED. IT WENT WELL FOR AWHILE, BUT I DISCOVERED I WAS TALKING TO MYSELF ALL THE TIME. LIKE I'M DOING NOW.
NO, NO, I'M LISTENING THE SECOND HEAD FROM THE MALL? I KNOW, THEY'RE SO EXPENSIVE.
HEY, GUYS, *WHUSSUP?*
THE USUAL-- MY LIFE SUCKS AND WILL'S *GA-GA* OVER HER GUITAR HERO.
BUFFY HAS A JOB AT THE MALL.
A *WHAT?*

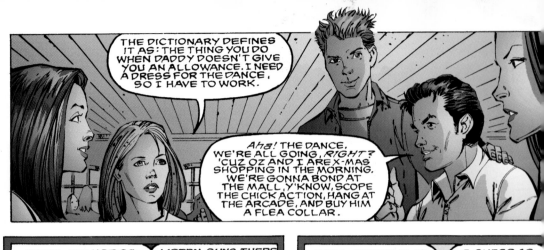

THE DICTIONARY DEFINES IT AS: THE THING YOU DO WHEN DADDY DOESN'T GIVE YOU AN ALLOWANCE. I NEED A DRESS FOR THE DANCE, SO I HAVE TO WORK.

AHA! THE DANCE. WE'RE ALL GOING, *RIGHT?* 'CUZ OZ AND I ARE X-MAS SHOPPING IN THE MORNING. WE'RE GONNA BOND AT THE MALL, Y'KNOW, SCOPE THE CHICK ACTION, HANG AT THE ARCADE, AND BUY HIM A FLEA COLLAR.

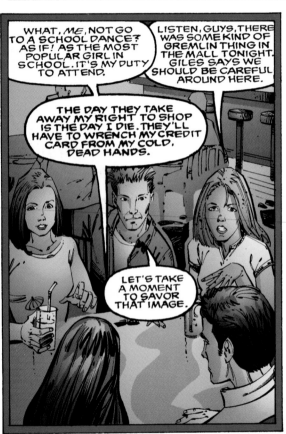

WHAT, *ME*, NOT GO TO A SCHOOL DANCE? AS IF! AS THE MOST POPULAR GIRL IN SCHOOL. IT'S MY DUTY TO ATTEND.

THE DAY THEY TAKE AWAY MY RIGHT TO SHOP IS THE DAY I DIE. THEY'LL HAVE TO WRENCH MY CREDIT CARD FROM MY COLD, DEAD HANDS.

LISTEN, GUYS, THERE WAS SOME KIND OF GREMLIN THING IN THE MALL TONIGHT. GILES SAYS WE SHOULD BE CAREFUL AROUND HERE.

LET'S TAKE A MOMENT TO SAVOR THAT IMAGE.

WELL, CORDELIA, IF YOU WANT MY GIFTS, YOU HAVE TO ACCOMPANY ME TO THE DANCE.

I GUESS AS A CHARITABLE CONTRIBUTION TO THE LESS POPULAR.

YOU COULD SHOP FOR A VERY EXPENSIVE DRESS THAT'LL STUN EVERYONE. SOMETHING SO EYE-CATCHING THEY DON'T EVEN NOTICE XANDER'S THERE.

OKAY, NOW SHE'S GOING WITH ME.

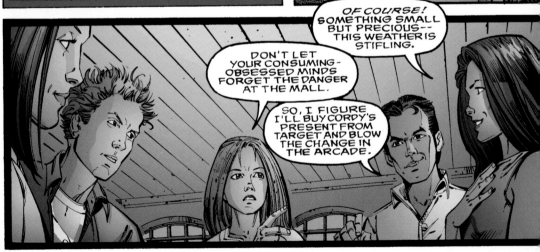

OF COURSE! SOMETHING SMALL BUT PRECIOUS-- THIS WEATHER IS STIFLING.

DON'T LET YOUR CONSUMING-OBSESSED MINDS FORGET THE DANGER AT THE MALL.

SO, I FIGURE I'LL BUY CORDY'S PRESENT FROM TARGET AND BLOW THE CHANGE IN THE ARCADE.

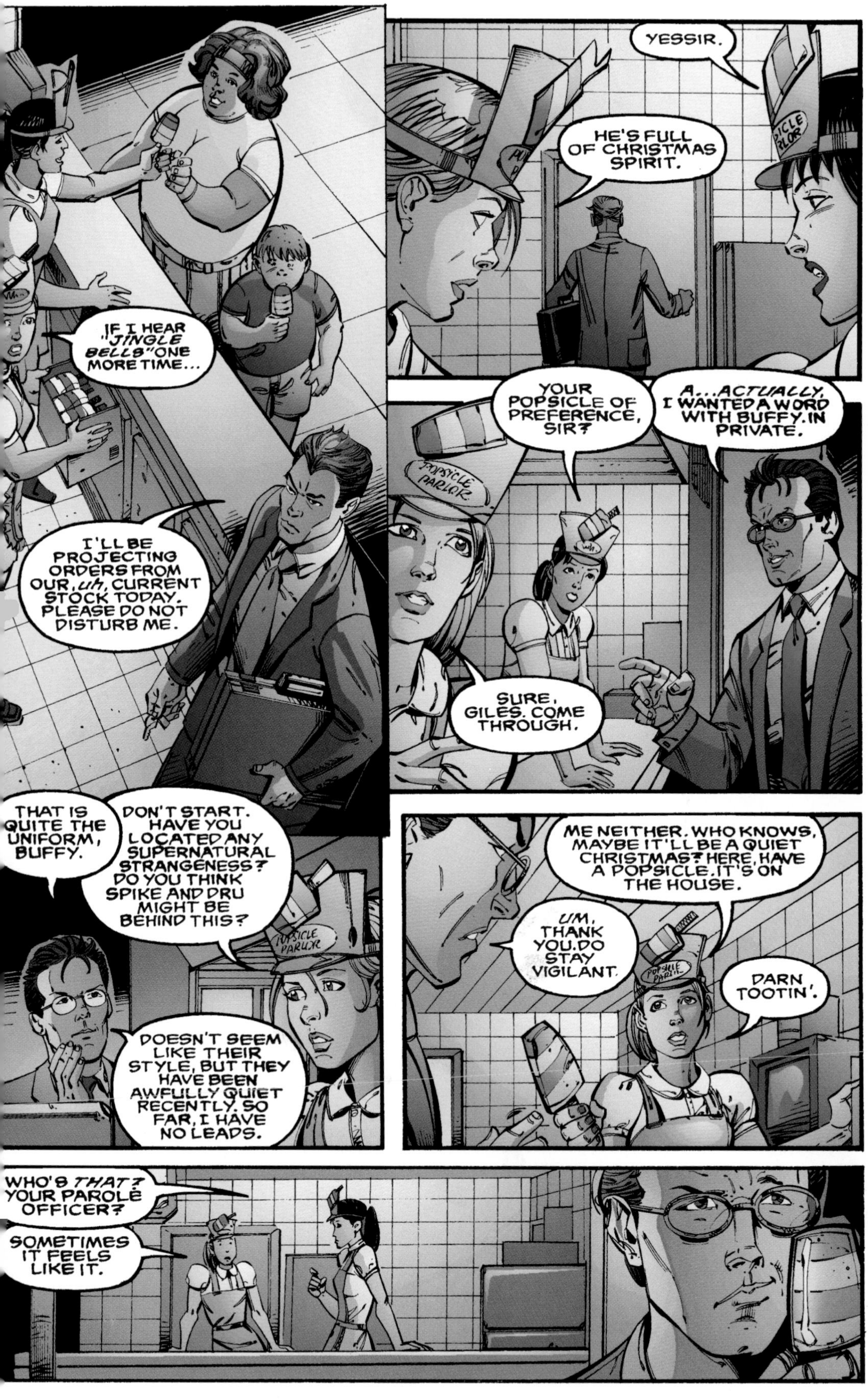
IF I HEAR "JINGLE BELLS" ONE MORE TIME...
I'LL BE PROJECTING ORDERS FROM OUR, uh, CURRENT STOCK TODAY. PLEASE DO NOT DISTURB ME.
YESSIR.
HE'S FULL OF CHRISTMAS SPIRIT.
YOUR POPSICLE OF PREFERENCE, SIR?
A...ACTUALLY, I WANTED A WORD WITH BUFFY. IN PRIVATE.
SURE, GILES. COME THROUGH.
THAT IS QUITE THE UNIFORM, BUFFY.
DON'T START. HAVE YOU LOCATED ANY SUPERNATURAL STRANGENESS? DO YOU THINK SPIKE AND DRU MIGHT BE BEHIND THIS?
DOESN'T SEEM LIKE THEIR STYLE, BUT THEY HAVE BEEN AWFULLY QUIET RECENTLY. SO FAR, I HAVE NO LEADS.
ME NEITHER. WHO KNOWS, MAYBE IT'LL BE A QUIET CHRISTMAS? HERE, HAVE A POPSICLE. IT'S ON THE HOUSE.
UM, THANK YOU. DO STAY VIGILANT.
DARN TOOTIN'.
WHO'S THAT? YOUR PAROLE OFFICER?
SOMETIMES IT FEELS LIKE IT.

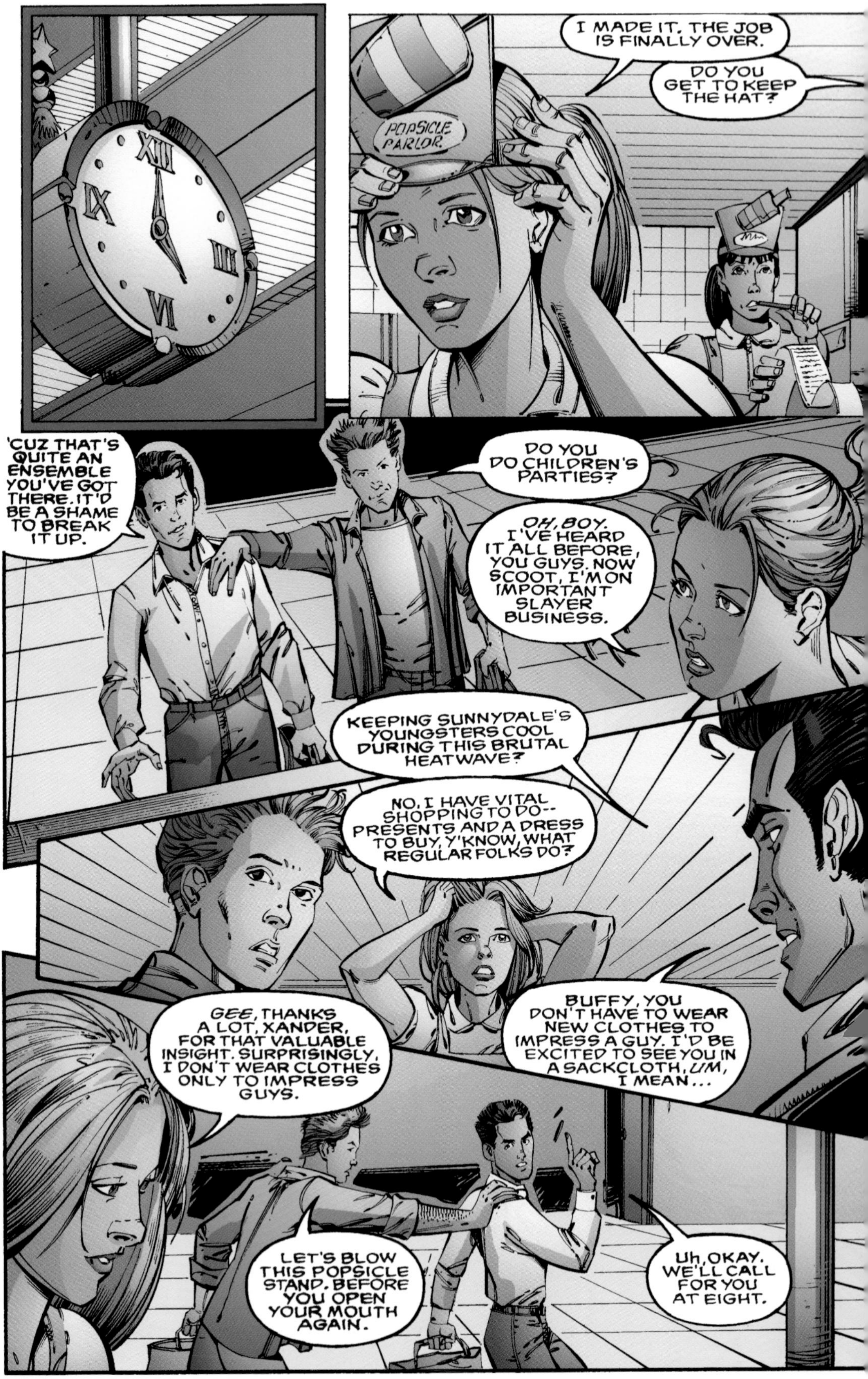
I MADE IT. THE JOB IS FINALLY OVER.
DO YOU GET TO KEEP THE HAT?
POPSICLE PARLOR
'CUZ THAT'S QUITE AN ENSEMBLE YOU'VE GOT THERE. IT'D BE A SHAME TO BREAK IT UP.
DO YOU DO CHILDREN'S PARTIES?
OH, BOY. I'VE HEARD IT ALL BEFORE, YOU GUYS. NOW SCOOT, I'M ON IMPORTANT SLAYER BUSINESS.
KEEPING SUNNYDALE'S YOUNGSTERS COOL DURING THIS BRUTAL HEATWAVE?
NO, I HAVE VITAL SHOPPING TO DO-- PRESENTS AND A DRESS TO BUY, Y'KNOW, WHAT REGULAR FOLKS DO?
BUFFY, YOU DON'T HAVE TO WEAR NEW CLOTHES TO IMPRESS A GUY. I'D BE EXCITED TO SEE YOU IN A SACKCLOTH, UM, I MEAN...
GEE, THANKS A LOT, XANDER, FOR THAT VALUABLE INSIGHT. SURPRISINGLY, I DON'T WEAR CLOTHES ONLY TO IMPRESS GUYS.
LET'S BLOW THIS POPSICLE STAND, BEFORE YOU OPEN YOUR MOUTH AGAIN.
UH, OKAY. WE'LL CALL FOR YOU AT EIGHT.

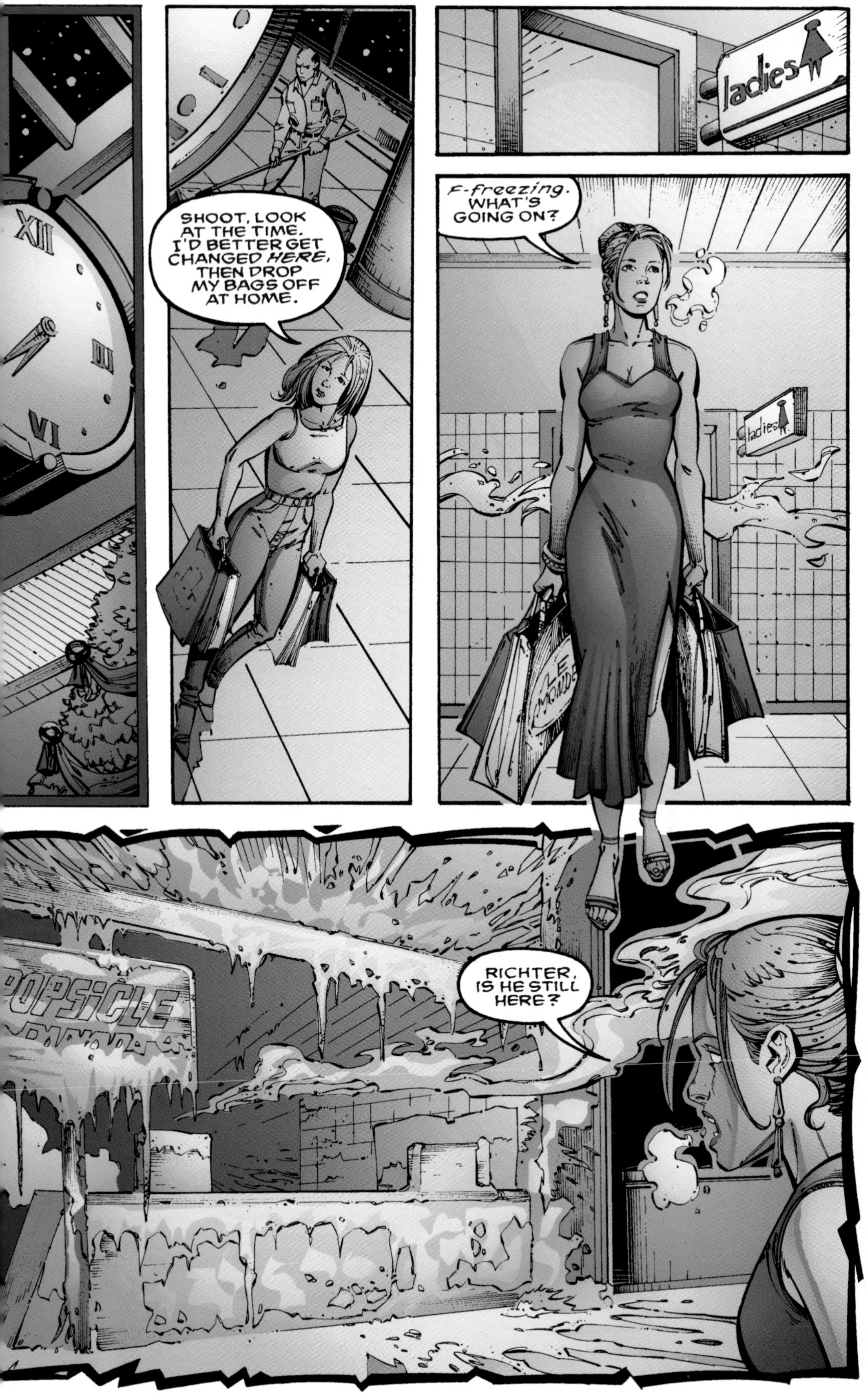
SHOOT, LOOK AT THE TIME. I'D BETTER GET CHANGED *HERE*, THEN DROP MY BAGS OFF AT HOME.
ladies
F-freezing. WHAT'S GOING ON?
ladies
LE MONDE
POPSICLE
RICHTER, IS HE STILL HERE?

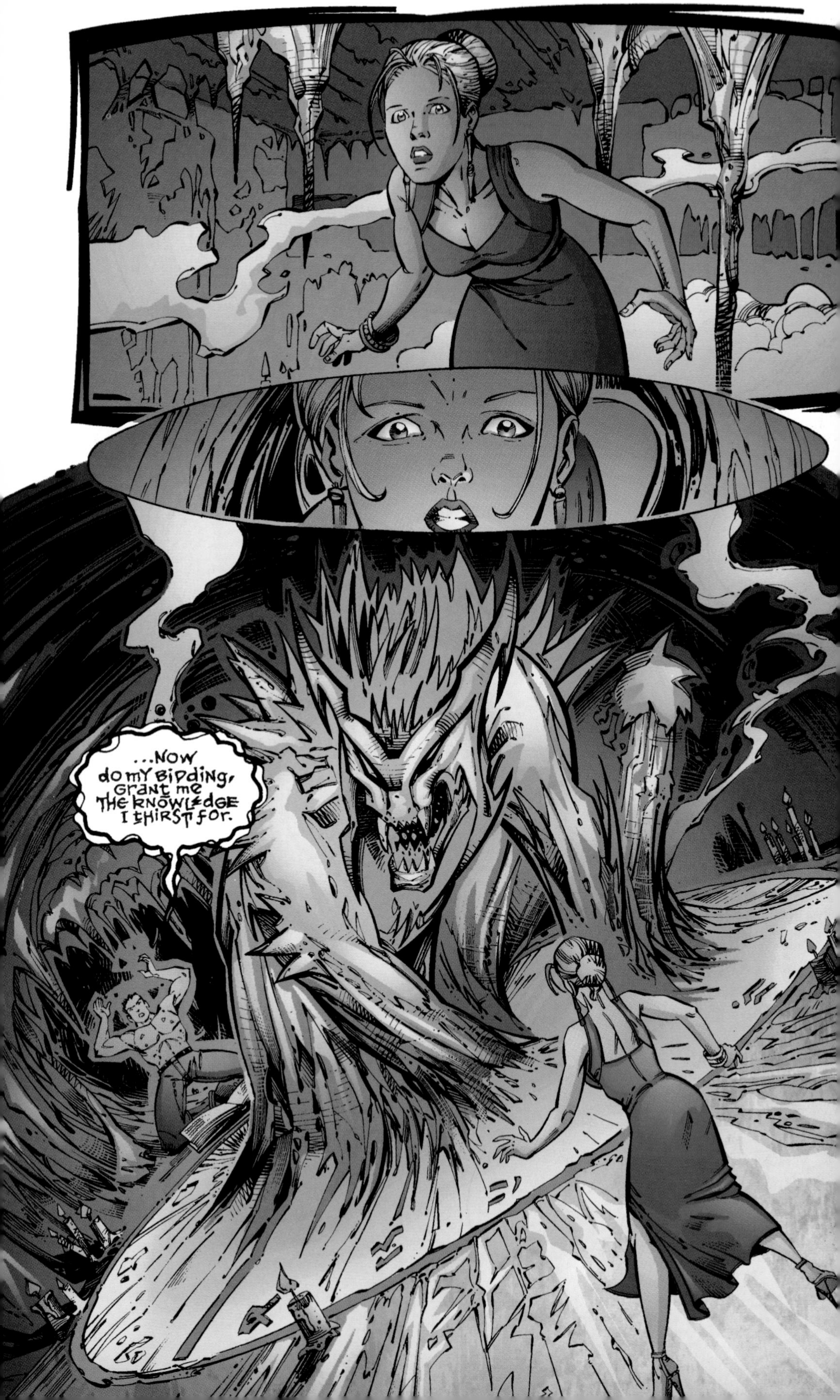
...NOW do MY BIDDING, GRANT ME THE KNOWLEDGE I THIRST FOR.

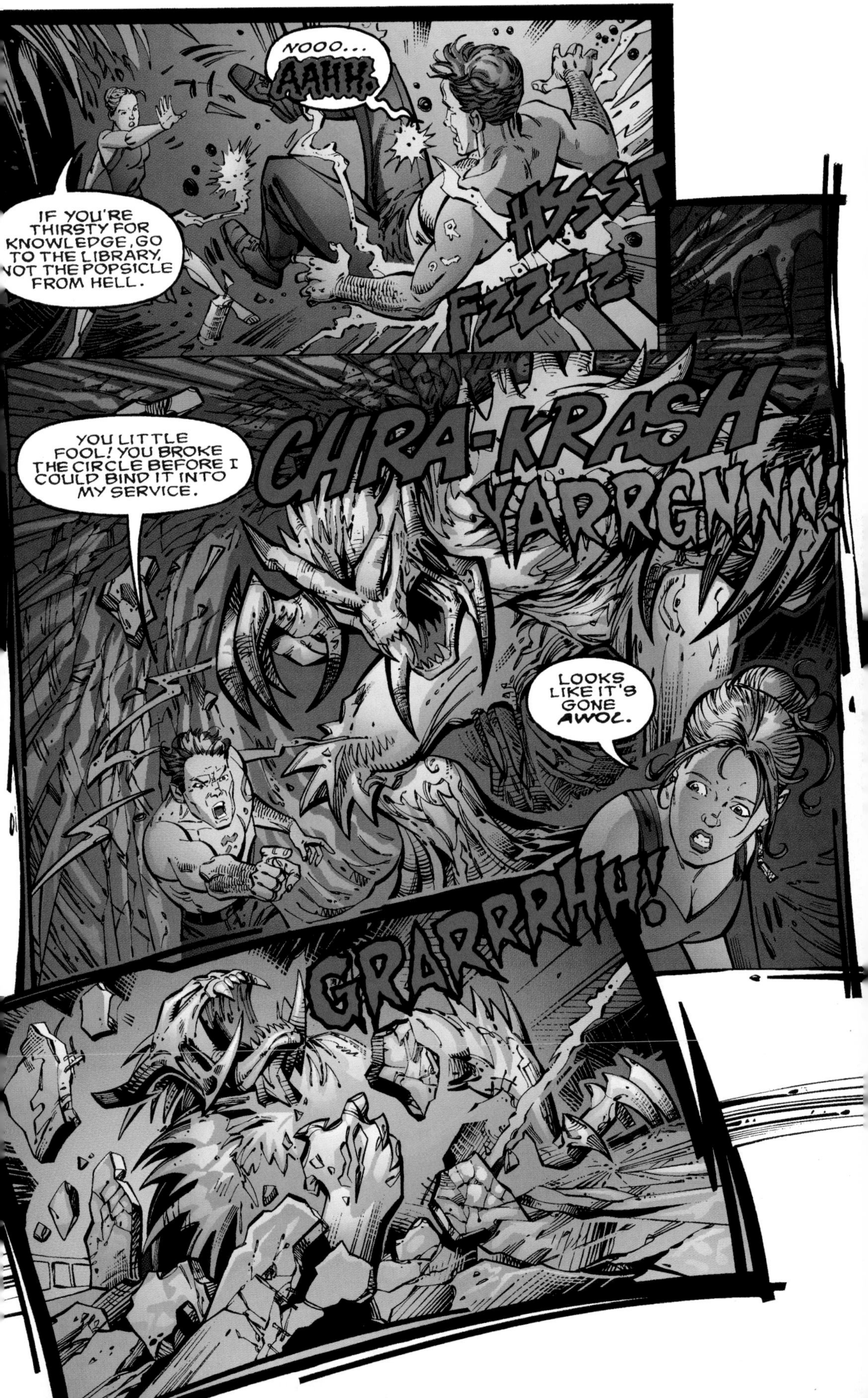
NOOO... AAHH.
IF YOU'RE THIRSTY FOR KNOWLEDGE, GO TO THE LIBRARY, NOT THE POPSICLE FROM HELL.
HSSST
FZZZZ
CHRA-KRASH
YOU LITTLE FOOL! YOU BROKE THE CIRCLE BEFORE I COULD BIND IT INTO MY SERVICE.
YARRGNNN!
LOOKS LIKE IT'S GONE AWOL.
GRARRRHH!

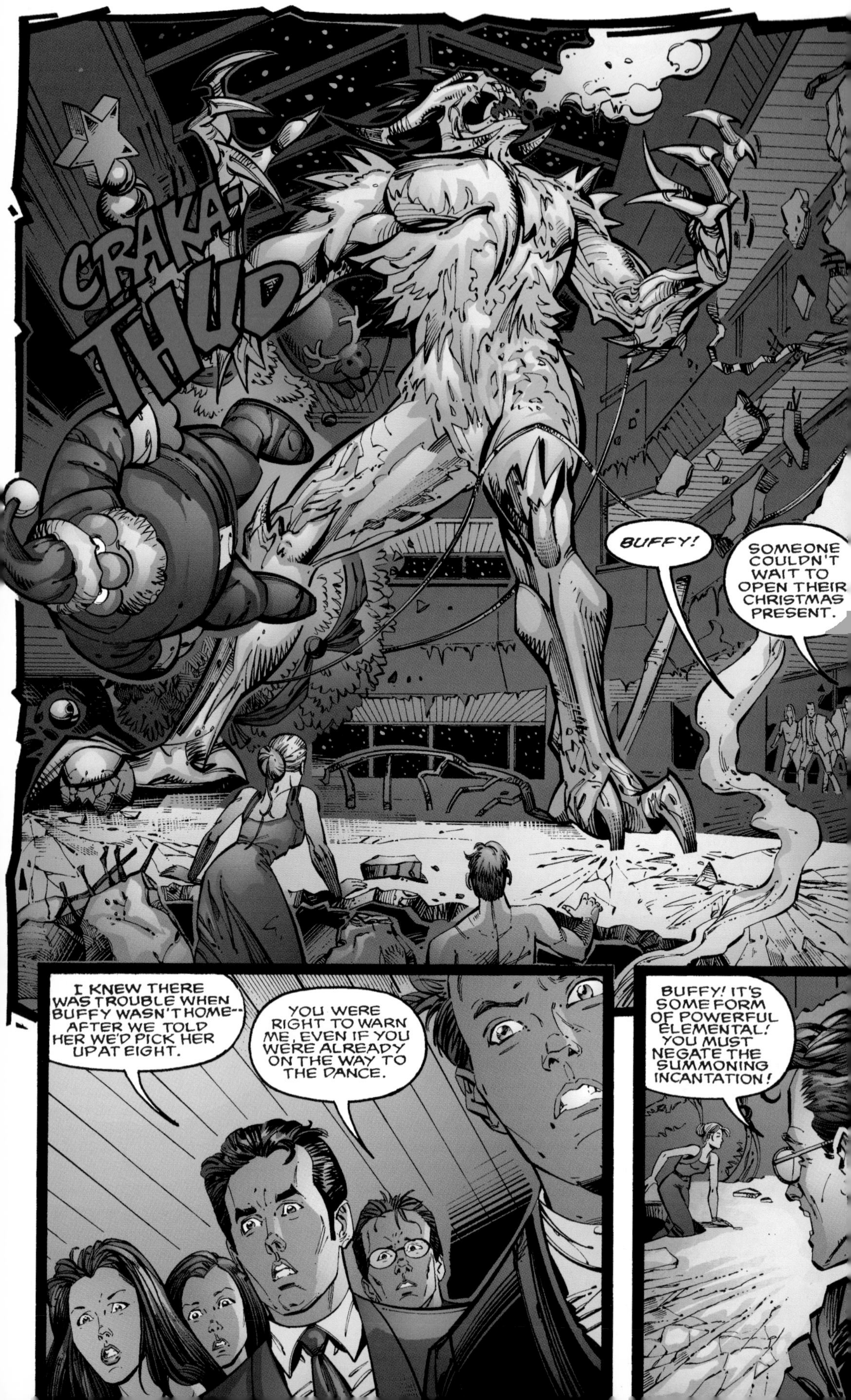
CRAKA-THUD
BUFFY!
SOMEONE COULDN'T WAIT TO OPEN THEIR CHRISTMAS PRESENT.
I KNEW THERE WAS TROUBLE WHEN BUFFY WASN'T HOME-- AFTER WE TOLD HER WE'D PICK HER UP AT EIGHT.
YOU WERE RIGHT TO WARN ME, EVEN IF YOU WERE ALREADY ON THE WAY TO THE DANCE.
BUFFY! IT'S SOME FORM OF POWERFUL ELEMENTAL! YOU MUST NEGATE THE SUMMONING INCANTATION!

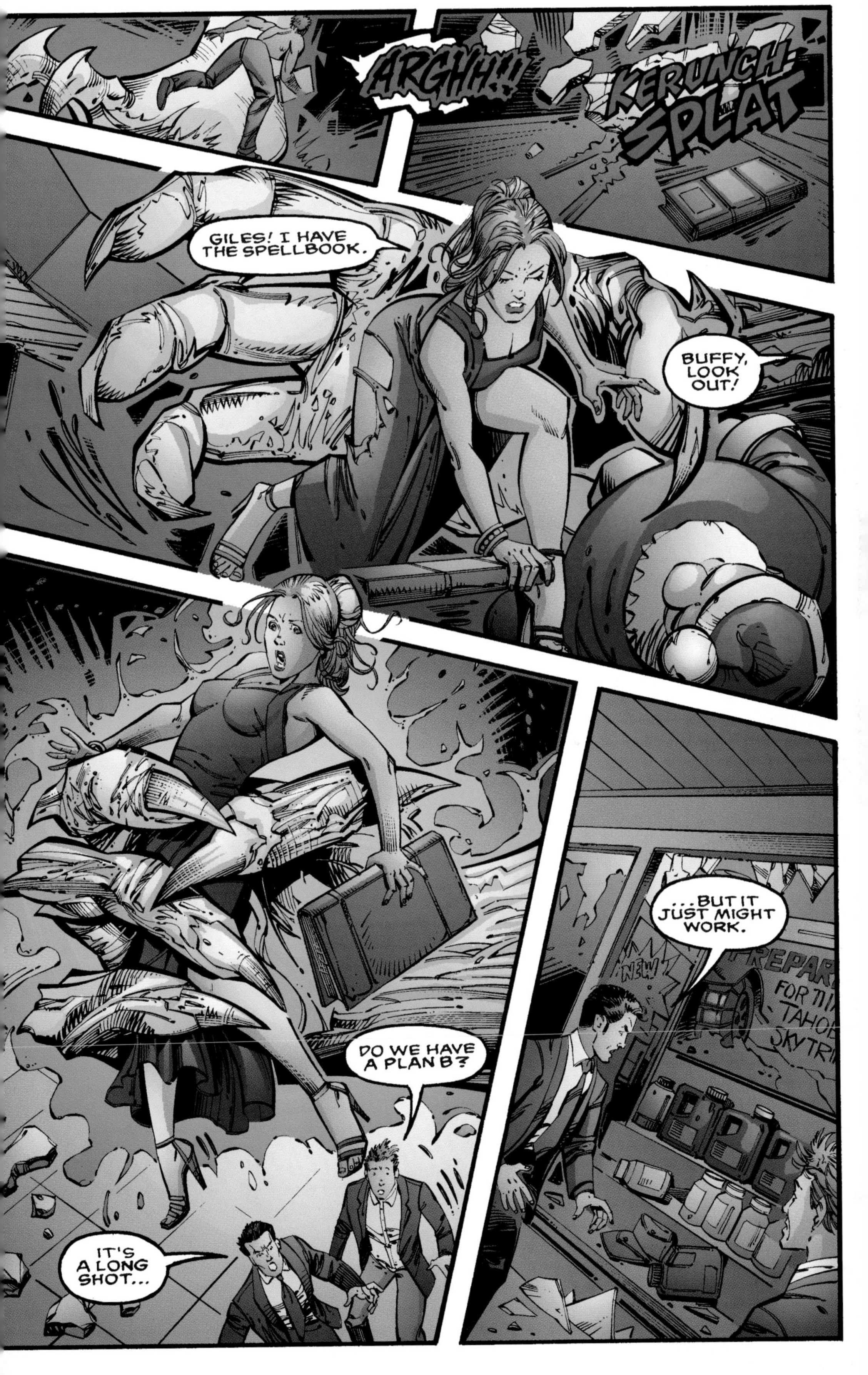
ARGHH!!
KERUNCH
SPLAT
GILES! I HAVE THE SPELLBOOK.
BUFFY, LOOK OUT!
DO WE HAVE A PLAN B?
IT'S A LONG SHOT...
...BUT IT JUST MIGHT WORK.

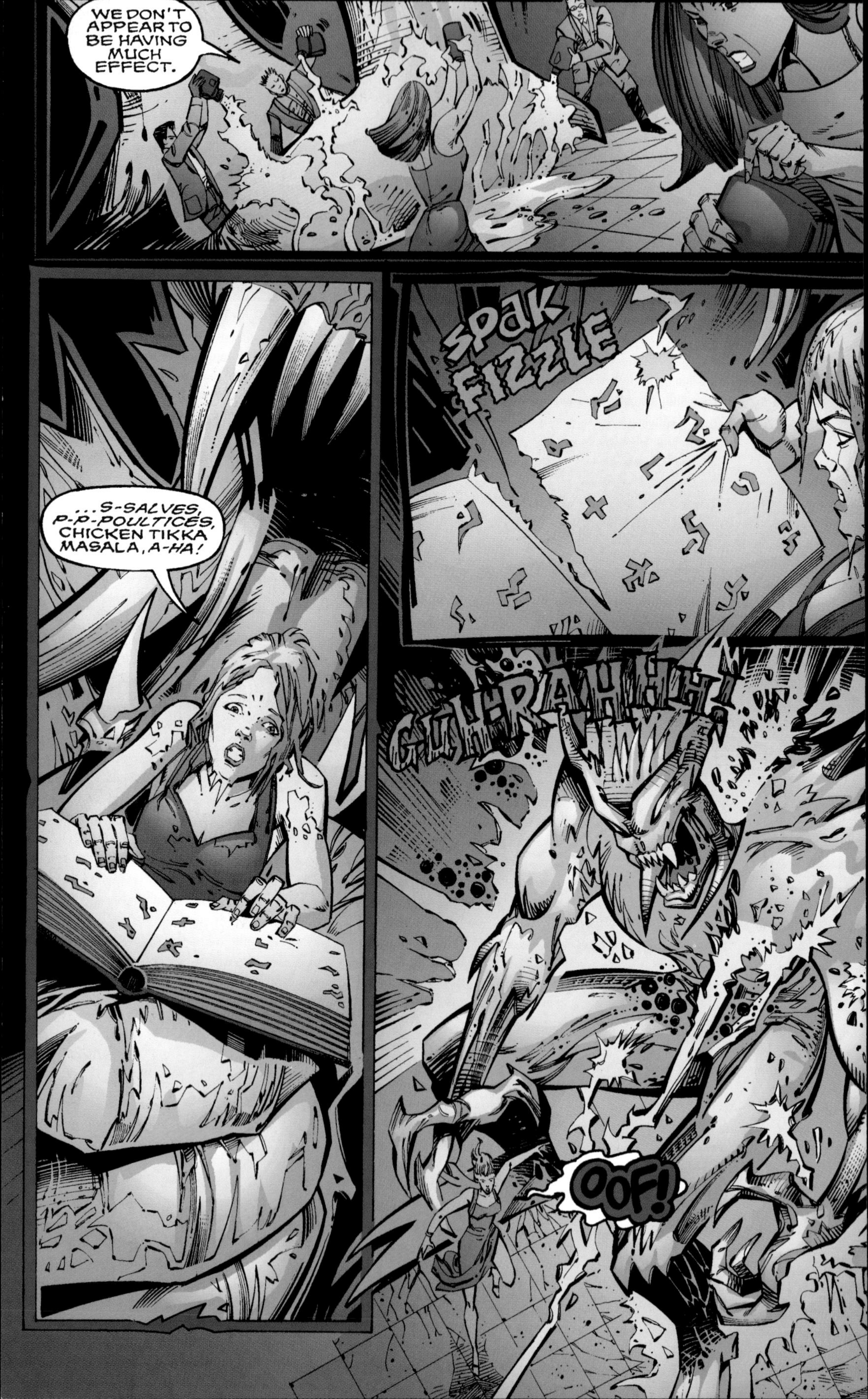
WE DON'T APPEAR TO BE HAVING MUCH EFFECT.
...S-SALVES, P-P-POULTICES, CHICKEN TIKKA MASALA, A-HA!
SPAK
FIZZLE
GUHRAHHHH!
OOF!

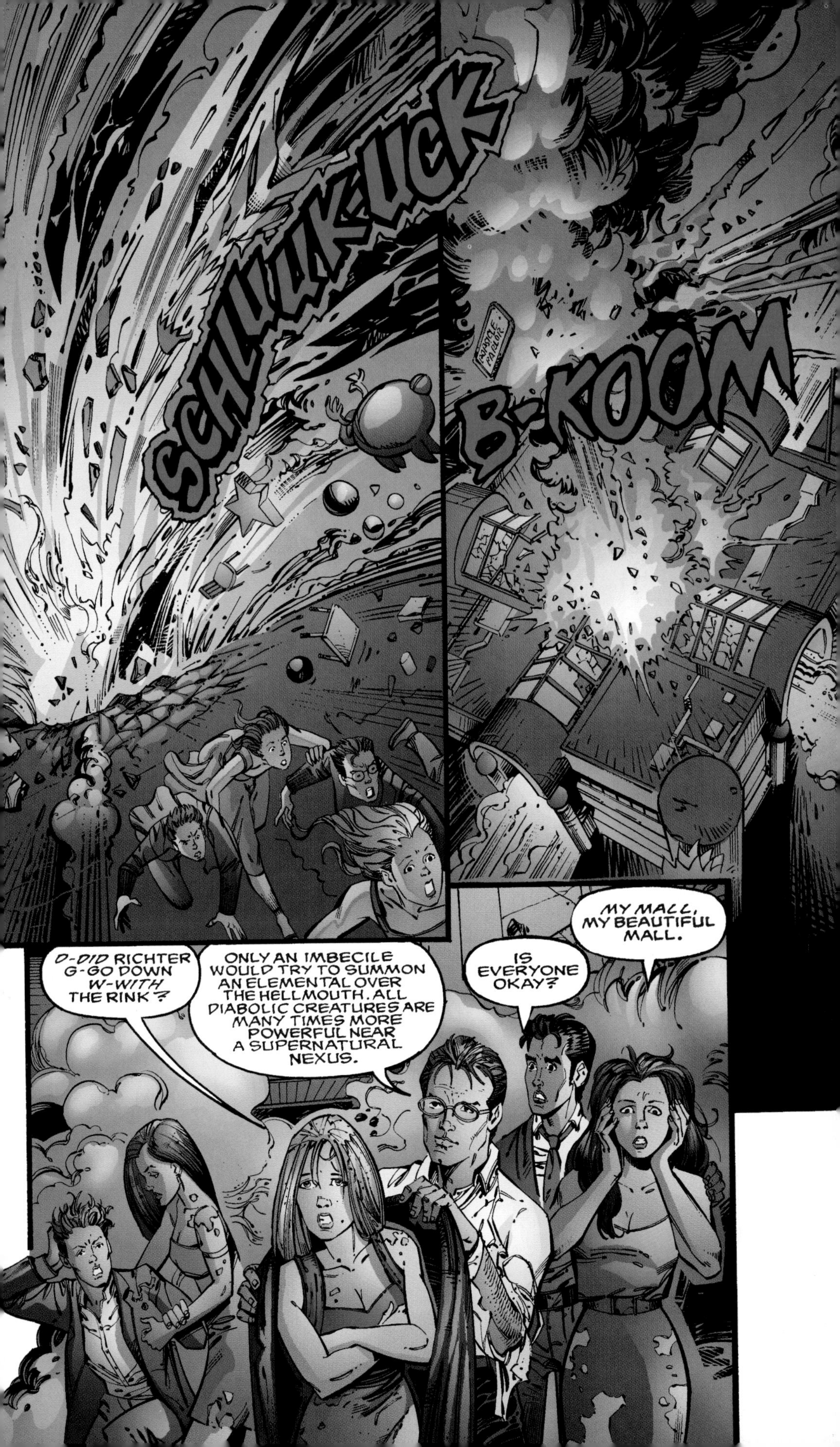
SCHLUUK-UCK
B-KOOM
D-DID RICHTER G-GO DOWN W-WITH THE RINK?
ONLY AN IMBECILE WOULD TRY TO SUMMON AN ELEMENTAL OVER THE HELLMOUTH. ALL DIABOLIC CREATURES ARE MANY TIMES MORE POWERFUL NEAR A SUPERNATURAL NEXUS.
IS EVERYONE OKAY?
MY MALL, MY BEAUTIFUL MALL.

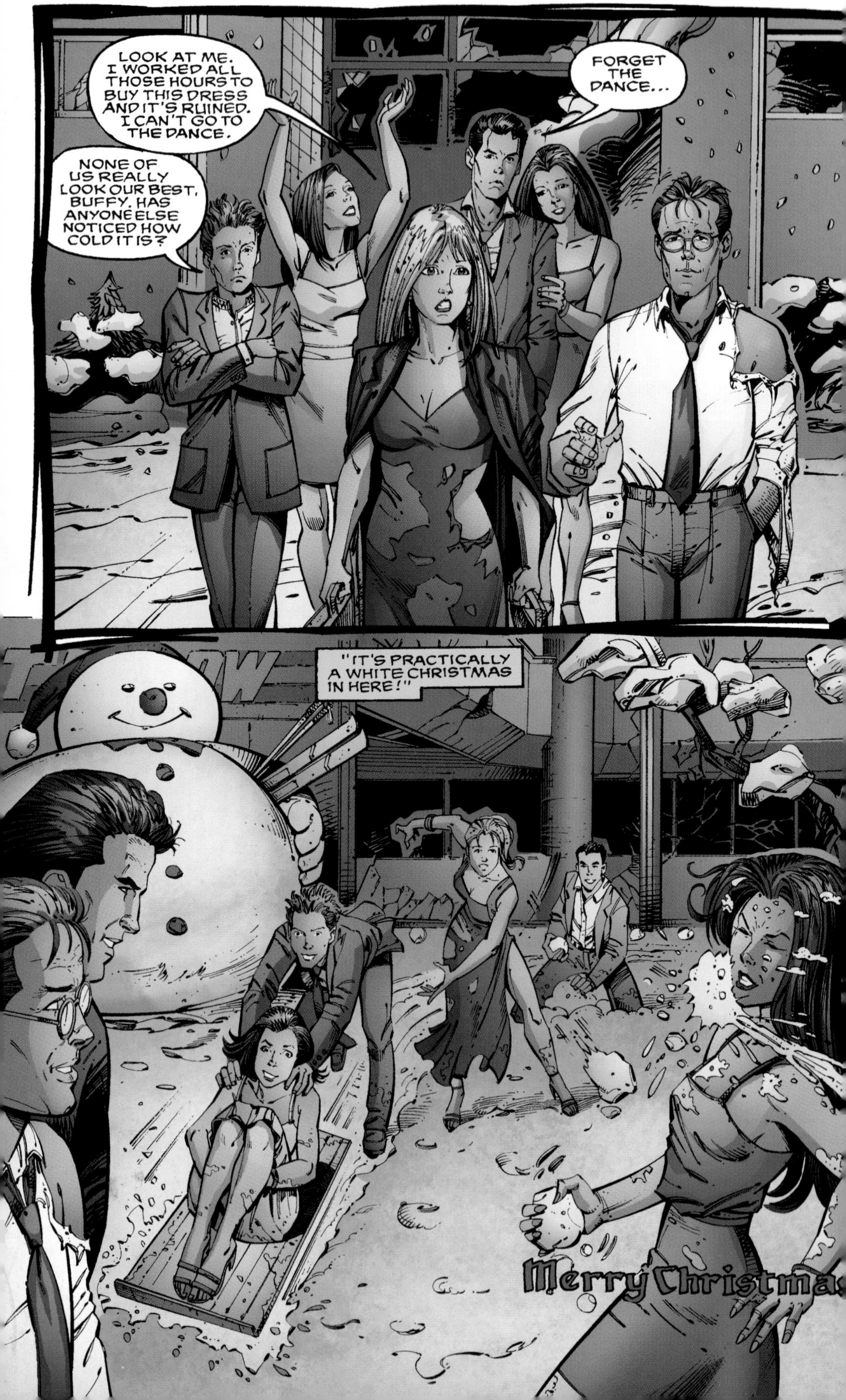

LOOK AT ME. I WORKED ALL THOSE HOURS TO BUY THIS DRESS AND IT'S RUINED. I CAN'T GO TO THE DANCE.
NONE OF US REALLY LOOK OUR BEST, BUFFY. HAS ANYONE ELSE NOTICED HOW COLD IT IS?
FORGET THE DANCE...
"IT'S PRACTICALLY A WHITE CHRISTMAS IN HERE!"
Merry Christmas

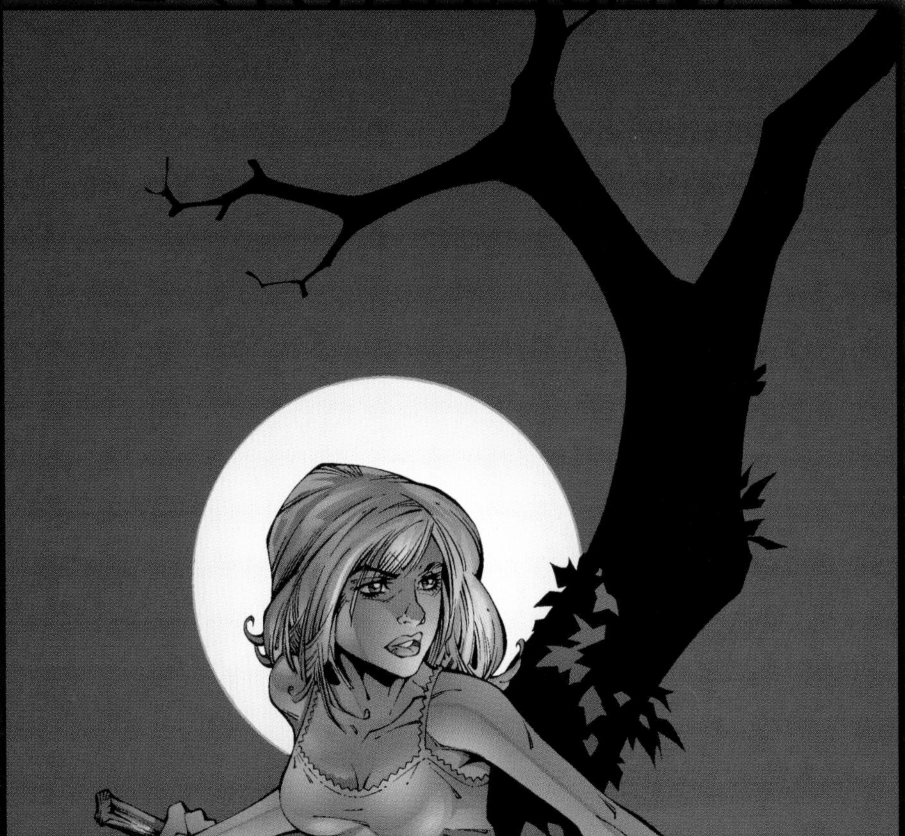
RLK.
the guy

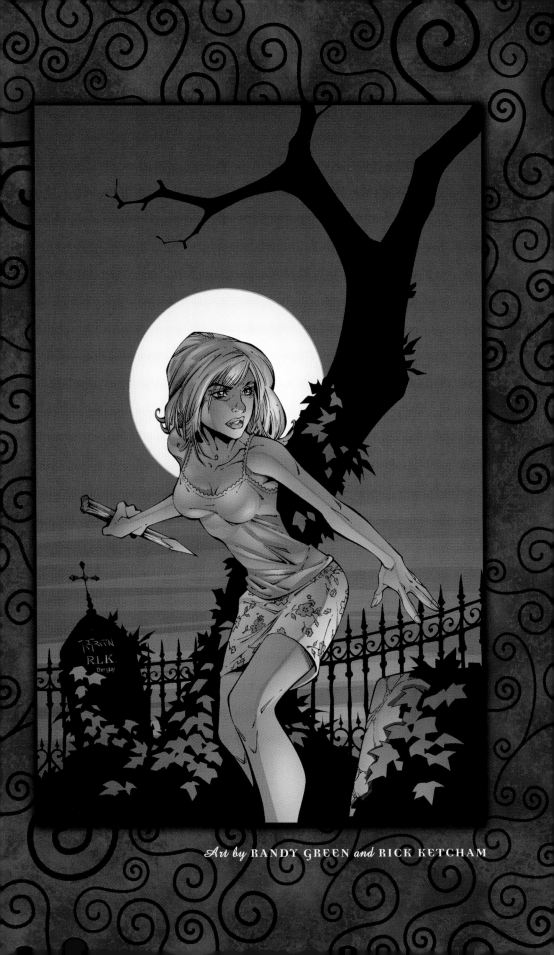

Art by RANDY GREEN *and* RICK KETCHAM

Happy
New Year

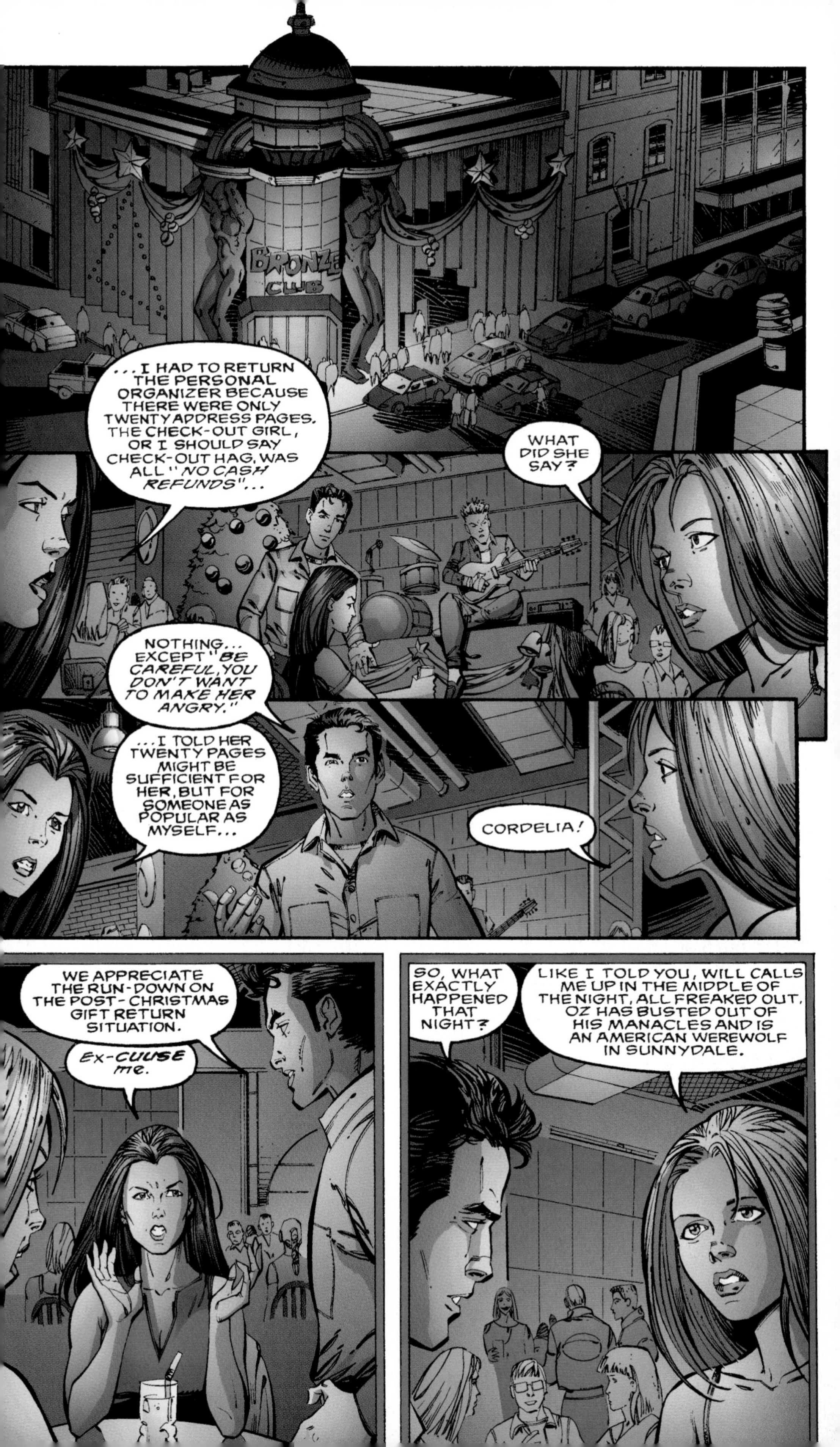
BRONZE CLUB
...I HAD TO RETURN THE PERSONAL ORGANIZER BECAUSE THERE WERE ONLY TWENTY ADDRESS PAGES. THE CHECK-OUT GIRL, OR I SHOULD SAY CHECK-OUT HAG, WAS ALL "NO CASH REFUNDS"...
WHAT DID SHE SAY?
NOTHING... EXCEPT "BE CAREFUL, YOU DON'T WANT TO MAKE HER ANGRY."
...I TOLD HER TWENTY PAGES MIGHT BE SUFFICIENT FOR HER, BUT FOR SOMEONE AS POPULAR AS MYSELF...
CORDELIA!
WE APPRECIATE THE RUN-DOWN ON THE POST-CHRISTMAS GIFT RETURN SITUATION.
Ex-CUUSE me.
SO, WHAT EXACTLY HAPPENED THAT NIGHT?
LIKE I TOLD YOU, WILL CALLS ME UP IN THE MIDDLE OF THE NIGHT, ALL FREAKED OUT. OZ HAS BUSTED OUT OF HIS MANACLES AND IS AN AMERICAN WEREWOLF IN SUNNYDALE.

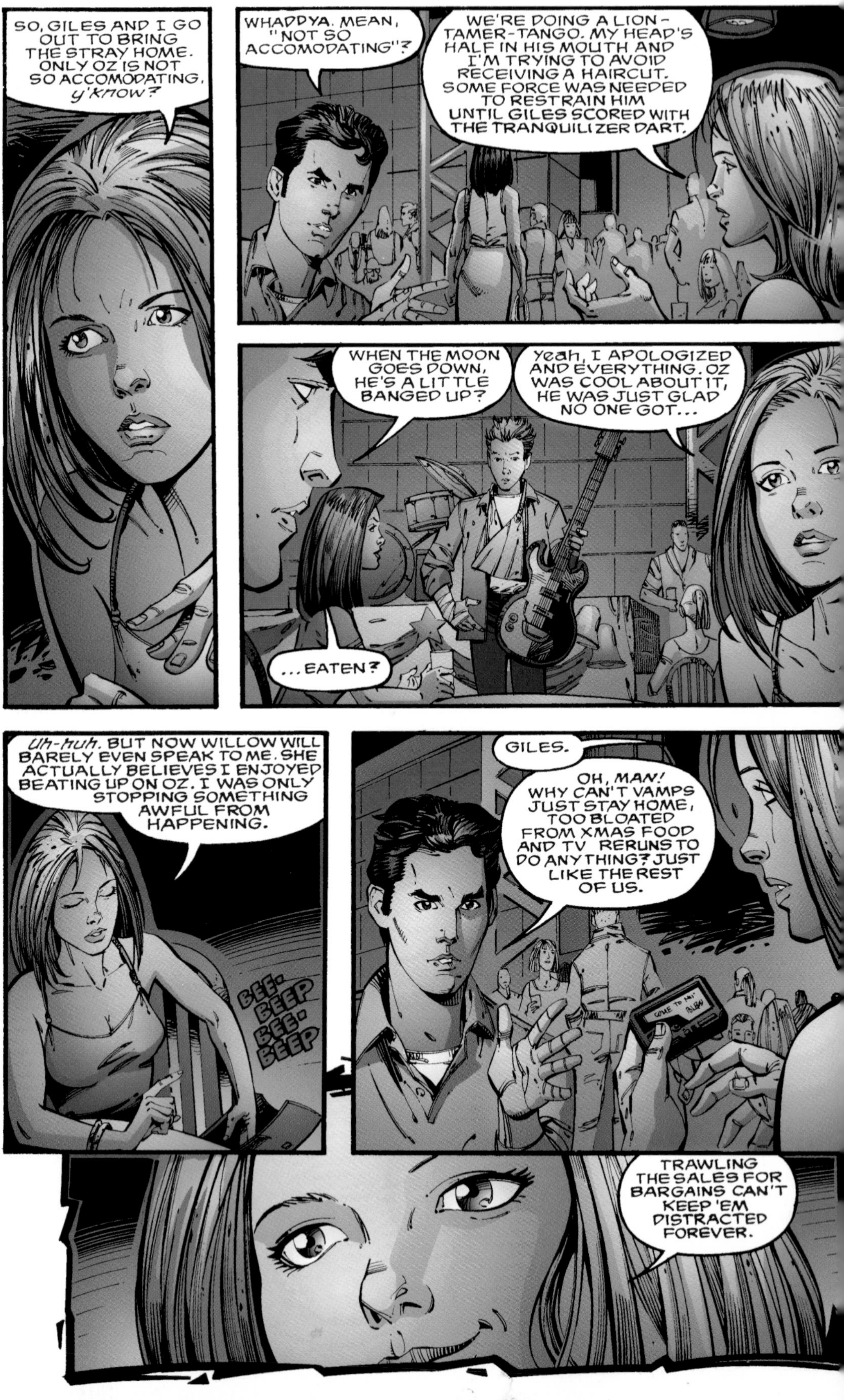
SO, GILES AND I GO OUT TO BRING THE STRAY HOME. ONLY OZ IS NOT SO ACCOMODATING, y'KNOW?
WHADDYA. MEAN, "NOT SO ACCOMODATING"?
WE'RE DOING A LION-TAMER-TANGO. MY HEAD'S HALF IN HIS MOUTH AND I'M TRYING TO AVOID RECEIVING A HAIRCUT. SOME FORCE WAS NEEDED TO RESTRAIN HIM UNTIL GILES SCORED WITH THE TRANQUILIZER DART.
WHEN THE MOON GOES DOWN, HE'S A LITTLE BANGED UP?
yeah, I APOLOGIZED AND EVERYTHING. OZ WAS COOL ABOUT IT, HE WAS JUST GLAD NO ONE GOT...
...EATEN?
Uh-huh. BUT NOW WILLOW WILL BARELY EVEN SPEAK TO ME. SHE ACTUALLY BELIEVES I ENJOYED BEATING UP ON OZ. I WAS ONLY STOPPING SOMETHING AWFUL FROM HAPPENING.
BEE-BEEP BEE-BEEP
GILES.
OH, MAN! WHY CAN'T VAMPS JUST STAY HOME, TOO BLOATED FROM XMAS FOOD AND TV RERUNS TO DO ANYTHING? JUST LIKE THE REST OF US.
TRAWLING THE SALES FOR BARGAINS CAN'T KEEP 'EM DISTRACTED FOREVER.

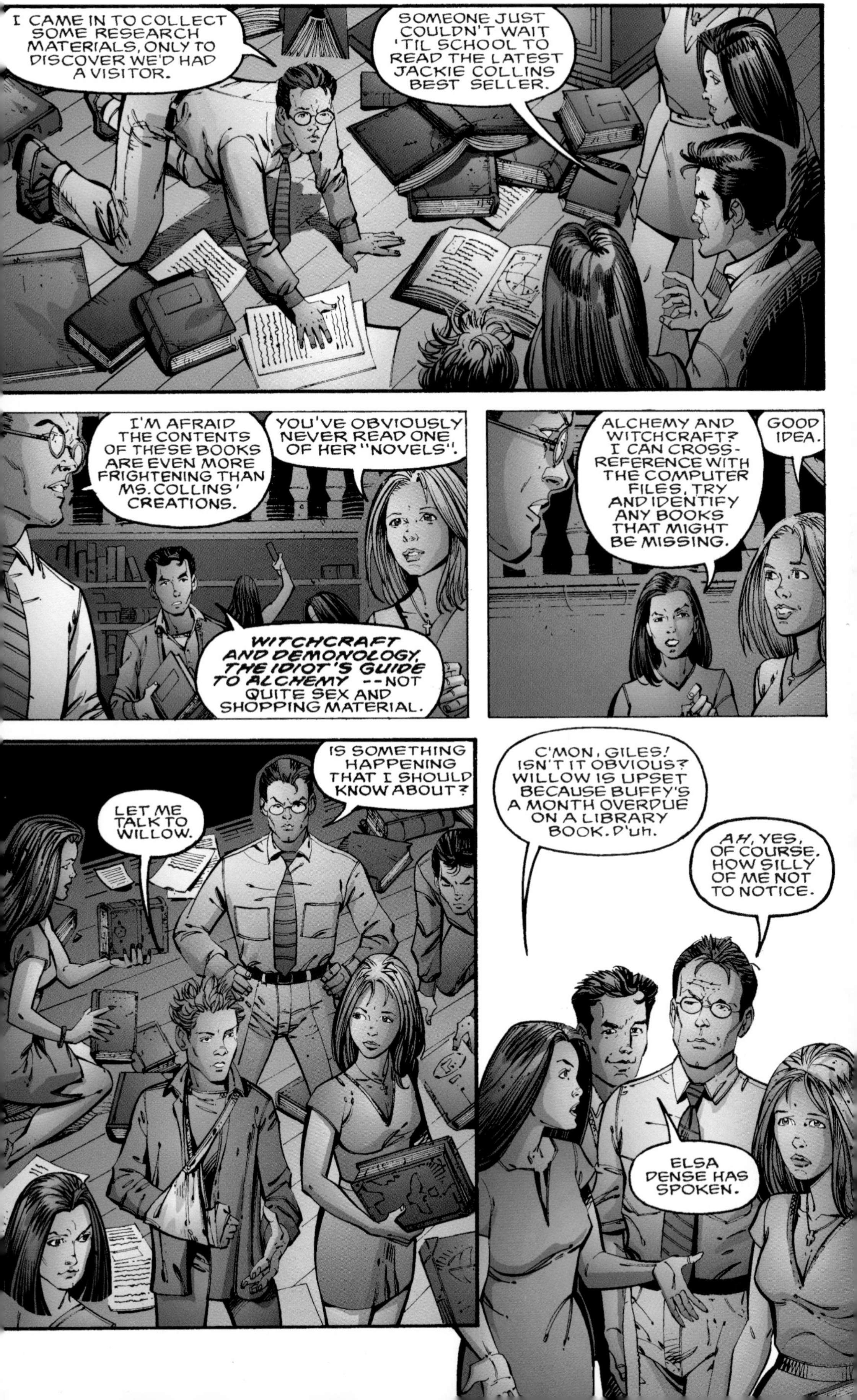

I CAME IN TO COLLECT SOME RESEARCH MATERIALS, ONLY TO DISCOVER WE'D HAD A VISITOR.
SOMEONE JUST COULDN'T WAIT 'TIL SCHOOL TO READ THE LATEST JACKIE COLLINS BEST SELLER.
I'M AFRAID THE CONTENTS OF THESE BOOKS ARE EVEN MORE FRIGHTENING THAN MS. COLLINS' CREATIONS.
YOU'VE OBVIOUSLY NEVER READ ONE OF HER "NOVELS".
WITCHCRAFT AND DEMONOLOGY, THE IDIOT'S GUIDE TO ALCHEMY --NOT QUITE SEX AND SHOPPING MATERIAL.
ALCHEMY AND WITCHCRAFT? I CAN CROSS-REFERENCE WITH THE COMPUTER FILES, TRY AND IDENTIFY ANY BOOKS THAT MIGHT BE MISSING.
GOOD IDEA.
IS SOMETHING HAPPENING THAT I SHOULD KNOW ABOUT?
LET ME TALK TO WILLOW.
C'MON, GILES! ISN'T IT OBVIOUS? WILLOW IS UPSET BECAUSE BUFFY'S A MONTH OVERDUE ON A LIBRARY BOOK. D'uh.
AH, YES, OF COURSE. HOW SILLY OF ME NOT TO NOTICE.
ELSA DENSE HAS SPOKEN.

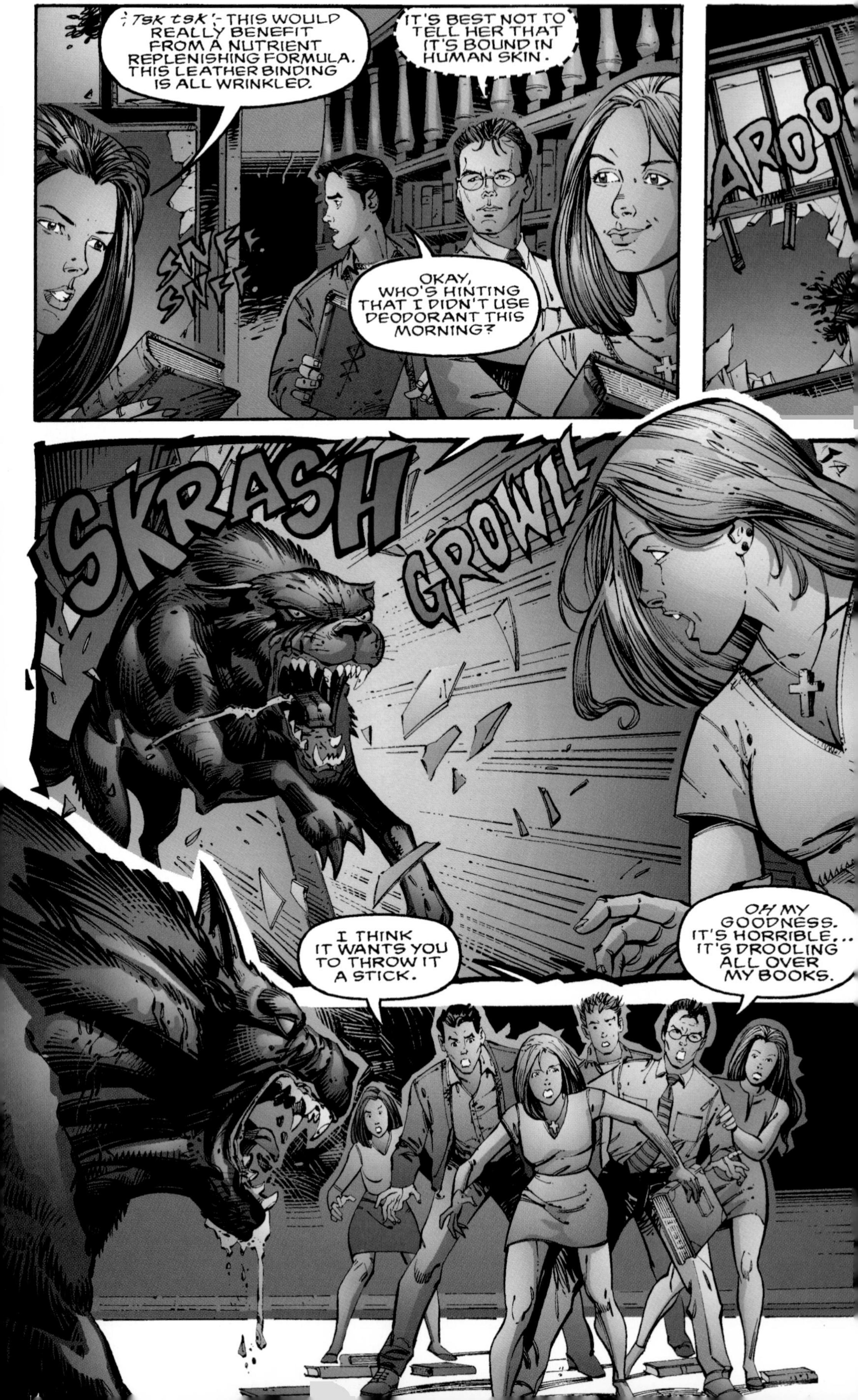

TSK TSK - THIS WOULD REALLY BENEFIT FROM A NUTRIENT REPLENISHING FORMULA. THIS LEATHER BINDING IS ALL WRINKLED.
IT'S BEST NOT TO TELL HER THAT IT'S BOUND IN HUMAN SKIN.
SNFF SNFF
OKAY, WHO'S HINTING THAT I DIDN'T USE DEODORANT THIS MORNING?
AROO
SKRASH
GROWLL
I THINK IT WANTS YOU TO THROW IT A STICK.
OH MY GOODNESS. IT'S HORRIBLE... IT'S DROOLING ALL OVER MY BOOKS.

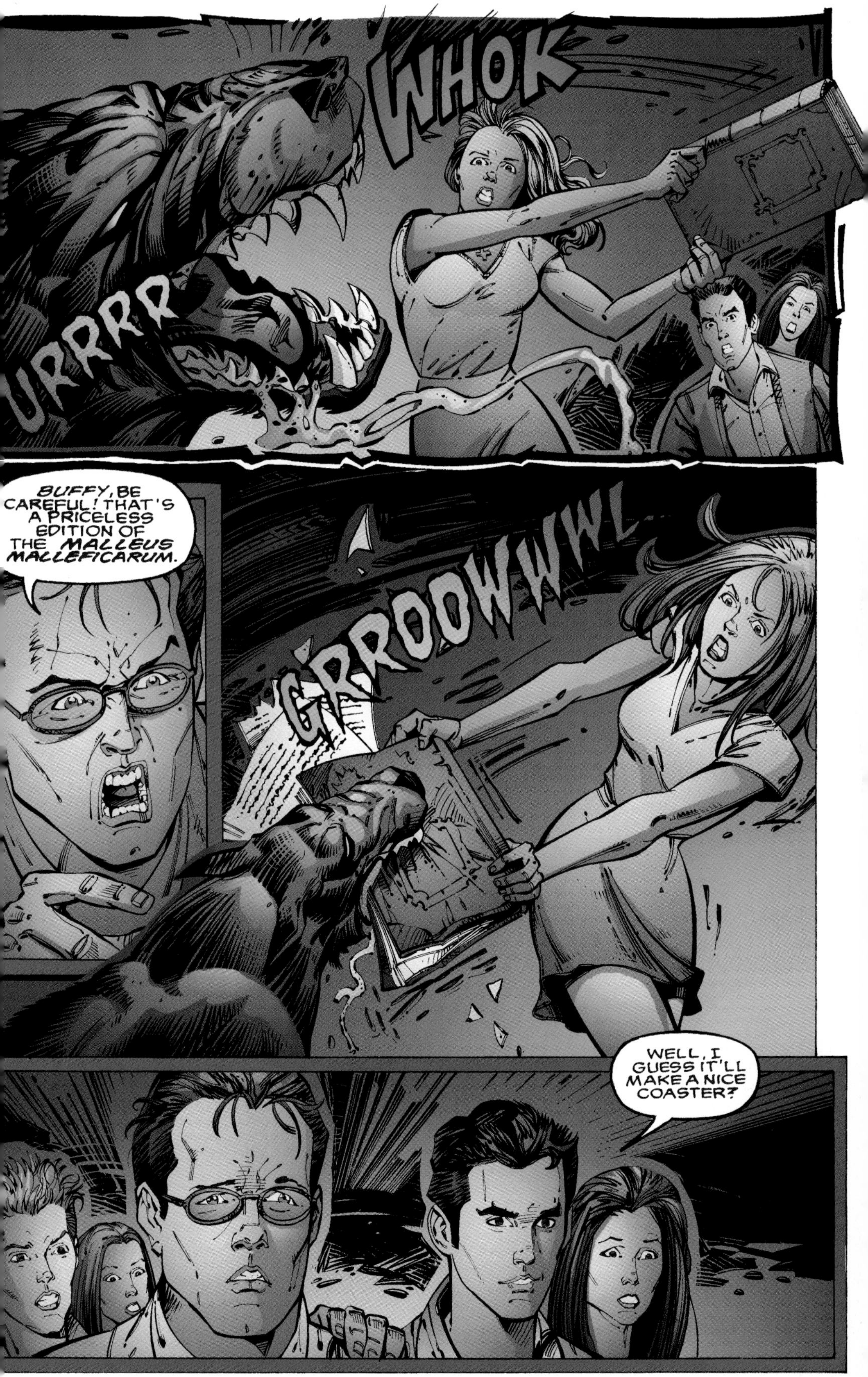
WHOK
URRRR
BUFFY, BE CAREFUL! THAT'S A PRICELESS EDITION OF THE MALLEUS MALLEFICARUM.
GRROOWWWL
WELL, I GUESS IT'LL MAKE A NICE COASTER?

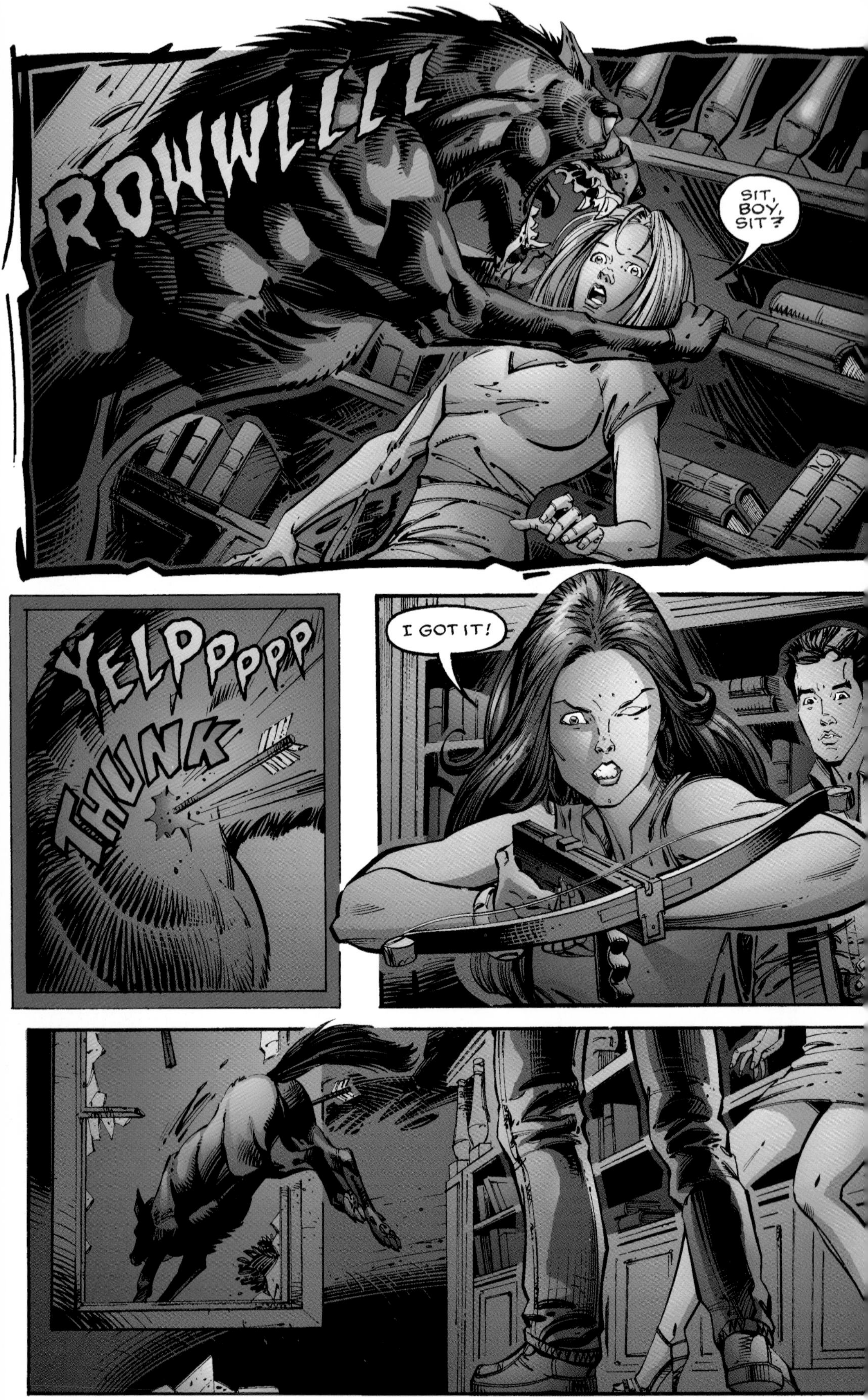
ROWWLLLL
SIT, BOY, SIT?
YELPPPPP
THUNK
I GOT IT!

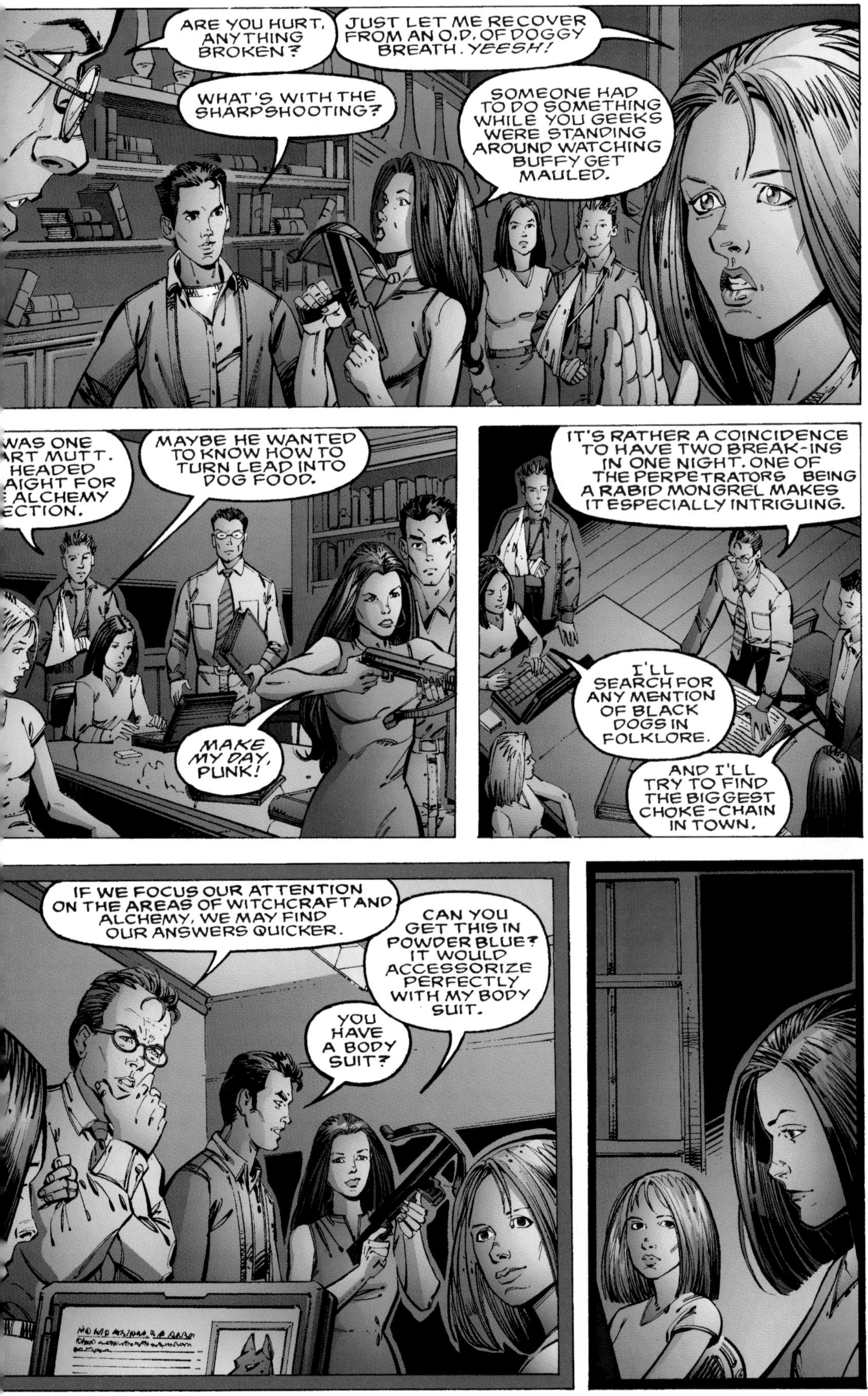

ARE YOU HURT, ANYTHING BROKEN?
JUST LET ME RECOVER FROM AN O.D. OF DOGGY BREATH. *YEESH!*
WHAT'S WITH THE SHARPSHOOTING?
SOMEONE HAD TO DO SOMETHING WHILE YOU GEEKS WERE STANDING AROUND WATCHING BUFFY GET MAULED.
WAS ONE ART MUTT. HEADED AIGHT FOR E ALCHEMY ECTION.
MAYBE HE WANTED TO KNOW HOW TO TURN LEAD INTO DOG FOOD.
MAKE MY DAY, PUNK!
IT'S RATHER A COINCIDENCE TO HAVE TWO BREAK-INS IN ONE NIGHT. ONE OF THE PERPETRATORS BEING A RABID MONGREL MAKES IT ESPECIALLY INTRIGUING.
I'LL SEARCH FOR ANY MENTION OF BLACK DOGS IN FOLKLORE.
AND I'LL TRY TO FIND THE BIGGEST CHOKE-CHAIN IN TOWN.
IF WE FOCUS OUR ATTENTION ON THE AREAS OF WITCHCRAFT AND ALCHEMY, WE MAY FIND OUR ANSWERS QUICKER.
CAN YOU GET THIS IN POWDER BLUE? IT WOULD ACCESSORIZE PERFECTLY WITH MY BODY SUIT.
YOU HAVE A BODY SUIT?

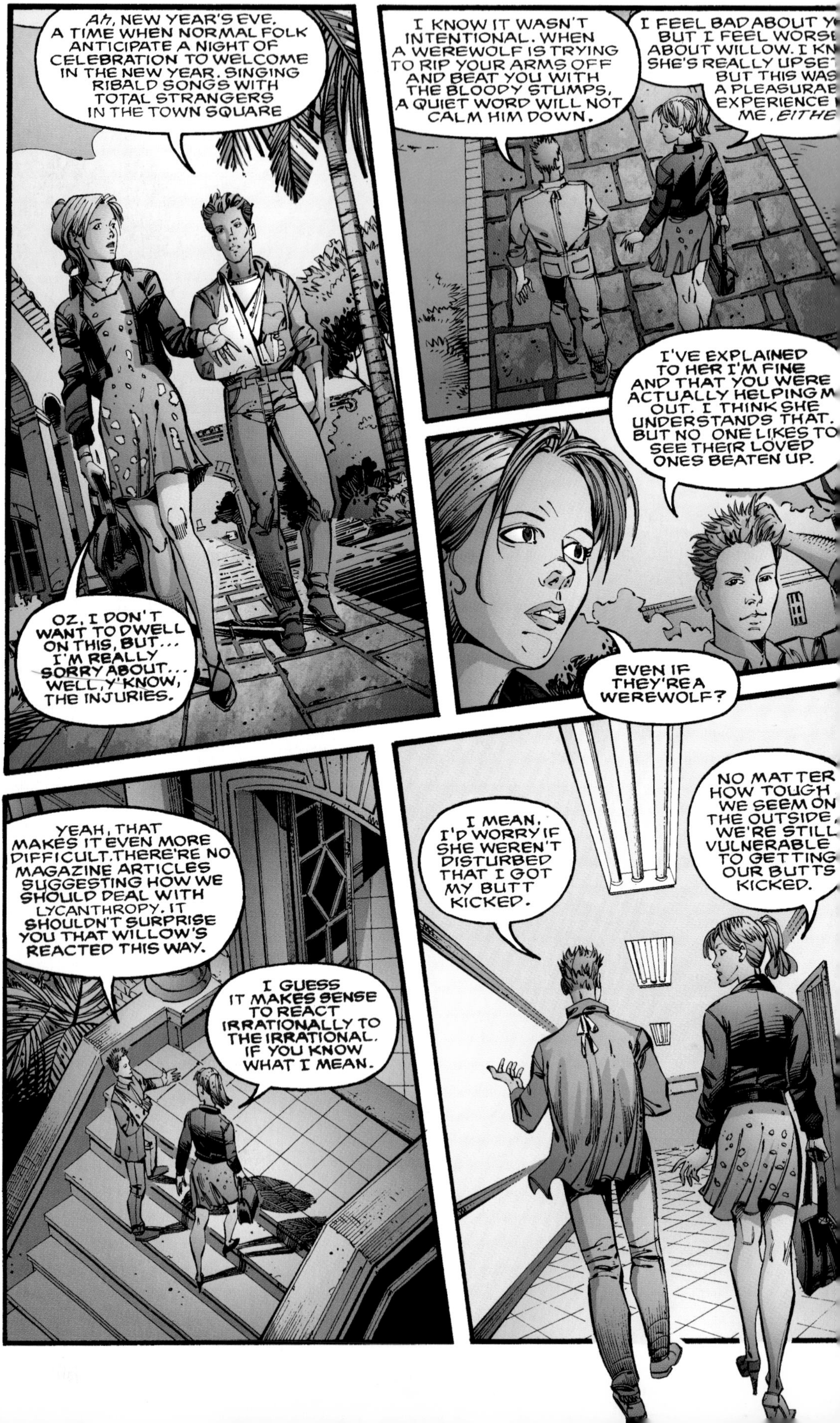
Ah, NEW YEAR'S EVE. A TIME WHEN NORMAL FOLK ANTICIPATE A NIGHT OF CELEBRATION TO WELCOME IN THE NEW YEAR. SINGING RIBALD SONGS WITH TOTAL STRANGERS IN THE TOWN SQUARE
OZ, I DON'T WANT TO DWELL ON THIS, BUT... I'M REALLY SORRY ABOUT... WELL, Y'KNOW, THE INJURIES.
I KNOW IT WASN'T INTENTIONAL. WHEN A WEREWOLF IS TRYING TO RIP YOUR ARMS OFF AND BEAT YOU WITH THE BLOODY STUMPS, A QUIET WORD WILL NOT CALM HIM DOWN.
I FEEL BAD ABOUT Y BUT I FEEL WORSE ABOUT WILLOW. I KN SHE'S REALLY UPSET BUT THIS WAS A PLEASURAB EXPERIENCE ME, EITHE
I'VE EXPLAINED TO HER I'M FINE AND THAT YOU WERE ACTUALLY HELPING M OUT. I THINK SHE UNDERSTANDS THAT. BUT NO ONE LIKES TO SEE THEIR LOVED ONES BEATEN UP.
EVEN IF THEY'RE A WEREWOLF?
YEAH, THAT MAKES IT EVEN MORE DIFFICULT. THERE'RE NO MAGAZINE ARTICLES SUGGESTING HOW WE SHOULD DEAL WITH LYCANTHROPY. IT SHOULDN'T SURPRISE YOU THAT WILLOW'S REACTED THIS WAY.
I GUESS IT MAKES SENSE TO REACT IRRATIONALLY TO THE IRRATIONAL. IF YOU KNOW WHAT I MEAN.
I MEAN, I'D WORRY IF SHE WEREN'T DISTURBED THAT I GOT MY BUTT KICKED.
NO MATTER HOW TOUGH WE SEEM ON THE OUTSIDE, WE'RE STILL VULNERABLE TO GETTING OUR BUTTS KICKED.

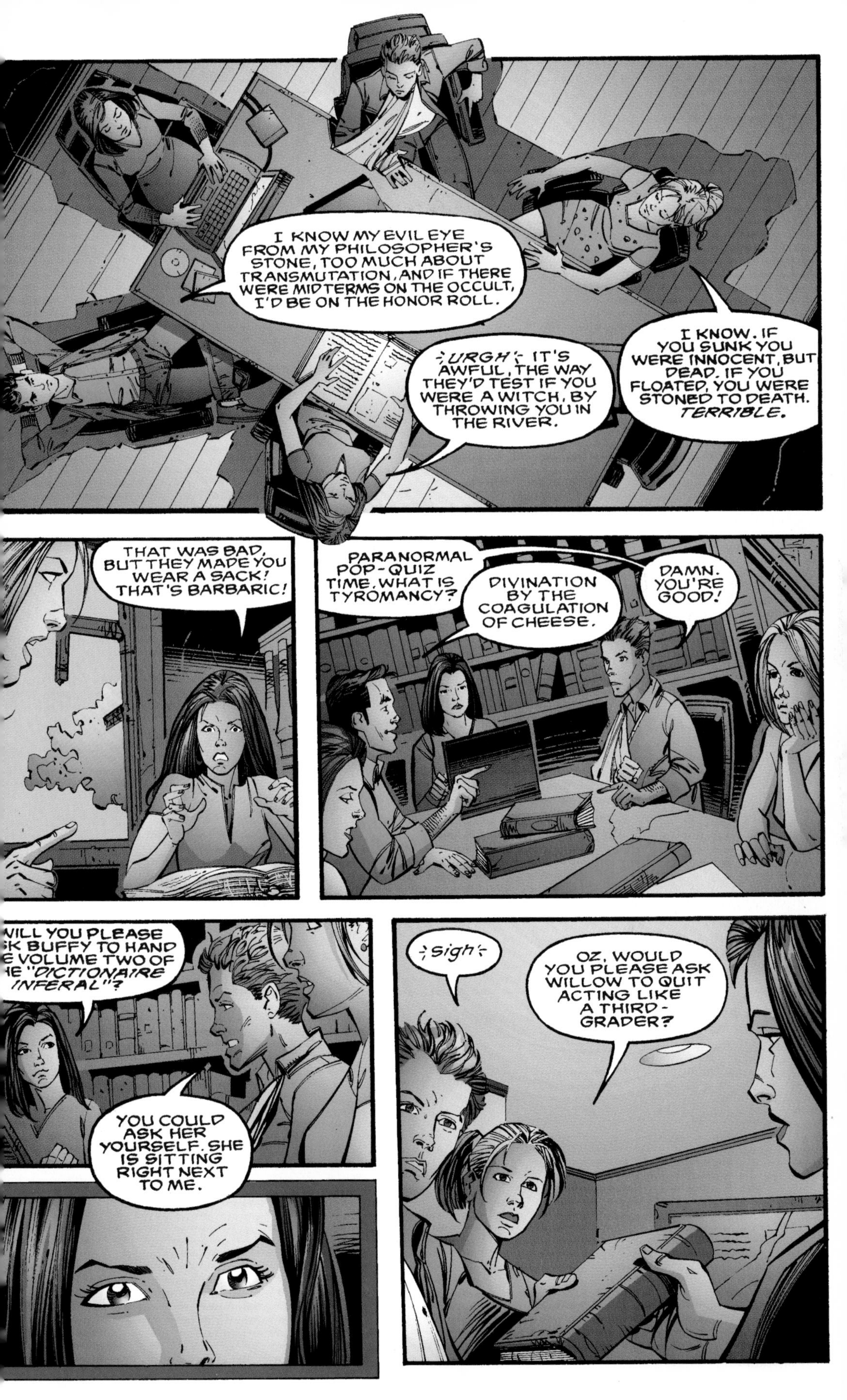

I KNOW MY EVIL EYE FROM MY PHILOSOPHER'S STONE, TOO MUCH ABOUT TRANSMUTATION, AND IF THERE WERE MIDTERMS ON THE OCCULT, I'D BE ON THE HONOR ROLL.
-URGH- IT'S AWFUL, THE WAY THEY'D TEST IF YOU WERE A WITCH, BY THROWING YOU IN THE RIVER.
I KNOW. IF YOU SUNK YOU WERE INNOCENT, BUT DEAD. IF YOU FLOATED, YOU WERE STONED TO DEATH. TERRIBLE.
THAT WAS BAD, BUT THEY MADE YOU WEAR A SACK! THAT'S BARBARIC!
PARANORMAL POP-QUIZ TIME. WHAT IS TYROMANCY?
DIVINATION BY THE COAGULATION OF CHEESE.
DAMN. YOU'RE GOOD!
WILL YOU PLEASE ASK BUFFY TO HAND ME VOLUME TWO OF THE "DICTIONAIRE INFERAL"?
YOU COULD ASK HER YOURSELF. SHE IS SITTING RIGHT NEXT TO ME.
-sigh-
OZ, WOULD YOU PLEASE ASK WILLOW TO QUIT ACTING LIKE A THIRD-GRADER?

OZ, *PLEASE* ASK BUFFY IF SHE INTENDS TO MAKE ME STOP. AFTER ALL, I WOULDN'T WANT TO CROSS THE *SLAYER*.

OZ, PLEASE INFORM WILLOW, IN CASE SHE ISN'T AWARE--SARCASM IS THE LOWEST FORM OF WIT.

WILL YOU TWO STOP THIS INFERNAL NONSENSE AT ONCE? OR DO I HAVE TO MAKE YOU BOTH STAND IN A CORNER? OR ARE WE GOING TO FIND THIS HELLHOUND AT LOOSE IN SUNNYVALE?

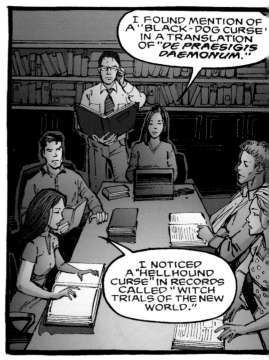

I FOUND MENTION OF A "BLACK-DOG CURSE" IN A TRANSLATION OF "*DE PRAESIGIS DAEMONUM.*"

I NOTICED A "HELLHOUND CURSE" IN RECORDS CALLED "WITCH TRIALS OF THE NEW WORLD."

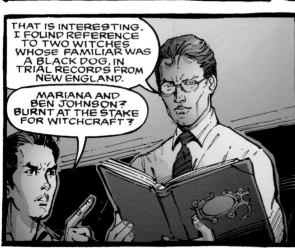

THAT IS INTERESTING. I FOUND REFERENCE TO TWO WITCHES WHOSE FAMILIAR WAS A BLACK DOG, IN TRIAL RECORDS FROM NEW ENGLAND.

MARIANA AND BEN JOHNSON? BURNT AT THE STAKE FOR WITCHCRAFT?

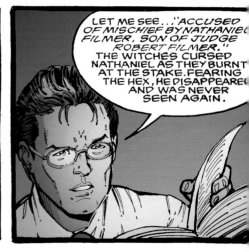

LET ME SEE..."ACCUSED OF MISCHIEF BY NATHANIEL FILMER, SON OF JUDGE ROBERT FILMER." THE WITCHES CURSED NATHANIEL AS THEY BURNT AT THE STAKE. FEARING THE HEX, HE DISAPPEARED AND WAS NEVER SEEN AGAIN.

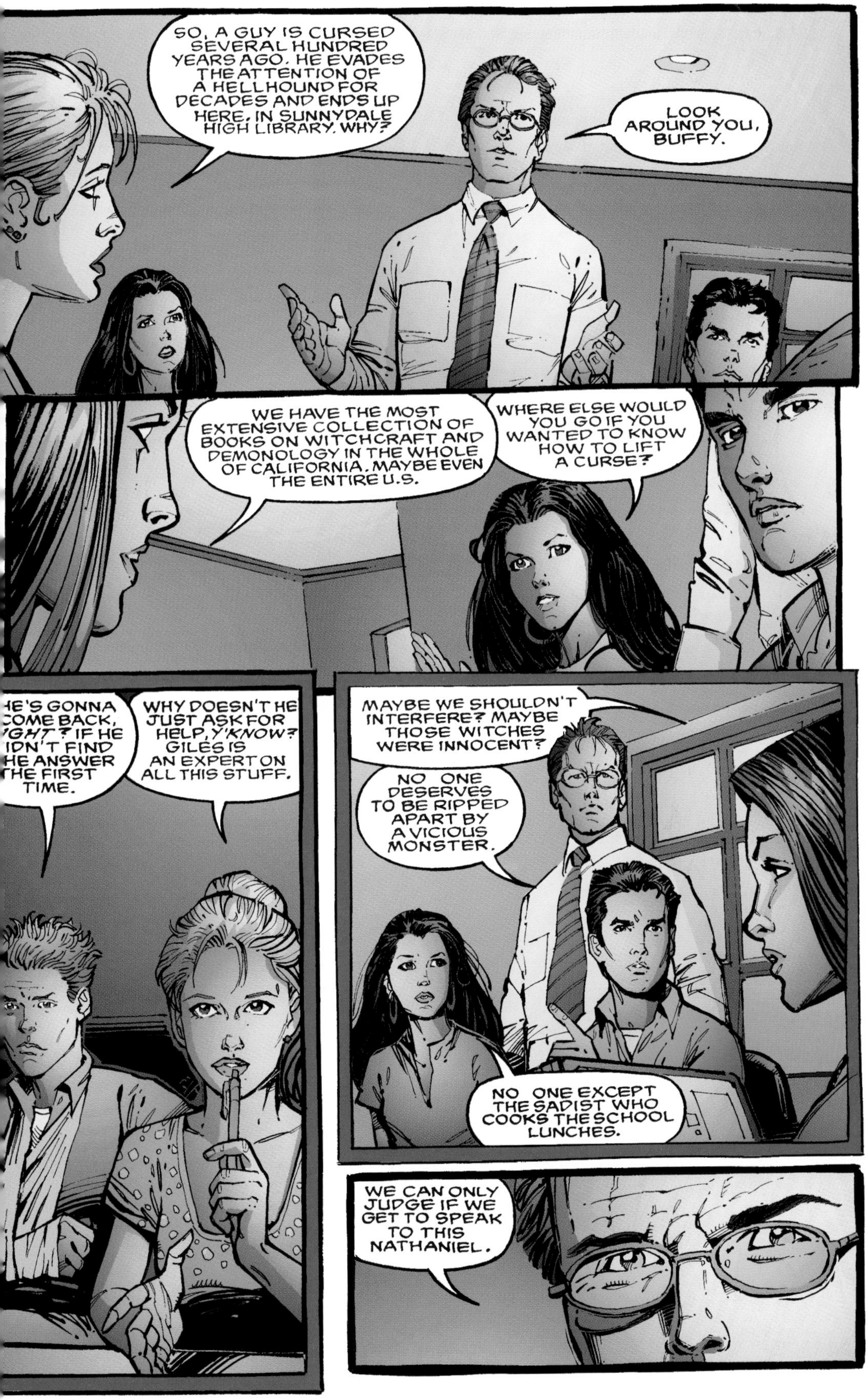
SO, A GUY IS CURSED SEVERAL HUNDRED YEARS AGO. HE EVADES THE ATTENTION OF A HELLHOUND FOR DECADES AND ENDS UP HERE, IN SUNNYDALE HIGH LIBRARY. WHY?
LOOK AROUND YOU, BUFFY.
WE HAVE THE MOST EXTENSIVE COLLECTION OF BOOKS ON WITCHCRAFT AND DEMONOLOGY IN THE WHOLE OF CALIFORNIA. MAYBE EVEN THE ENTIRE U.S.
WHERE ELSE WOULD YOU GO IF YOU WANTED TO KNOW HOW TO LIFT A CURSE?
E'S GONNA COME BACK, IGHT? IF HE IDN'T FIND HE ANSWER THE FIRST TIME.
WHY DOESN'T HE JUST ASK FOR HELP, Y'KNOW? GILES IS AN EXPERT ON ALL THIS STUFF.
MAYBE WE SHOULDN'T INTERFERE? MAYBE THOSE WITCHES WERE INNOCENT?
NO ONE DESERVES TO BE RIPPED APART BY A VICIOUS MONSTER.
NO ONE EXCEPT THE SADIST WHO COOKS THE SCHOOL LUNCHES.
WE CAN ONLY JUDGE IF WE GET TO SPEAK TO THIS NATHANIEL.

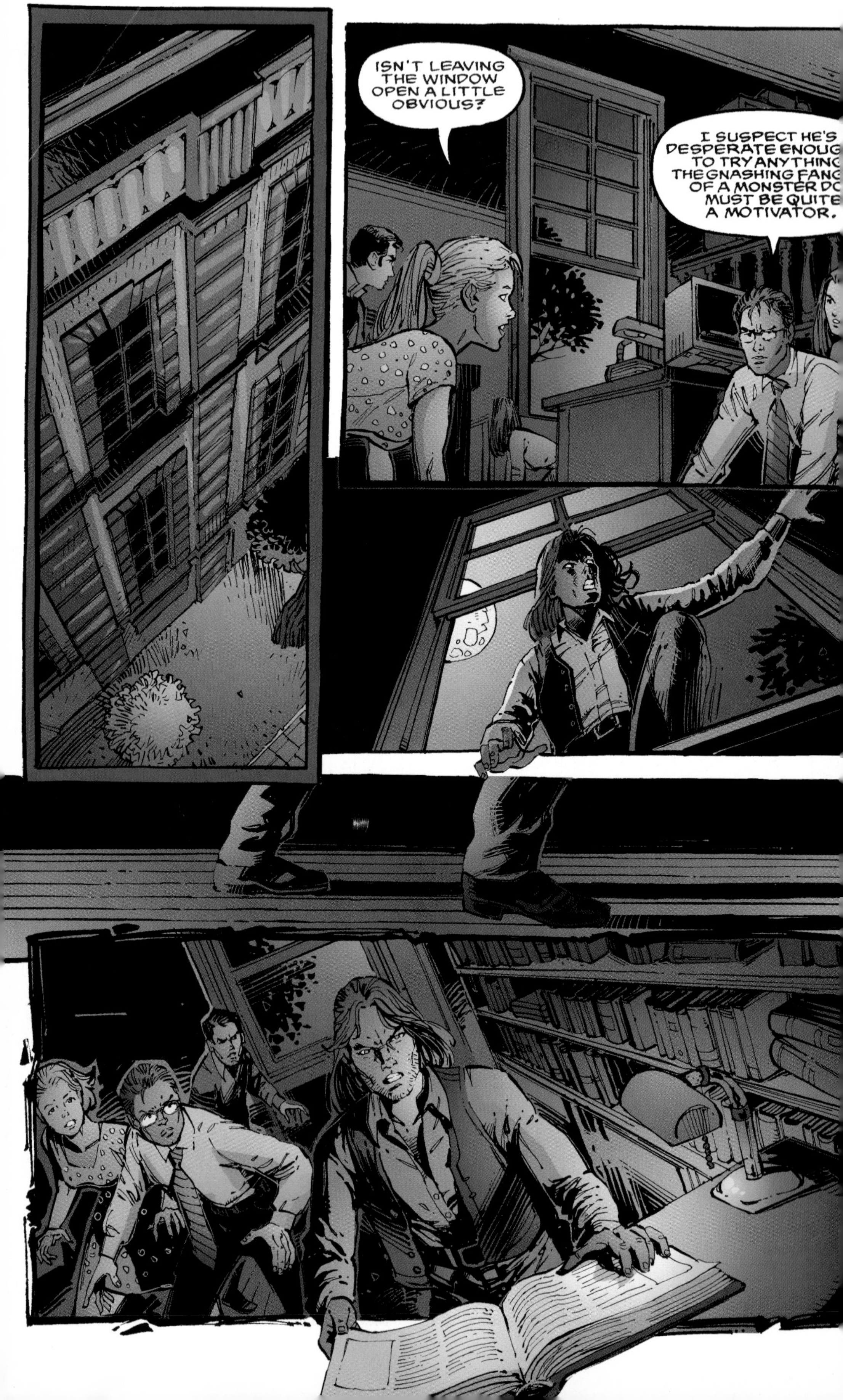
ISN'T LEAVING THE WINDOW OPEN A LITTLE OBVIOUS?
I SUSPECT HE'S DESPERATE ENOUG TO TRY ANYTHING THE GNASHING FANG OF A MONSTER DO MUST BE QUITE A MOTIVATOR.

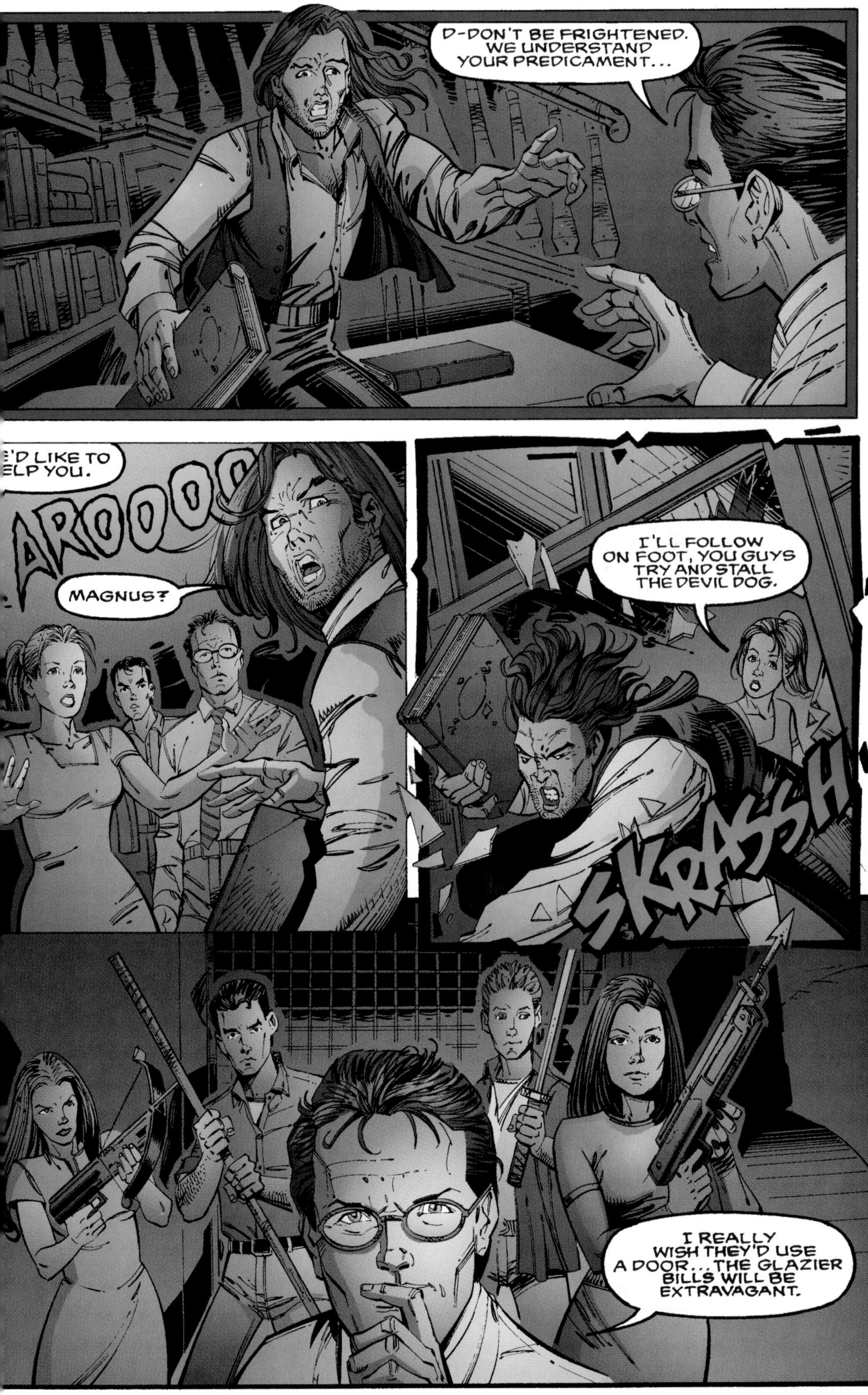
D-DON'T BE FRIGHTENED. WE UNDERSTAND YOUR PREDICAMENT...
'D LIKE TO ELP YOU.
AROOOO
MAGNUS?
I'LL FOLLOW ON FOOT, YOU GUYS TRY AND STALL THE DEVIL DOG.
SKRASSH!
I REALLY WISH THEY'D USE A DOOR... THE GLAZIER BILLS WILL BE EXTRAVAGANT.

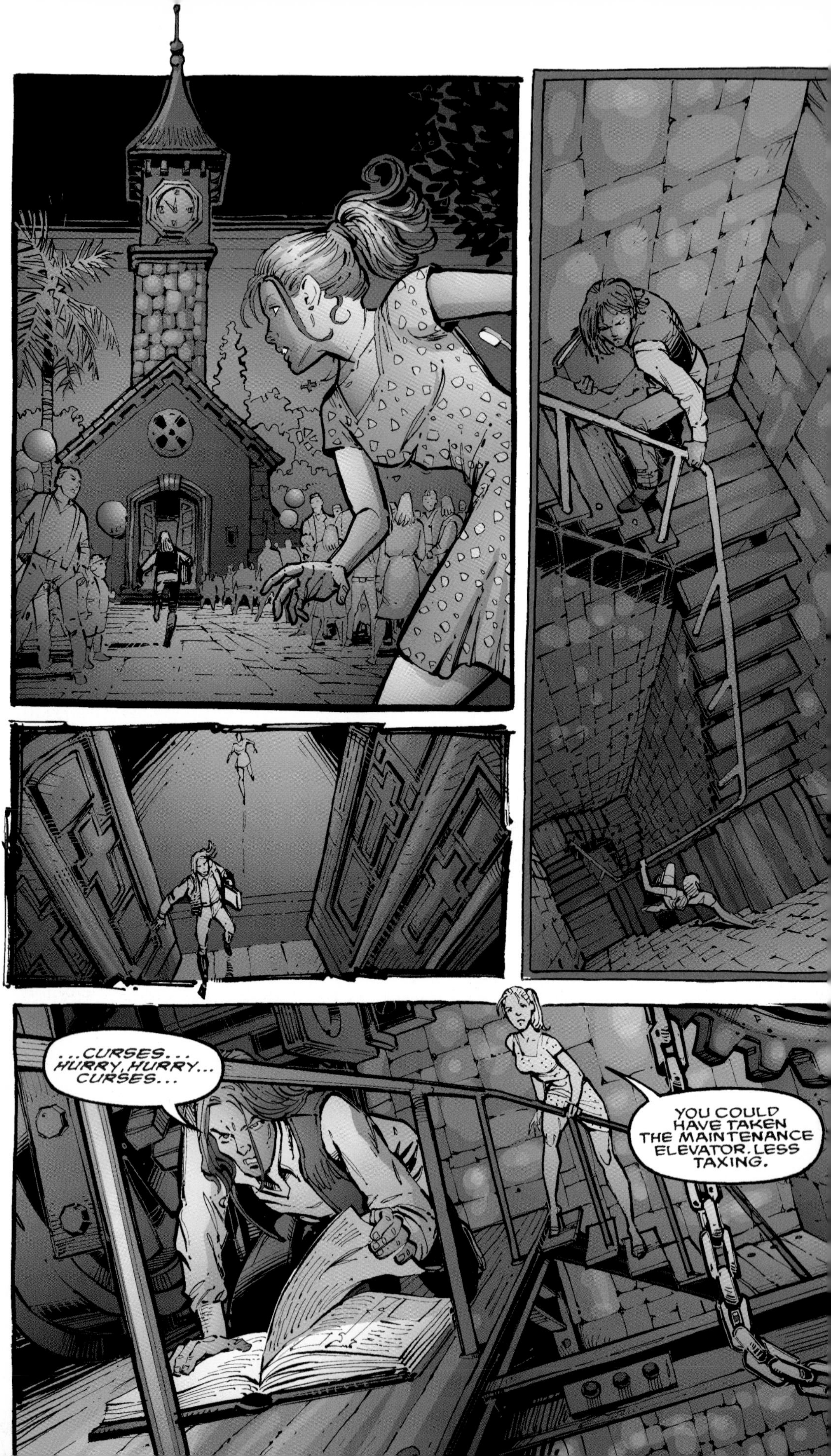
...CURSES...
HURRY, HURRY...
CURSES...
YOU COULD HAVE TAKEN THE MAINTENANCE ELEVATOR. LESS TAXING.

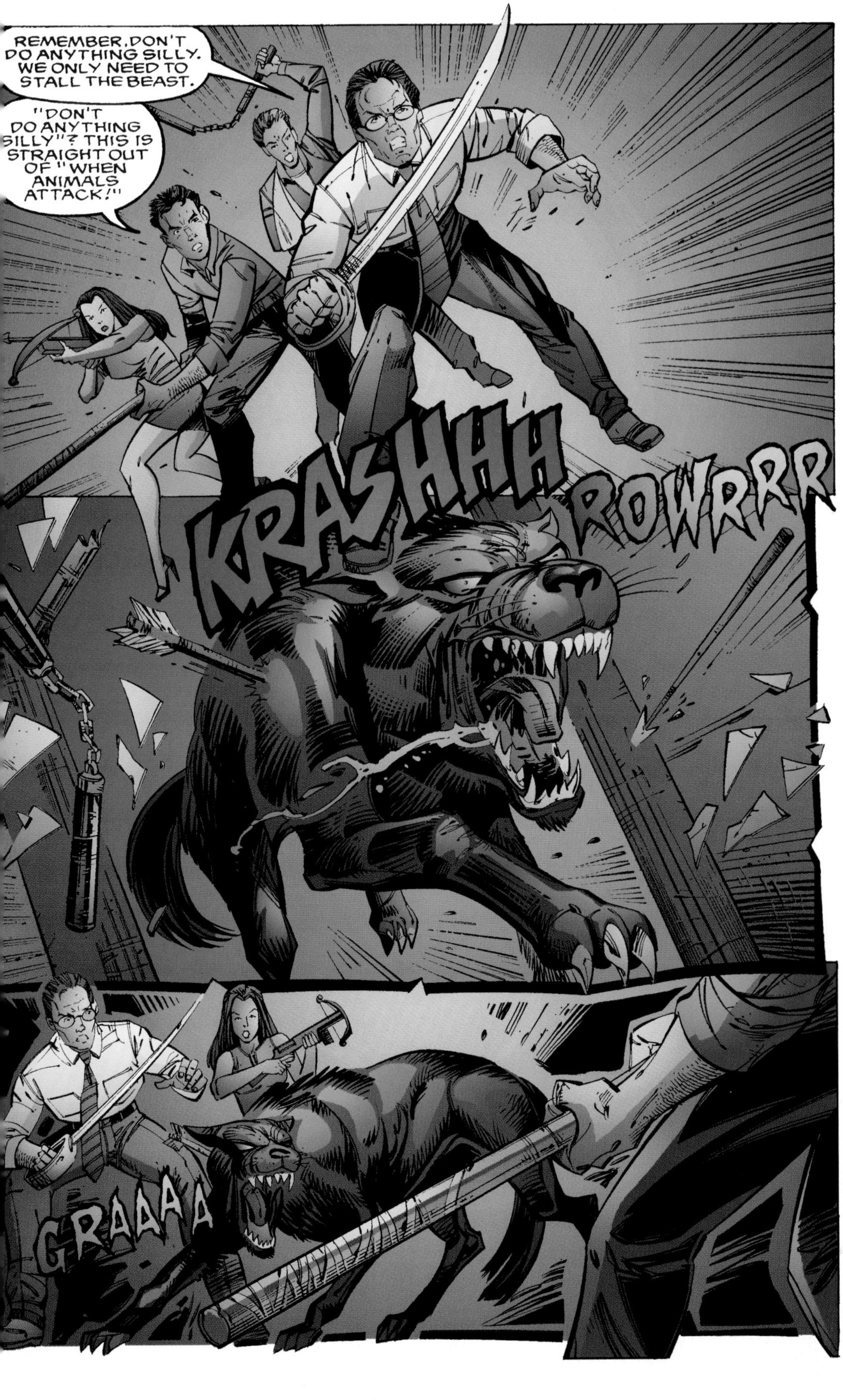
REMEMBER, DON'T DO ANYTHING SILLY. WE ONLY NEED TO STALL THE BEAST.
"DON'T DO ANYTHING SILLY"? THIS IS STRAIGHT OUT OF "WHEN ANIMALS ATTACK!"
KRASHHH
ROWRRR
GRAAAA

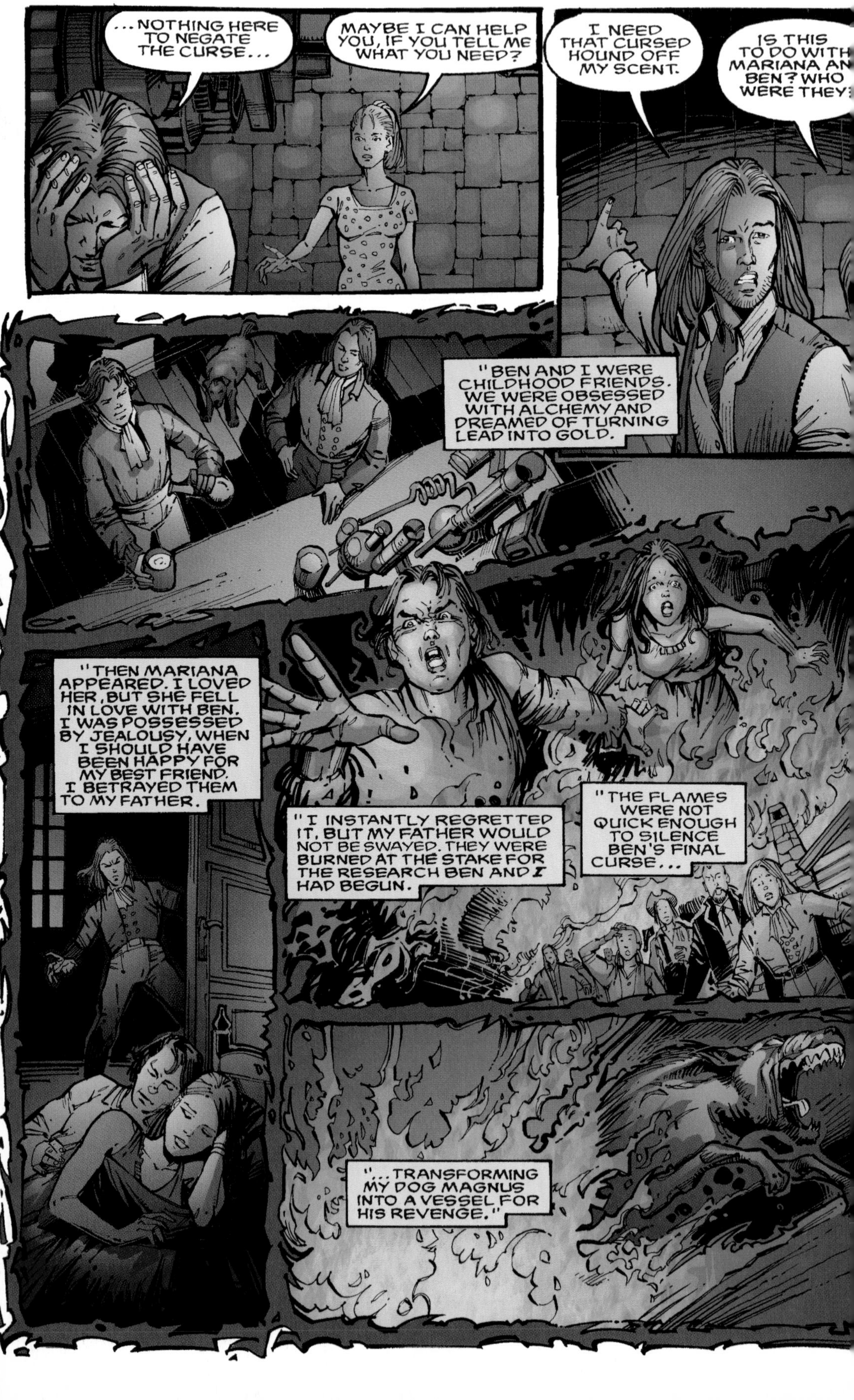
...NOTHING HERE TO NEGATE THE CURSE...
MAYBE I CAN HELP YOU, IF YOU TELL ME WHAT YOU NEED?
I NEED THAT CURSED HOUND OFF MY SCENT.
IS THIS TO DO WITH MARIANA AN BEN? WHO WERE THEY?
"BEN AND I WERE CHILDHOOD FRIENDS. WE WERE OBSESSED WITH ALCHEMY AND DREAMED OF TURNING LEAD INTO GOLD.
"THEN MARIANA APPEARED. I LOVED HER, BUT SHE FELL IN LOVE WITH BEN. I WAS POSSESSED BY JEALOUSY, WHEN I SHOULD HAVE BEEN HAPPY FOR MY BEST FRIEND. I BETRAYED THEM TO MY FATHER.
"I INSTANTLY REGRETTED IT, BUT MY FATHER WOULD NOT BE SWAYED. THEY WERE BURNED AT THE STAKE FOR THE RESEARCH BEN AND I HAD BEGUN.
"THE FLAMES WERE NOT QUICK ENOUGH TO SILENCE BEN'S FINAL CURSE...
"...TRANSFORMING MY DOG MAGNUS INTO A VESSEL FOR HIS REVENGE."

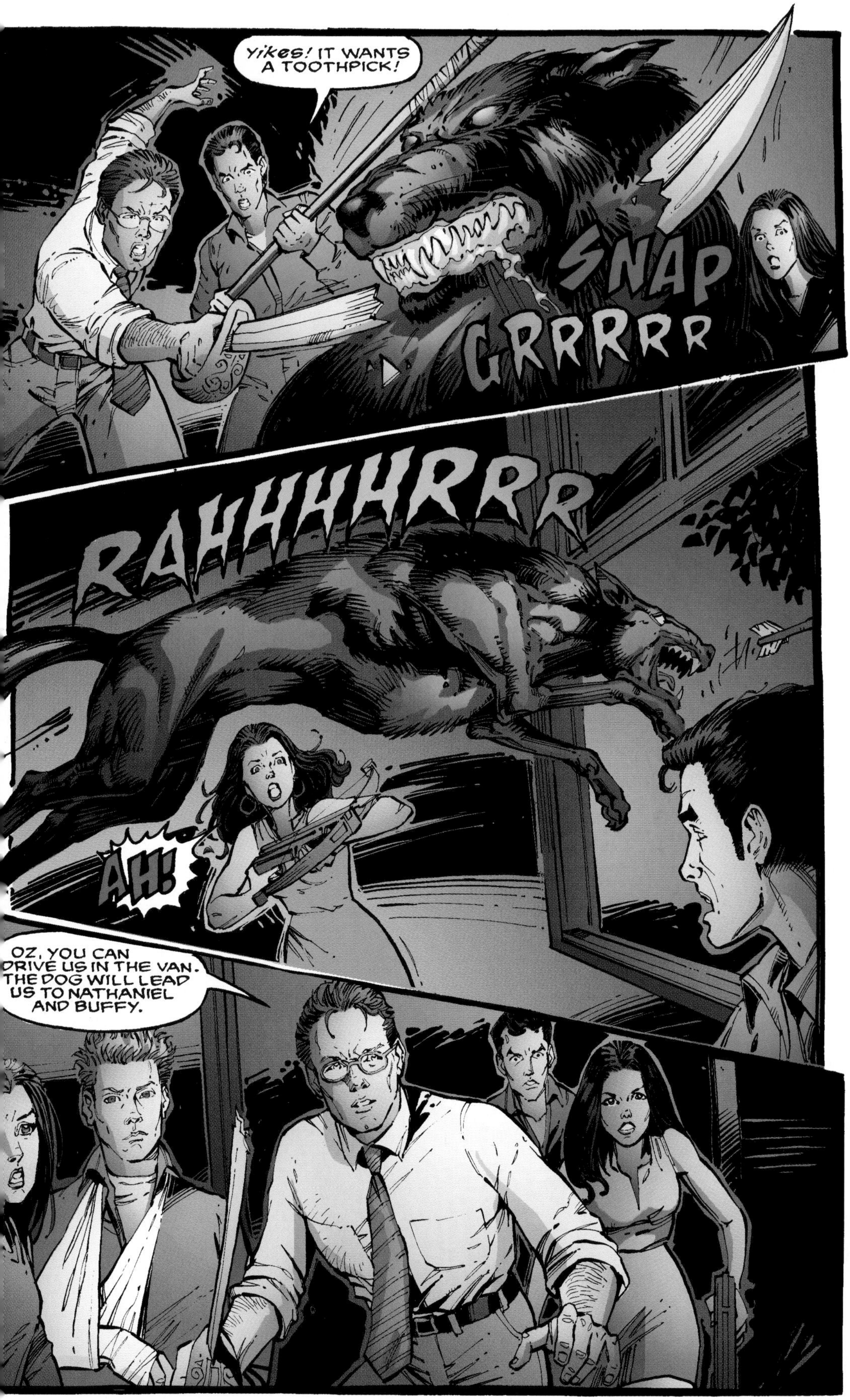
YIKES! IT WANTS A TOOTHPICK!
SNAP
GRRRRRR
RAHHHHRRRR
AH!
OZ, YOU CAN DRIVE US IN THE VAN. THE DOG WILL LEAD US TO NATHANIEL AND BUFFY.

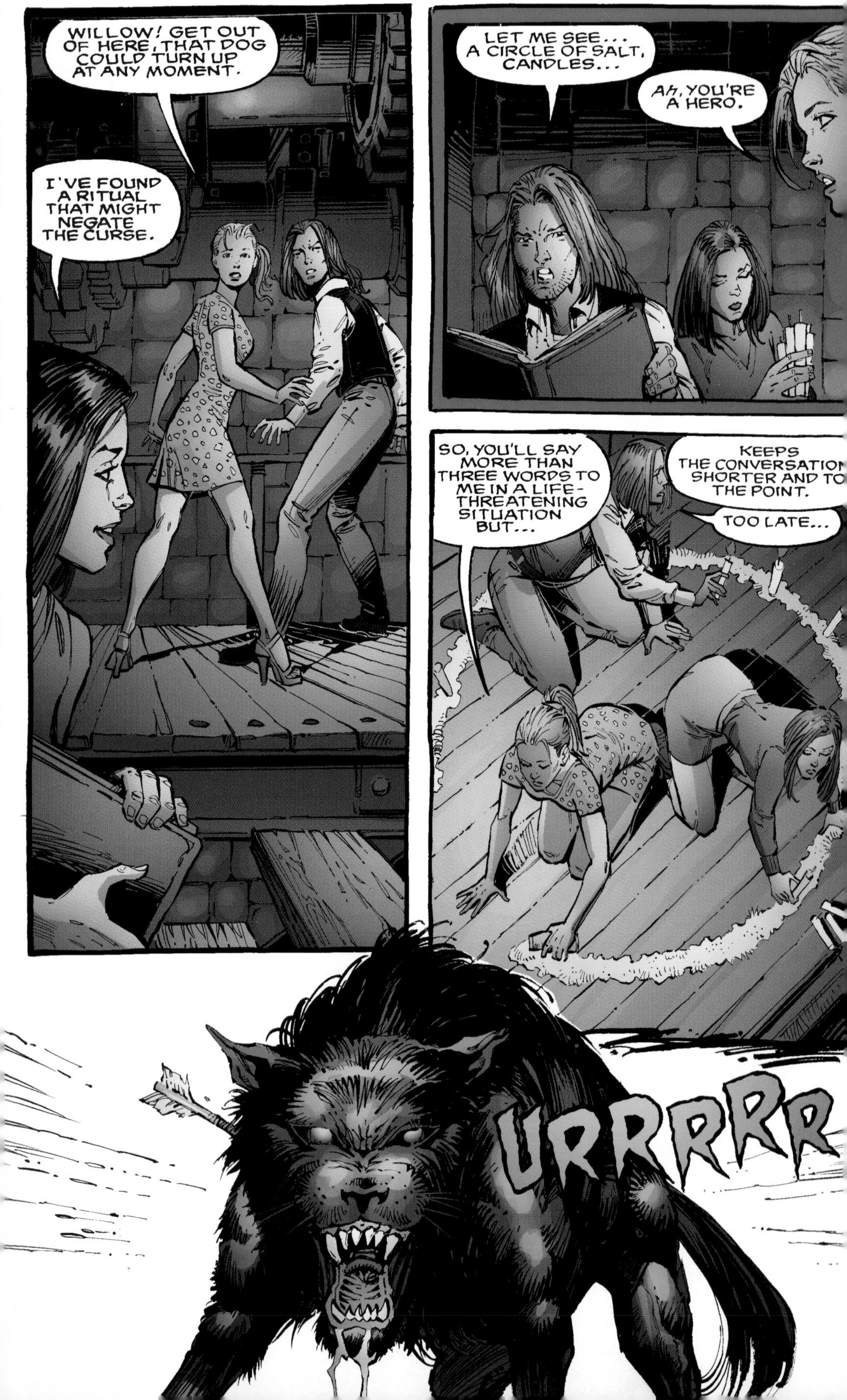
WILLOW! GET OUT OF HERE, THAT DOG COULD TURN UP AT ANY MOMENT.
I'VE FOUND A RITUAL THAT MIGHT NEGATE THE CURSE.
LET ME SEE... A CIRCLE OF SALT, CANDLES...
Ah, YOU'RE A HERO.
SO, YOU'LL SAY MORE THAN THREE WORDS TO ME IN A LIFE-THREATENING SITUATION BUT...
KEEPS THE CONVERSATION SHORTER AND TO THE POINT.
TOO LATE...
URRRRR

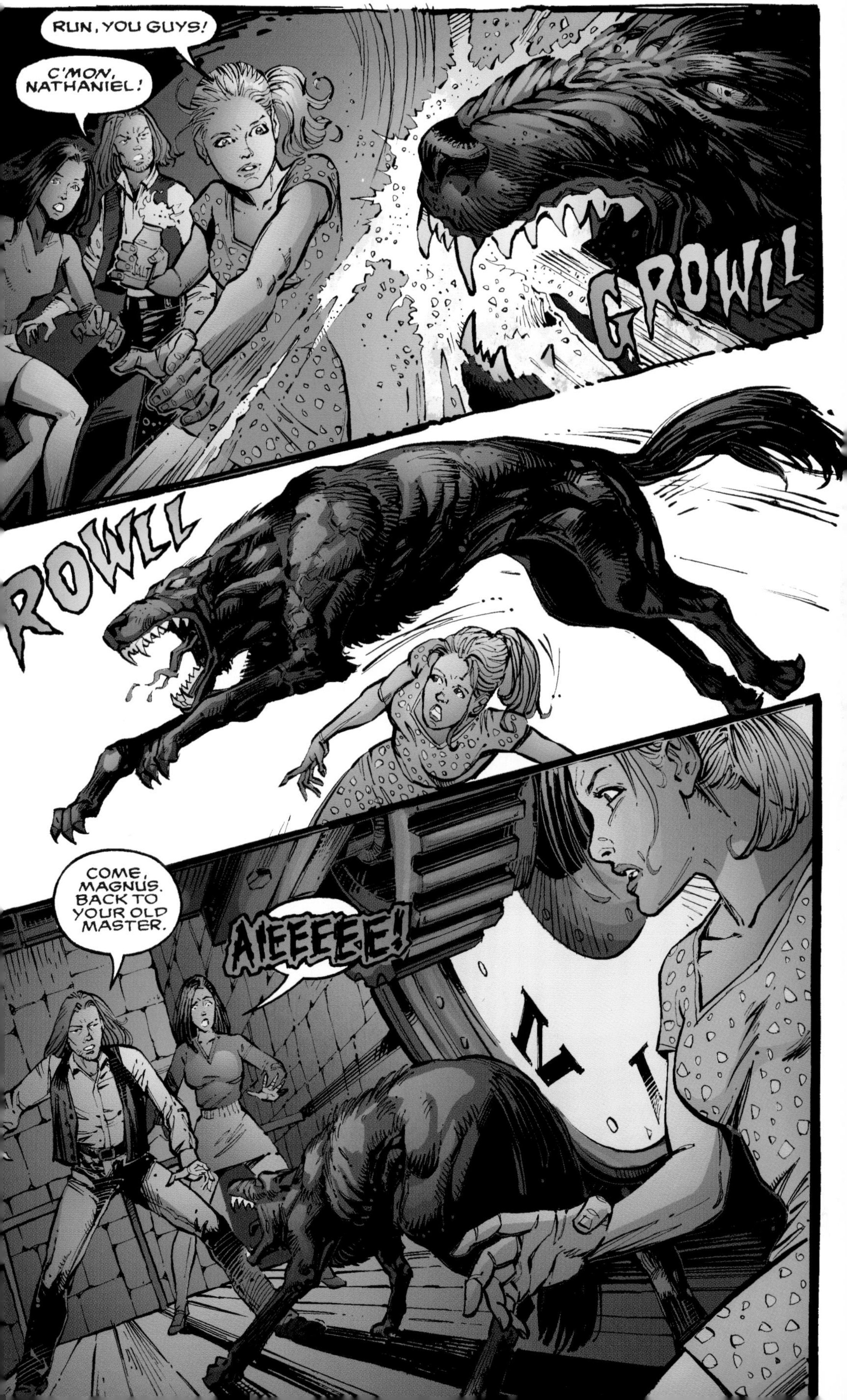
RUN, YOU GUYS!
C'MON, NATHANIEL!
GROWL
ROWLL
COME, MAGNUS. BACK TO YOUR OLD MASTER.
AIEEEEE!

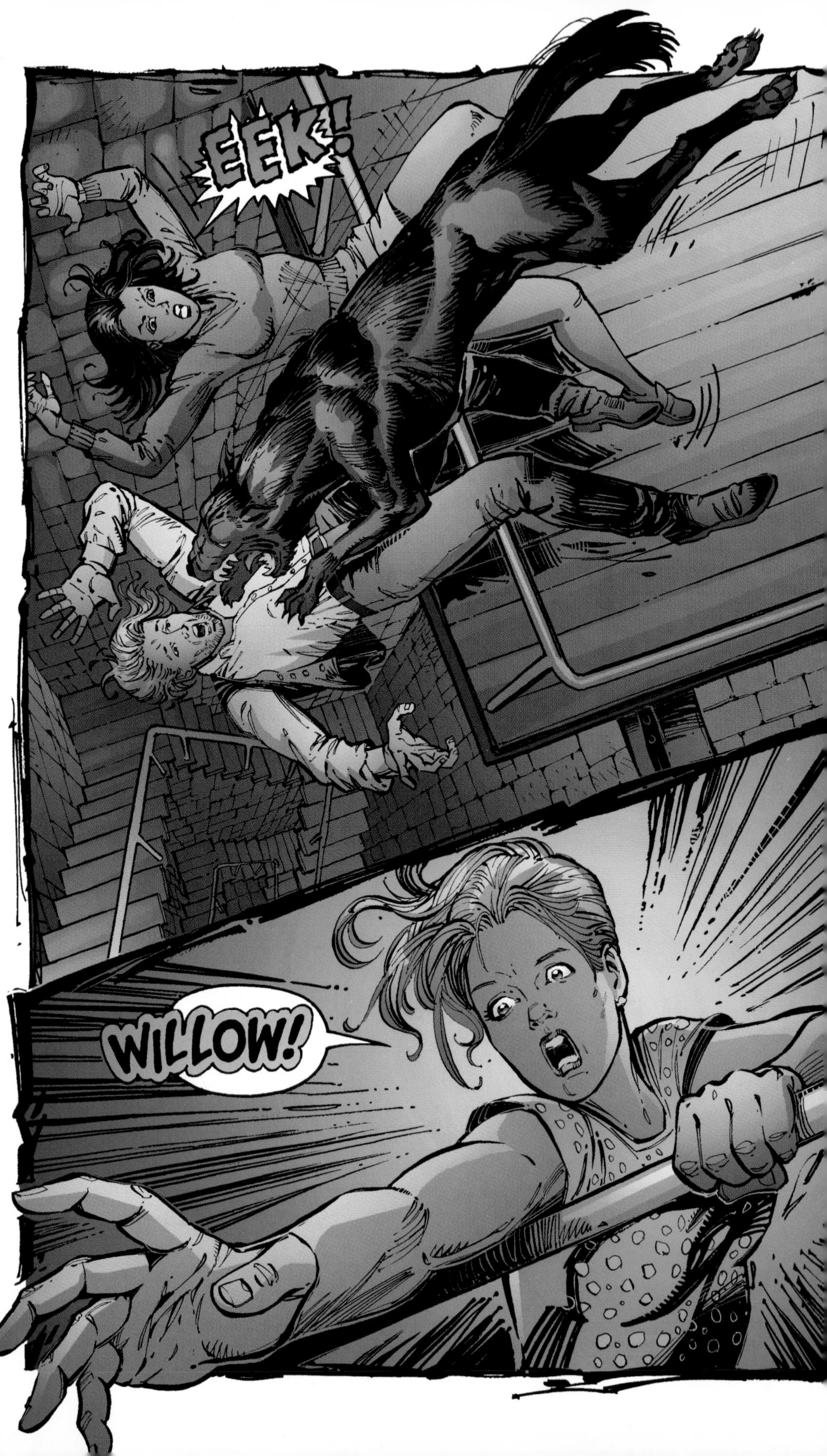
EEK!
WILLOW!

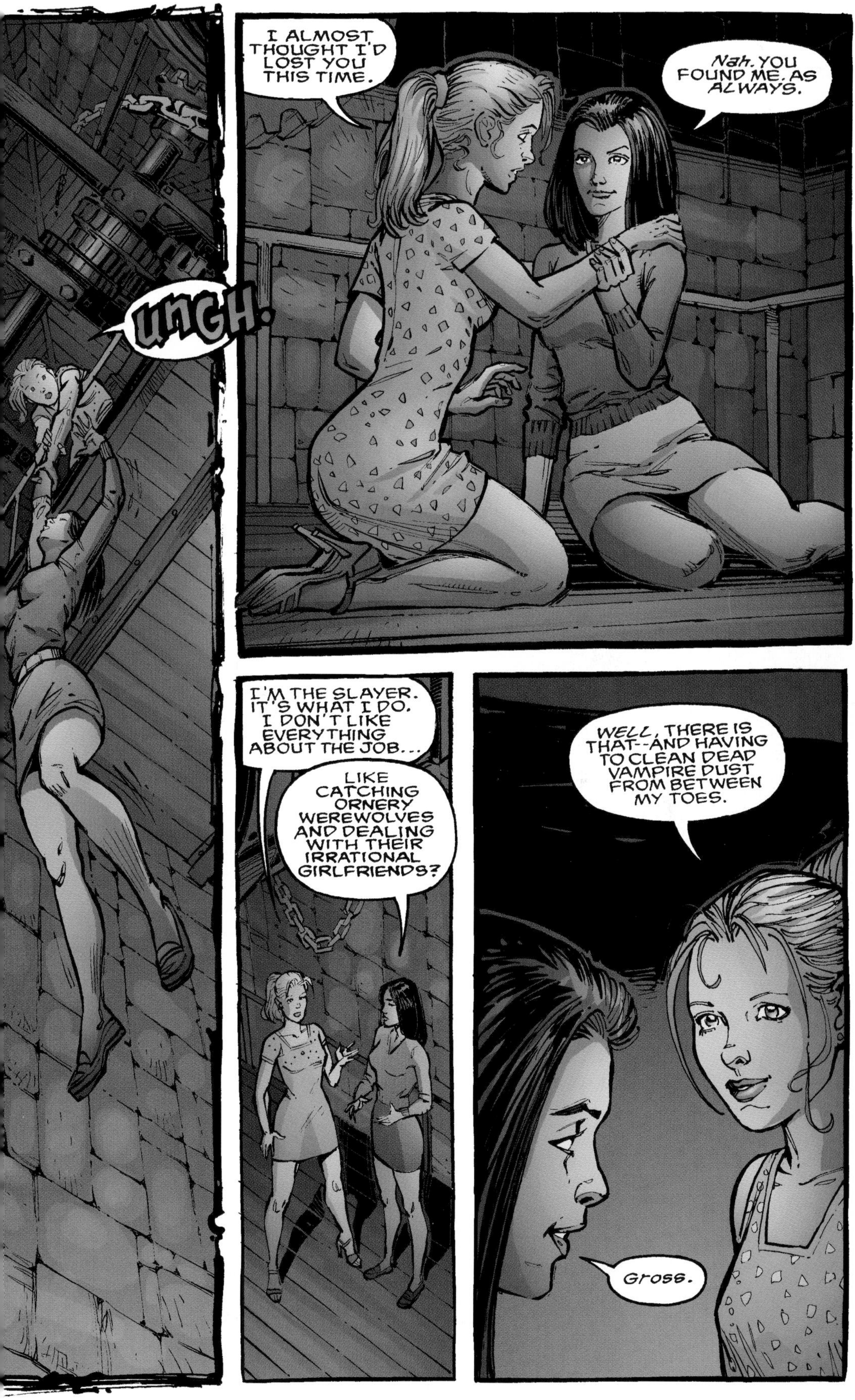
UNGH.
I ALMOST THOUGHT I'D LOST YOU THIS TIME.
Nah. YOU FOUND ME. AS ALWAYS.
I'M THE SLAYER. IT'S WHAT I DO. I DON'T LIKE EVERYTHING ABOUT THE JOB...
LIKE CATCHING ORNERY WEREWOLVES AND DEALING WITH THEIR IRRATIONAL GIRLFRIENDS?
WELL, THERE IS THAT--AND HAVING TO CLEAN DEAD VAMPIRE DUST FROM BETWEEN MY TOES.
Gross.

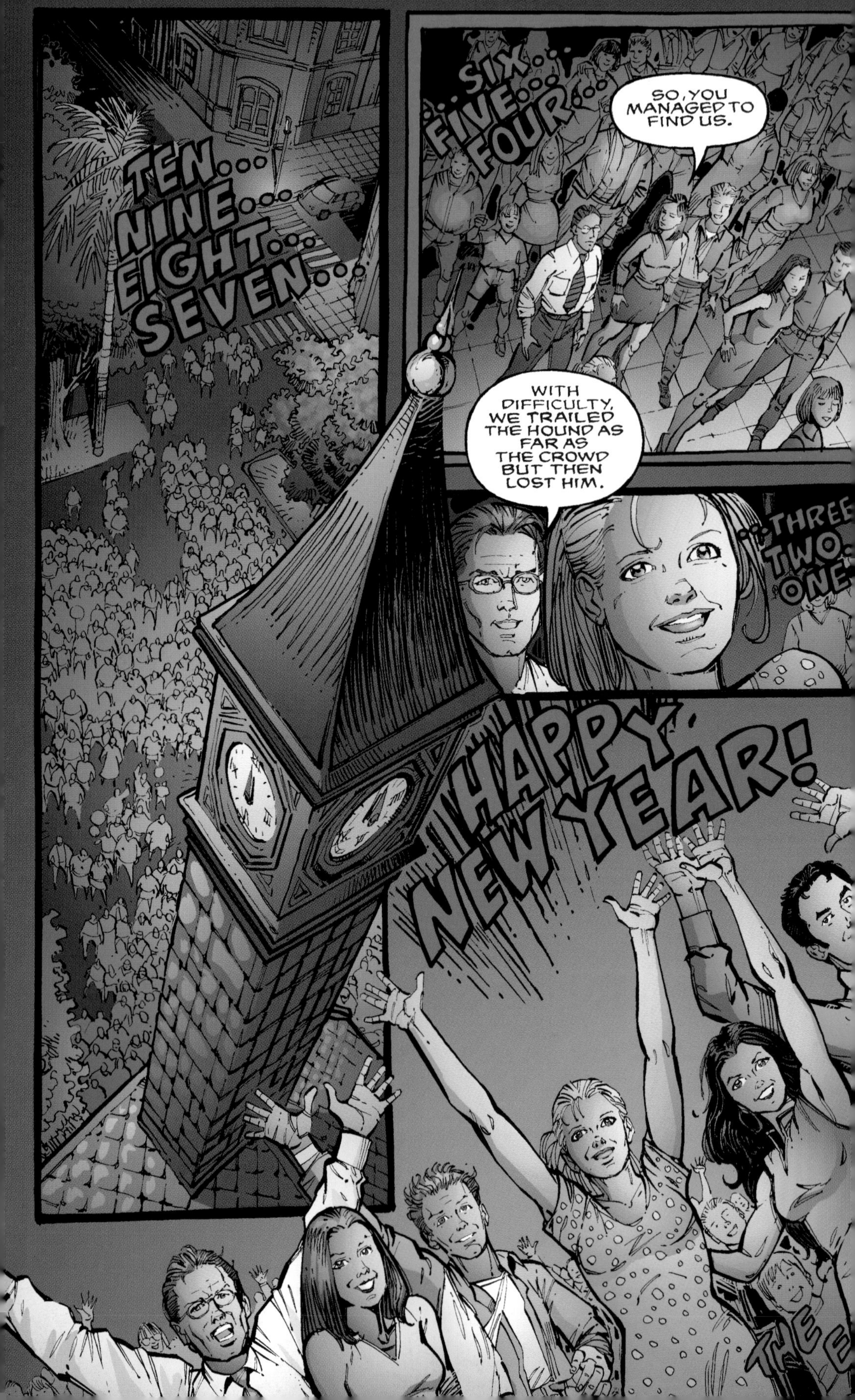
TEN... NINE... EIGHT... SEVEN...
...SIX... FIVE... FOUR...
SO, YOU MANAGED TO FIND US.
WITH DIFFICULTY. WE TRAILED THE HOUND AS FAR AS THE CROWD BUT THEN LOST HIM.
HAPPY NEW YEAR!

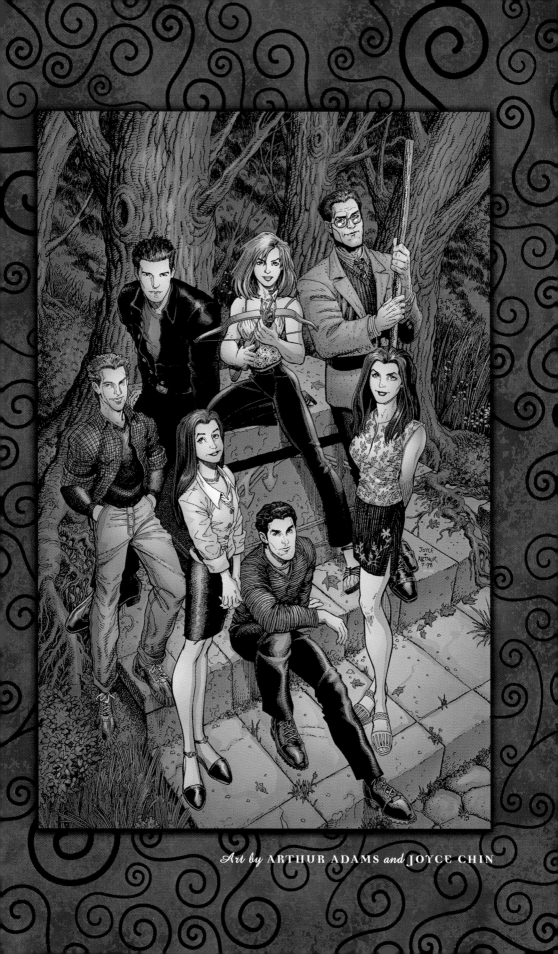

Art by ARTHUR ADAMS *and* JOYCE CHIN

New Kid
on the Block

chapter 1

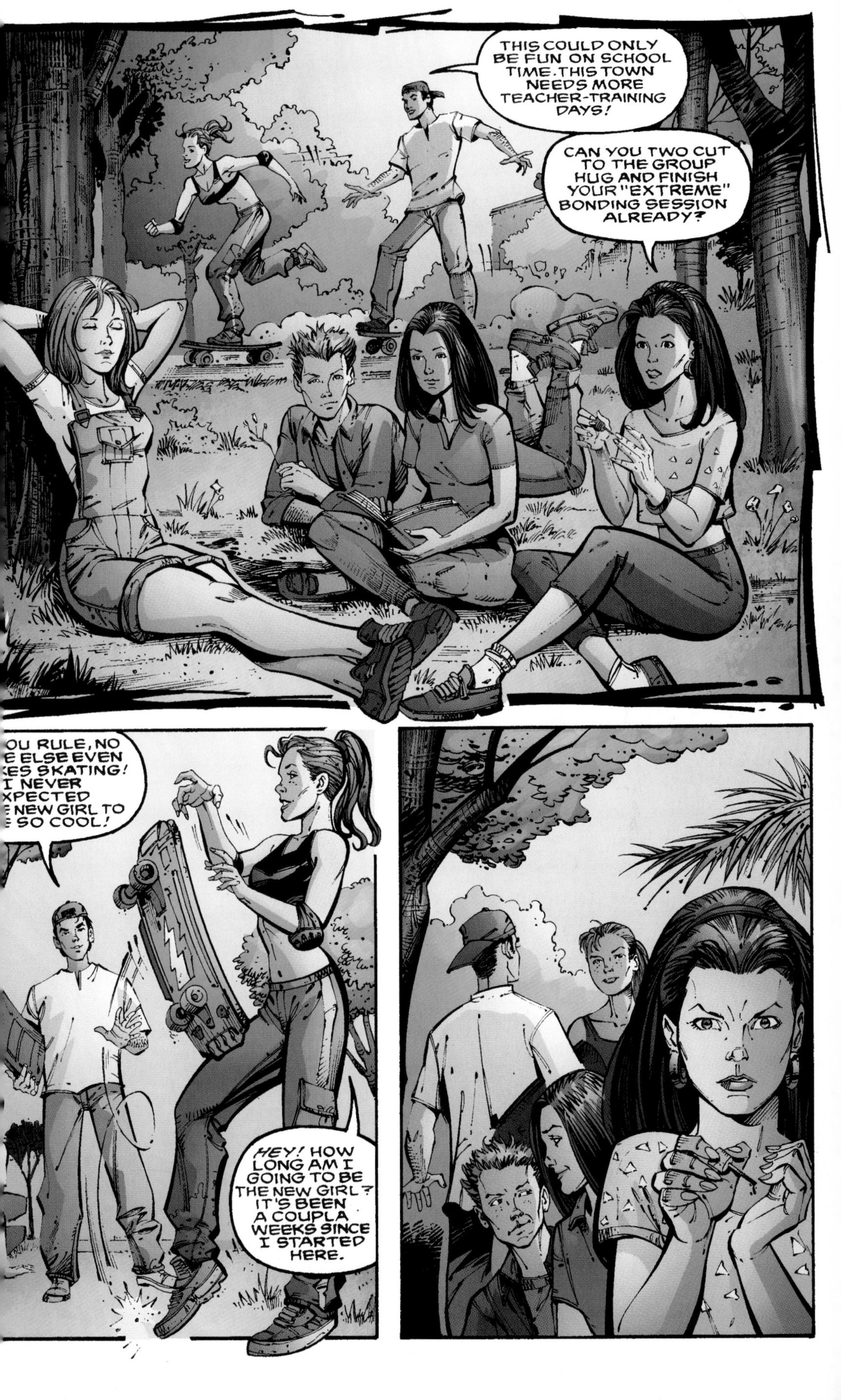
THIS COULD ONLY BE FUN ON SCHOOL TIME. THIS TOWN NEEDS MORE TEACHER-TRAINING DAYS!
CAN YOU TWO CUT TO THE GROUP HUG AND FINISH YOUR "EXTREME" BONDING SESSION ALREADY?
OU RULE, NO E ELSE EVEN KES SKATING! I NEVER XPECTED E NEW GIRL TO E SO COOL!
HEY! HOW LONG AM I GOING TO BE THE NEW GIRL? IT'S BEEN A COUPLA WEEKS SINCE I STARTED HERE.

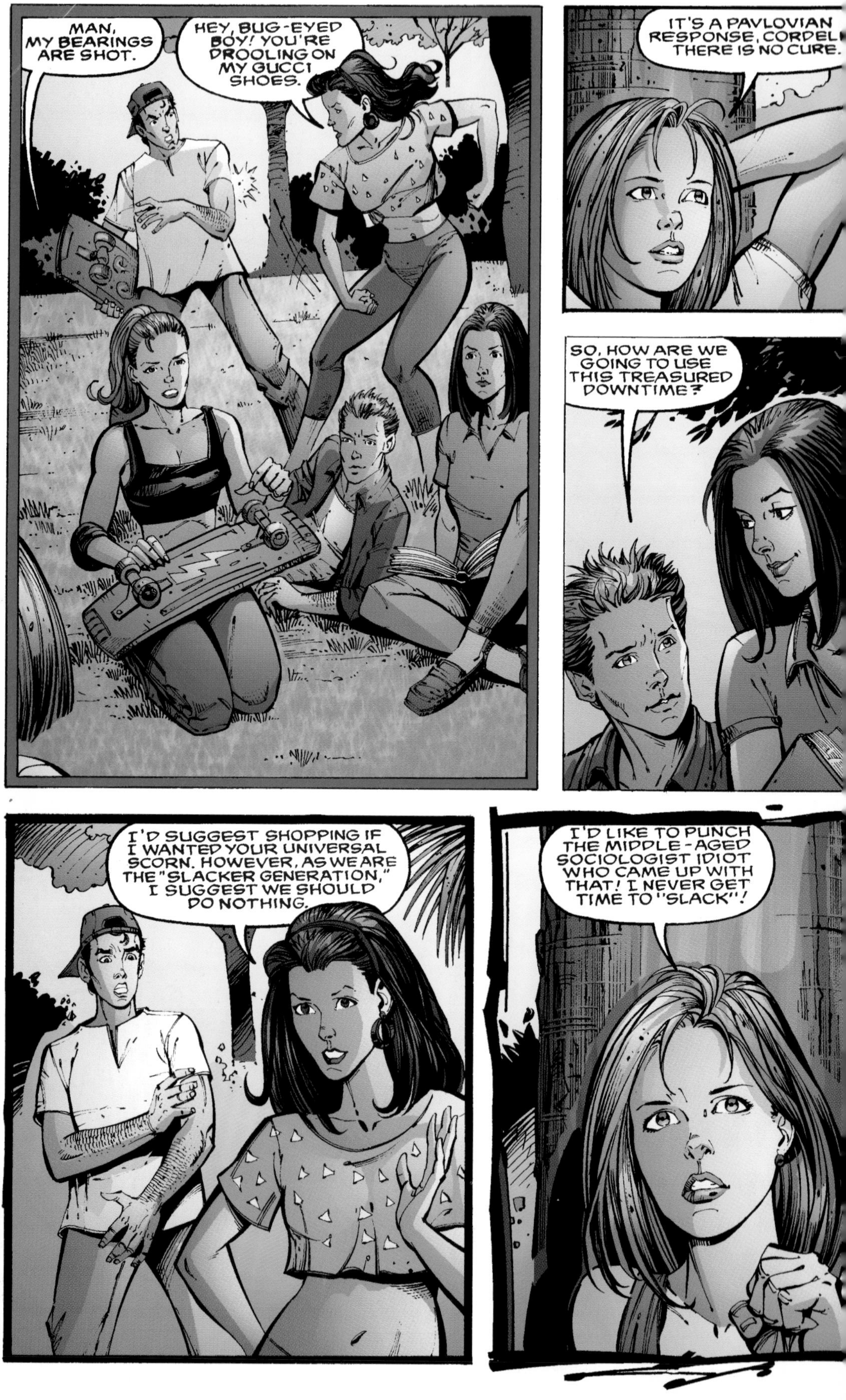
MAN, MY BEARINGS ARE SHOT.
HEY, BUG-EYED BOY! YOU'RE DROOLING ON MY GUCCI SHOES.
IT'S A PAVLOVIAN RESPONSE, CORDEL THERE IS NO CURE.
SO, HOW ARE WE GOING TO USE THIS TREASURED DOWNTIME?
I'D SUGGEST SHOPPING IF I WANTED YOUR UNIVERSAL SCORN. HOWEVER, AS WE ARE THE "SLACKER GENERATION," I SUGGEST WE SHOULD DO NOTHING.
I'D LIKE TO PUNCH THE MIDDLE-AGED SOCIOLOGIST IDIOT WHO CAME UP WITH THAT! I NEVER GET TIME TO "SLACK"!

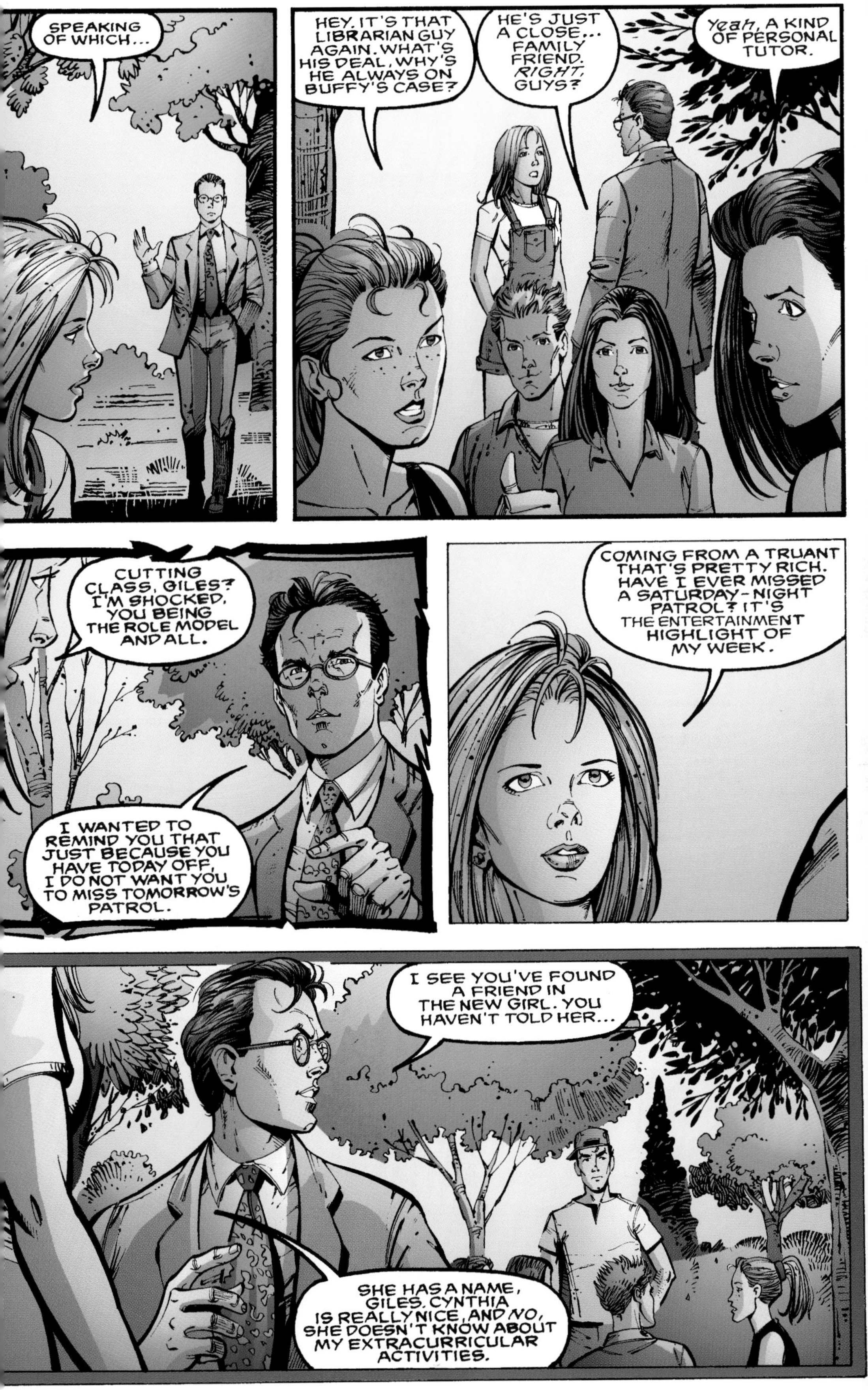
SPEAKING OF WHICH...
HEY, IT'S THAT LIBRARIAN GUY AGAIN. WHAT'S HIS DEAL, WHY'S HE ALWAYS ON BUFFY'S CASE?
HE'S JUST A CLOSE... FAMILY FRIEND. RIGHT, GUYS?
Yeah, A KIND OF PERSONAL TUTOR.
CUTTING CLASS, GILES? I'M SHOCKED, YOU BEING THE ROLE MODEL AND ALL.
I WANTED TO REMIND YOU THAT JUST BECAUSE YOU HAVE TODAY OFF, I DO NOT WANT YOU TO MISS TOMORROW'S PATROL.
COMING FROM A TRUANT THAT'S PRETTY RICH. HAVE I EVER MISSED A SATURDAY-NIGHT PATROL? IT'S THE ENTERTAINMENT HIGHLIGHT OF MY WEEK.
I SEE YOU'VE FOUND A FRIEND IN THE NEW GIRL. YOU HAVEN'T TOLD HER...
SHE HAS A NAME, GILES. CYNTHIA IS REALLY NICE, AND NO, SHE DOESN'T KNOW ABOUT MY EXTRACURRICULAR ACTIVITIES.

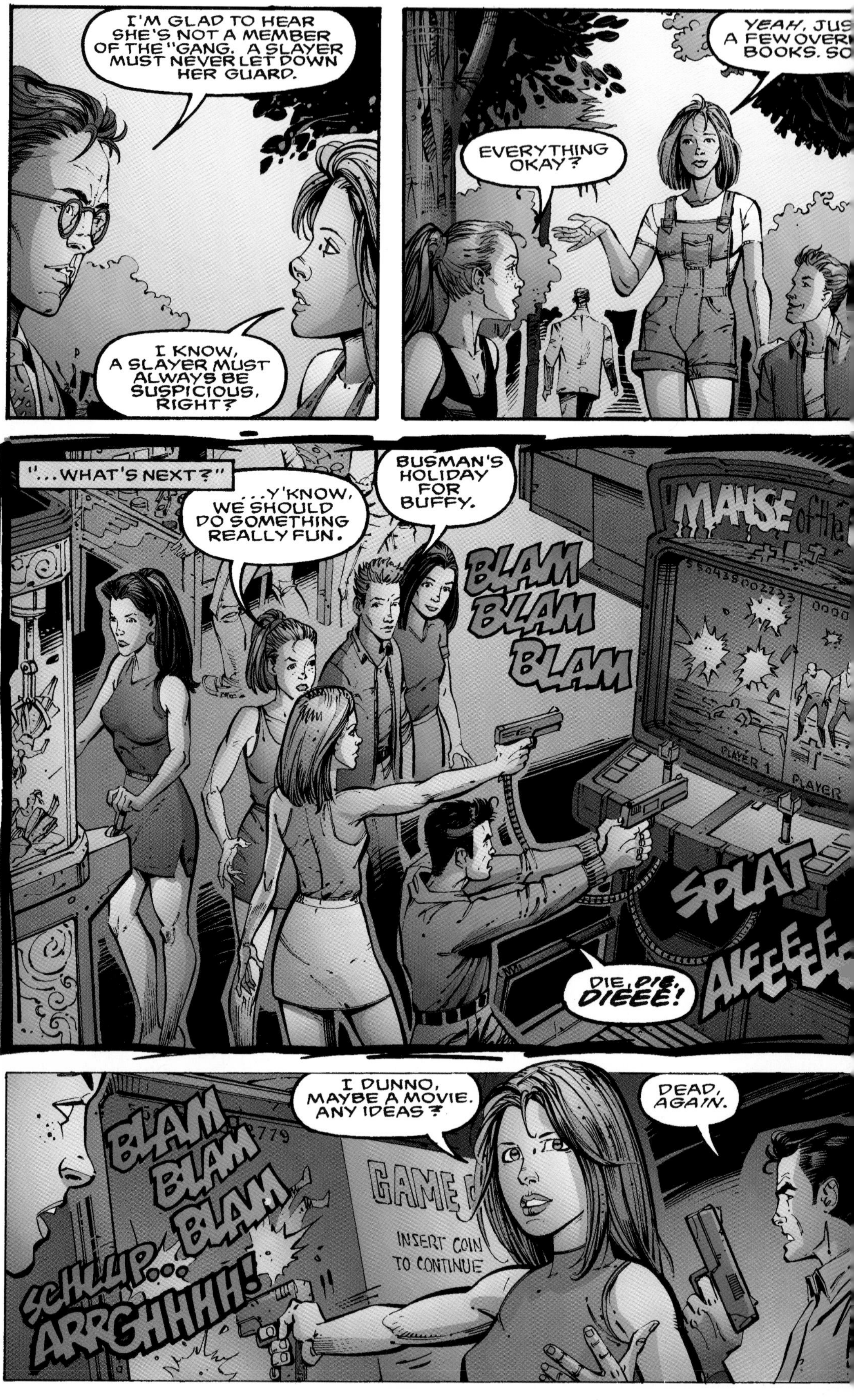
I'M GLAD TO HEAR SHE'S NOT A MEMBER OF THE "GANG. A SLAYER MUST NEVER LET DOWN HER GUARD.
I KNOW, A SLAYER MUST ALWAYS BE SUSPICIOUS, RIGHT?
YEAH, JUS
A FEW OVER
BOOKS. SO
EVERYTHING OKAY?
"...WHAT'S NEXT?"
...Y'KNOW, WE SHOULD DO SOMETHING REALLY FUN.
BUSMAN'S HOLIDAY FOR BUFFY.
BLAM BLAM BLAM
PLAYER 1
PLAYER
SPLAT
DIE, DIE, DIEEE!
I DUNNO, MAYBE A MOVIE. ANY IDEAS?
DEAD, AGAIN.
BLAM BLAM BLAM BLAM
SCHLLLP...
ARRGHHHH!
GAME
INSERT COIN TO CONTINUE

Y'KNOW THIS [MI]GHT SOUND WEIRD, [BUT] IT'S SOMETHING [I H]AVEN'T DONE [IN Y]EARS. IT'D BE [SO] MUCH FUN, I [AL]WAYS LOVED [TH]EM AS A KID...

OH REALLY, WHAT?

...MY GUN WAS BUSTED, THAT'S THE ONLY REASON...

YEAH, I'VE HEARD THAT EXCUSE BEFORE.

BACK TO YOUR WEIRD IDEA.

I THOUGHT IT'D BE COOL TO HAVE A SLUMBER PARTY?

A SLUMBER PARTY? AWESOME IDEA!

A SLUMBER PARTY SOUNDS GREAT! MY PARENTS ARE AWAY THIS WEEKEND, SO WE COULD ALL HANG OUT AT MY PLACE.

WE SHOULD INVITE ANOTHER FRIEND EACH, TO REACH THAT PERFECT SLUMBER PARTY NUMBER.

SO, DO WE ALL HAVE TO WEAR LIKE, OUR "JAMMIES" AND STUFF?

Uh, sure--

NO GUYS ALLOWED!

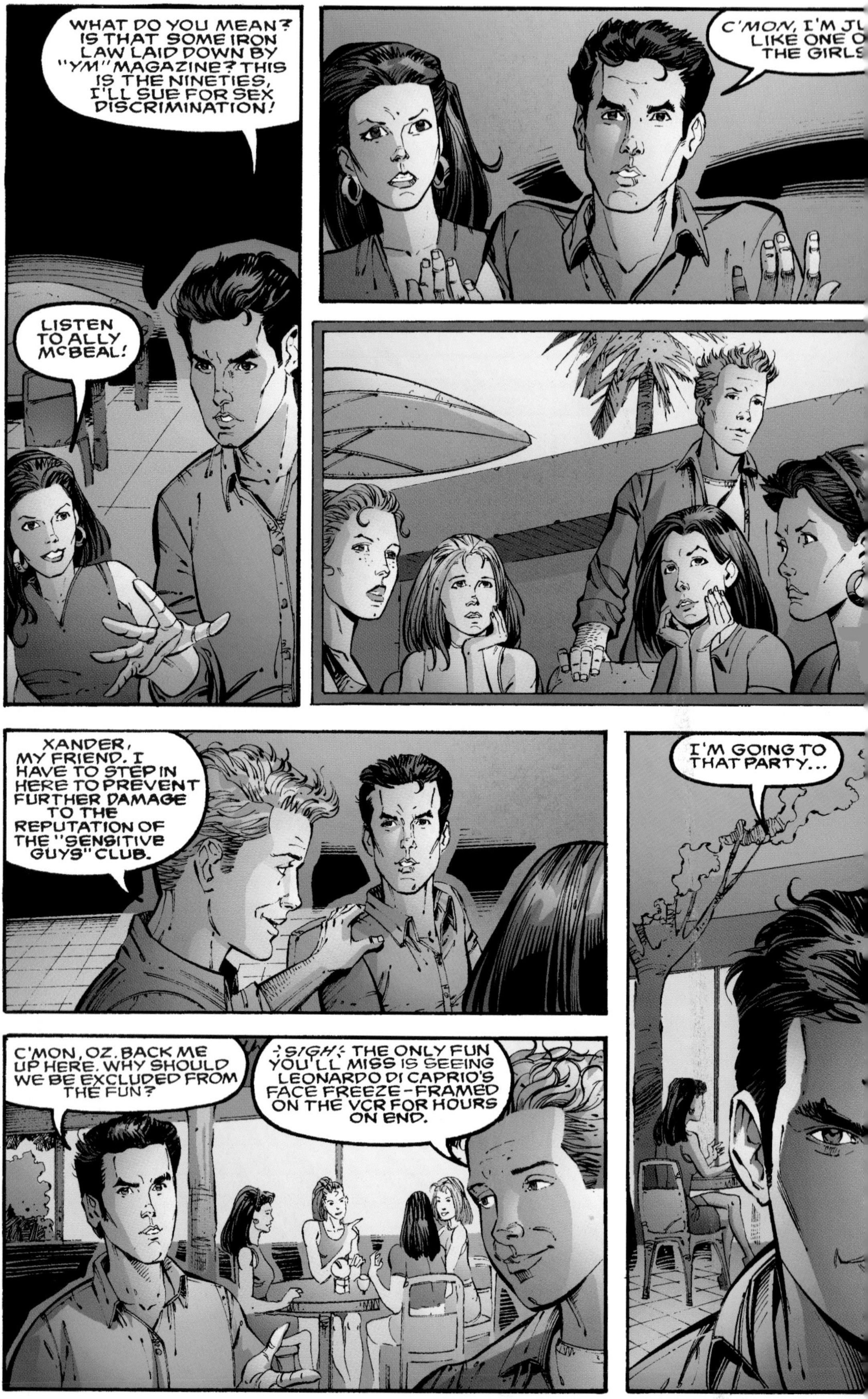
WHAT DO YOU MEAN? IS THAT SOME IRON LAW LAID DOWN BY "YM" MAGAZINE? THIS IS THE NINETIES, I'LL SUE FOR SEX DISCRIMINATION!
LISTEN TO ALLY McBEAL!
C'MON, I'M JU LIKE ONE O THE GIRLS
XANDER, MY FRIEND. I HAVE TO STEP IN HERE TO PREVENT FURTHER DAMAGE TO THE REPUTATION OF THE "SENSITIVE GUYS" CLUB.
C'MON, OZ. BACK ME UP HERE. WHY SHOULD WE BE EXCLUDED FROM THE FUN?
-SIGH- THE ONLY FUN YOU'LL MISS IS SEEING LEONARDO DI CAPRIO'S FACE FREEZE-FRAMED ON THE VCR FOR HOURS ON END.
I'M GOING TO THAT PARTY...

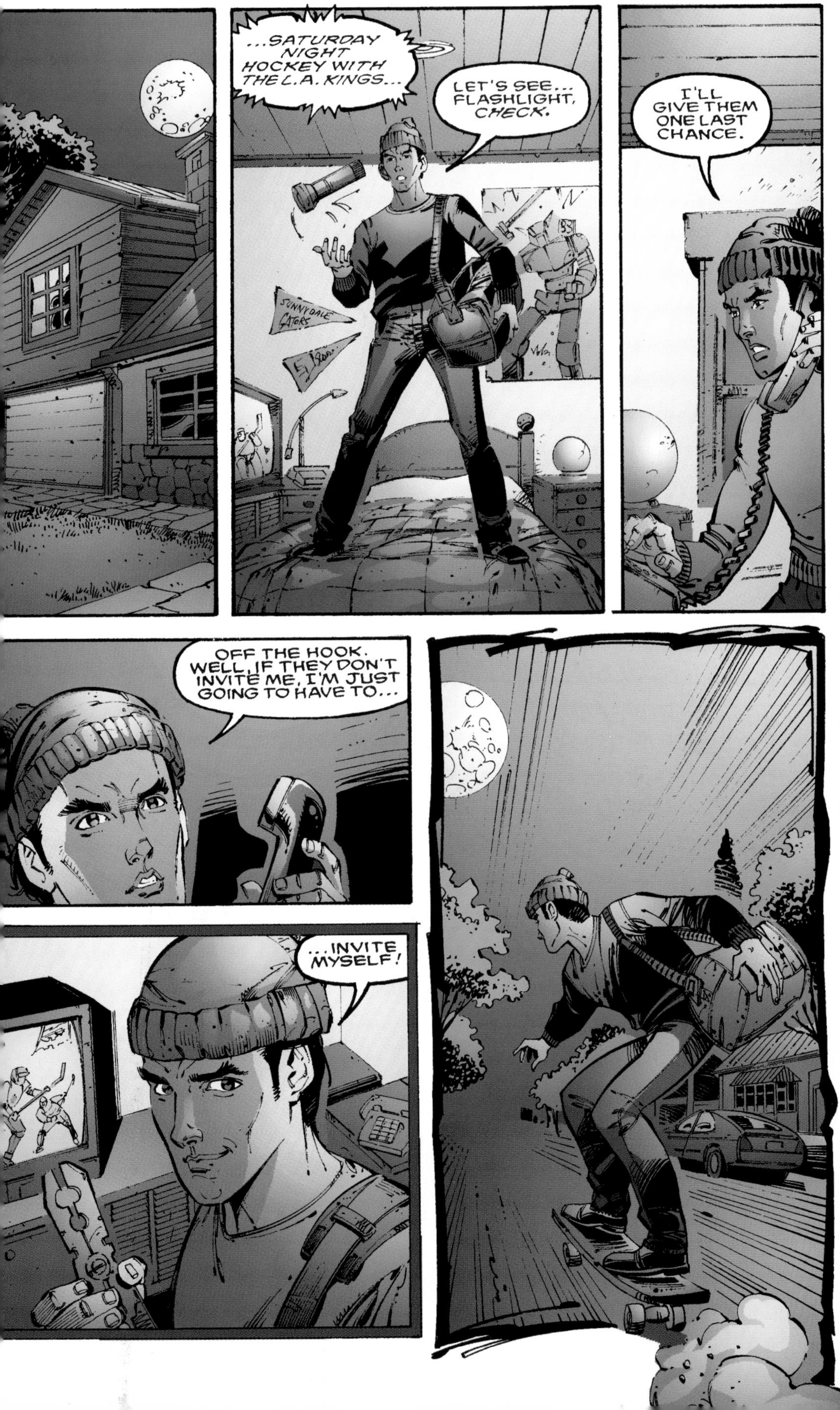
...SATURDAY NIGHT HOCKEY WITH THE L.A. KINGS...
LET'S SEE... FLASHLIGHT, CHECK.
SUNNYDALE GATORS
I'LL GIVE THEM ONE LAST CHANCE.
OFF THE HOOK. WELL, IF THEY DON'T INVITE ME, I'M JUST GOING TO HAVE TO...
...INVITE MYSELF!

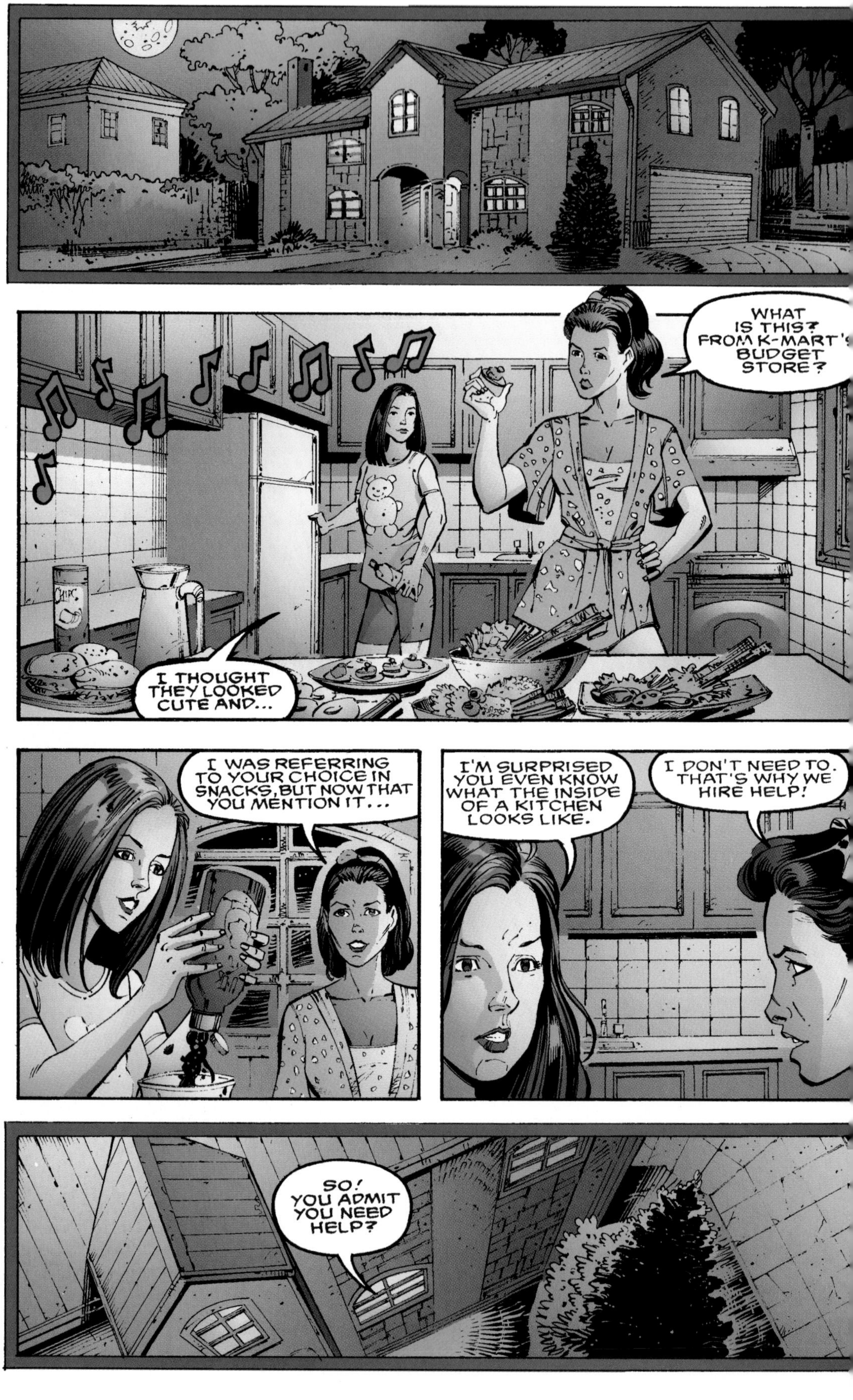
WHAT IS THIS? FROM K-MART'S BUDGET STORE?
I THOUGHT THEY LOOKED CUTE AND...
I WAS REFERRING TO YOUR CHOICE IN SNACKS, BUT NOW THAT YOU MENTION IT...
I'M SURPRISED YOU EVEN KNOW WHAT THE INSIDE OF A KITCHEN LOOKS LIKE.
I DON'T NEED TO. THAT'S WHY WE HIRE HELP!
SO! YOU ADMIT YOU NEED HELP?

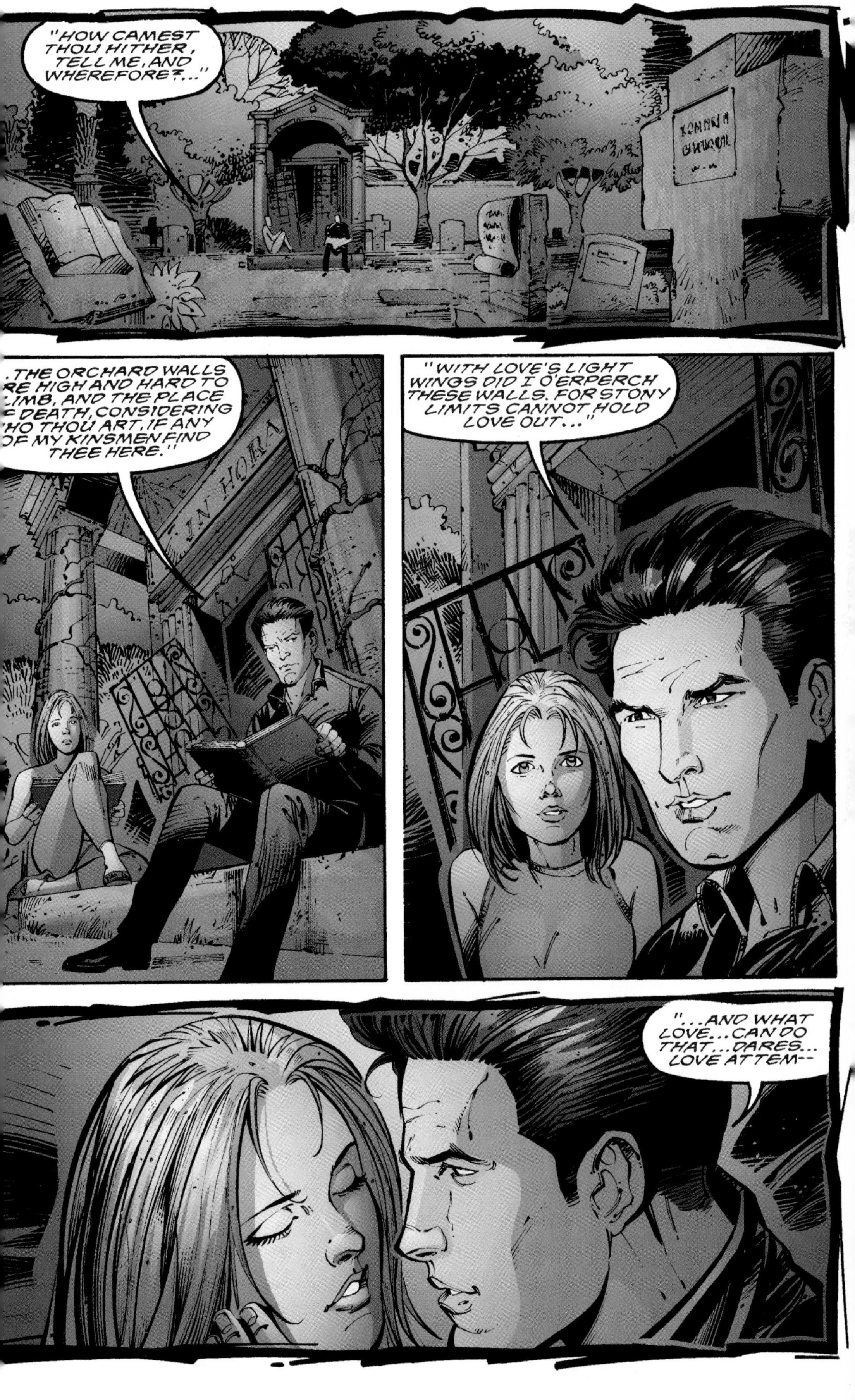
"HOW CAMEST THOU HITHER, TELL ME, AND WHEREFORE?..."
. THE ORCHARD WALLS RE HIGH AND HARD TO LIMB, AND THE PLACE F DEATH, CONSIDERING HO THOU ART, IF ANY OF MY KINSMEN FIND THEE HERE."
IN HORA
"WITH LOVE'S LIGHT WINGS DID I O'ERPERCH THESE WALLS. FOR STONY LIMITS CANNOT HOLD LOVE OUT..."
"...AND WHAT LOVE...CAN DO THAT...DARES... LOVE ATTEM--

Y'KNOW, MAYBE ENG. LIT. ISN'T QUITE THE SUBJECT TO KEEP OUR MINDS OFF... YOU KNOW.

Ur-hmm! I HAD NOTHING BUT POETRY ON MY MIND!

IF GUYS SPENT ALL THEIR TIME PAINTING EACH OTHERS' TOENAILS INSTEAD OF WATCHING FOOTBALL, IT'D THROW OUR ENTIRE CULTURE INTO A TAILSPIN TO OBLIVION.

WE HAVE A VISITOR.

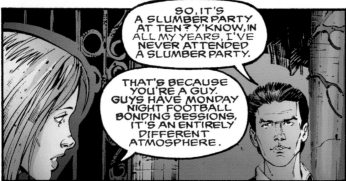

SO, IT'S A SLUMBER PARTY AT TEN? Y'KNOW, IN ALL MY YEARS, I'VE NEVER ATTENDED A SLUMBER PARTY.

THAT'S BECAUSE YOU'RE A GUY. GUYS HAVE MONDAY NIGHT FOOTBALL BONDING SESSIONS, IT'S AN ENTIRELY DIFFERENT ATMOSPHERE.

THAT'S CYNTHIA. SHE MUST BE HEADING TO THE PARTY. THOSE GUYS KINDA LOOK WEIRD.

THE NEW GIRL, DOES SHE HAVE A DEATH WISH?

RUN, CYNTHIA! *RUN!*

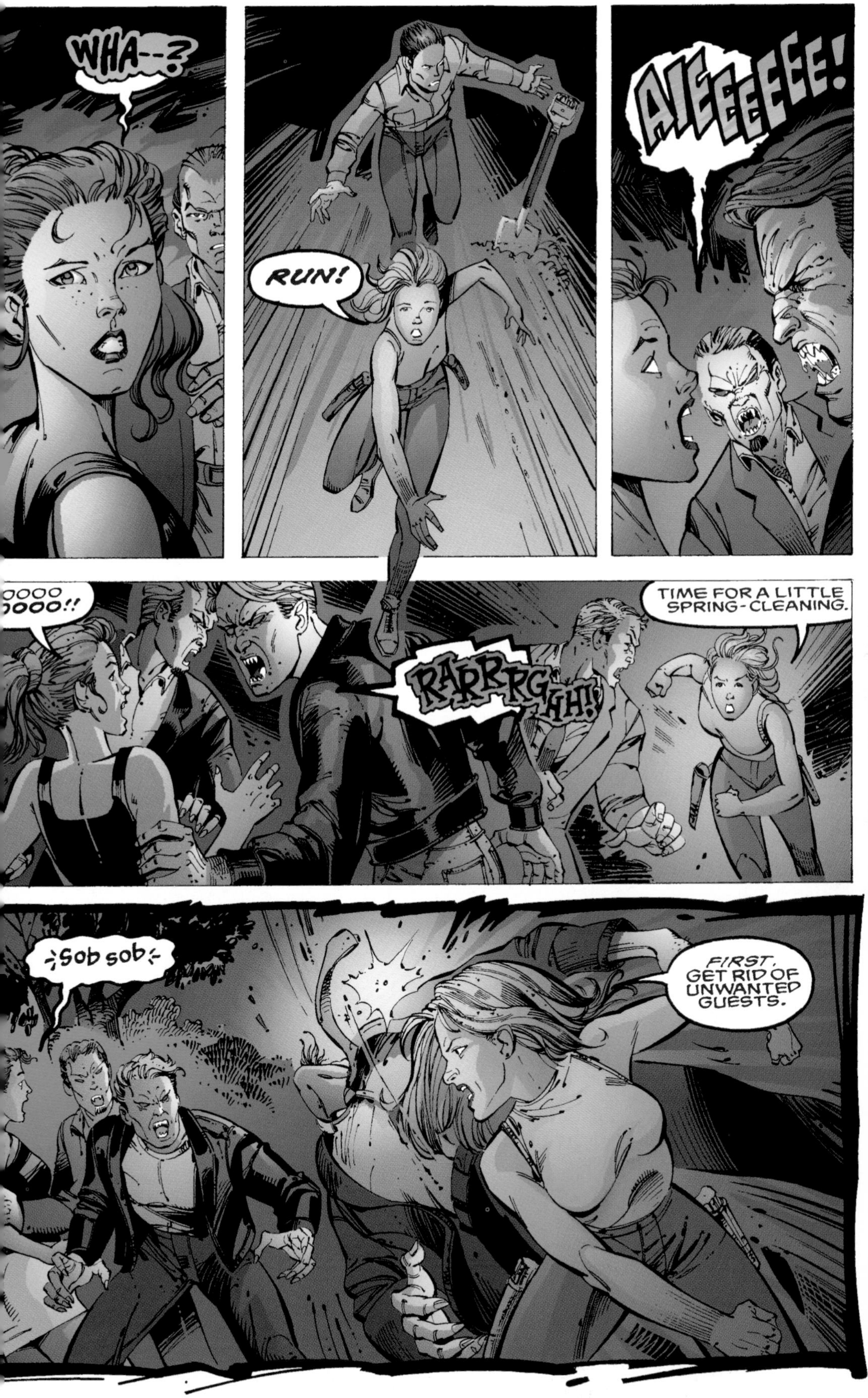
WHA--?
RUN!
AIEEEEEEE!
OOOO OOOO!!
RARRRGHH!
TIME FOR A LITTLE SPRING-CLEANING.
Sob sob
FIRST, GET RID OF UNWANTED GUESTS.

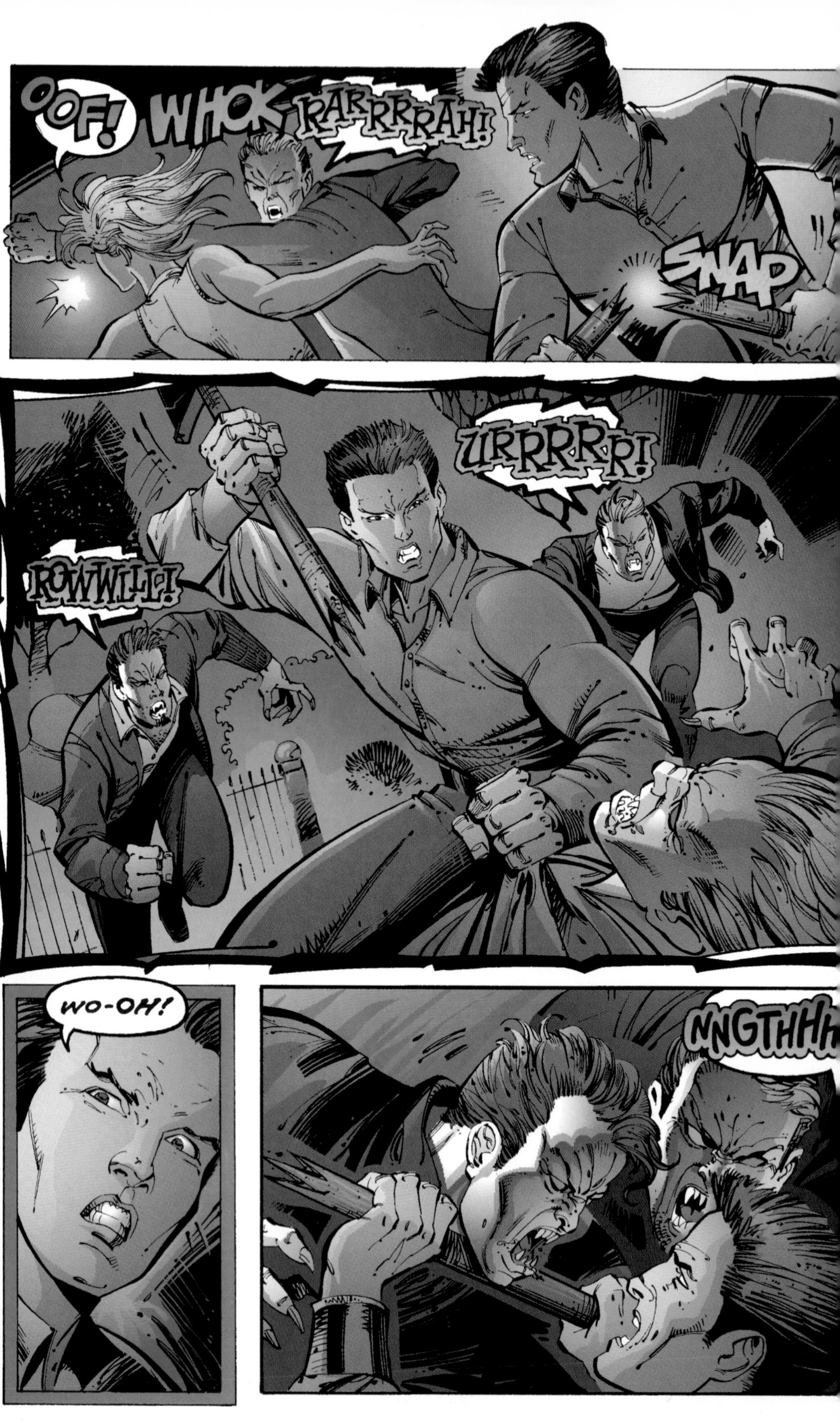
OOF!
WHOK
RARRRRAH!
SNAP
URRRRR!
ROWWLLL!
WO-OH!
NNGTHHH

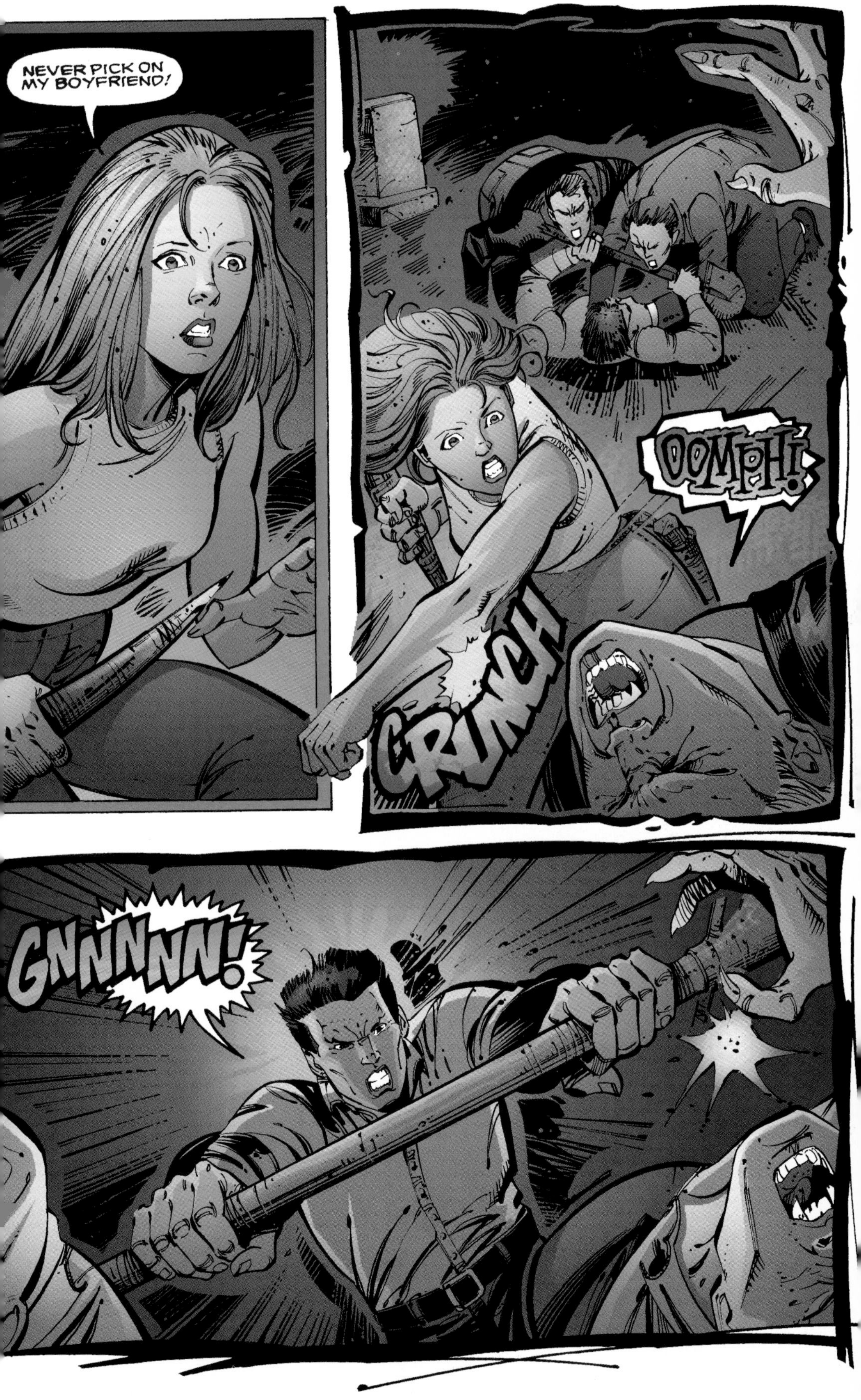
NEVER PICK ON MY BOYFRIEND!
OOMPH!
CRUNCH
GNNNNN!

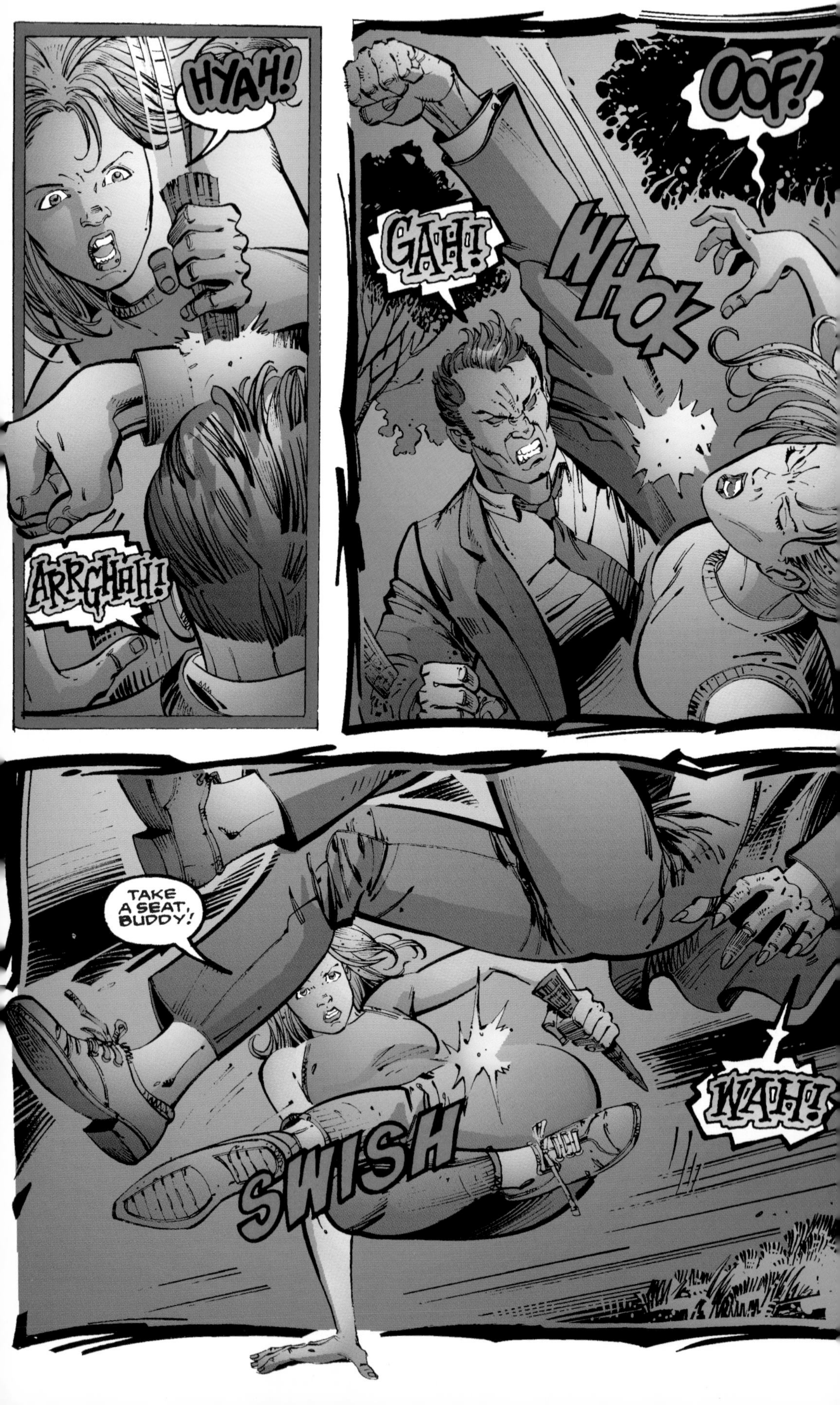
HYAH!
ARRGHHH!
GAH!
WHOK
OOF!
TAKE A SEAT, BUDDY!
SWISH
WAH!

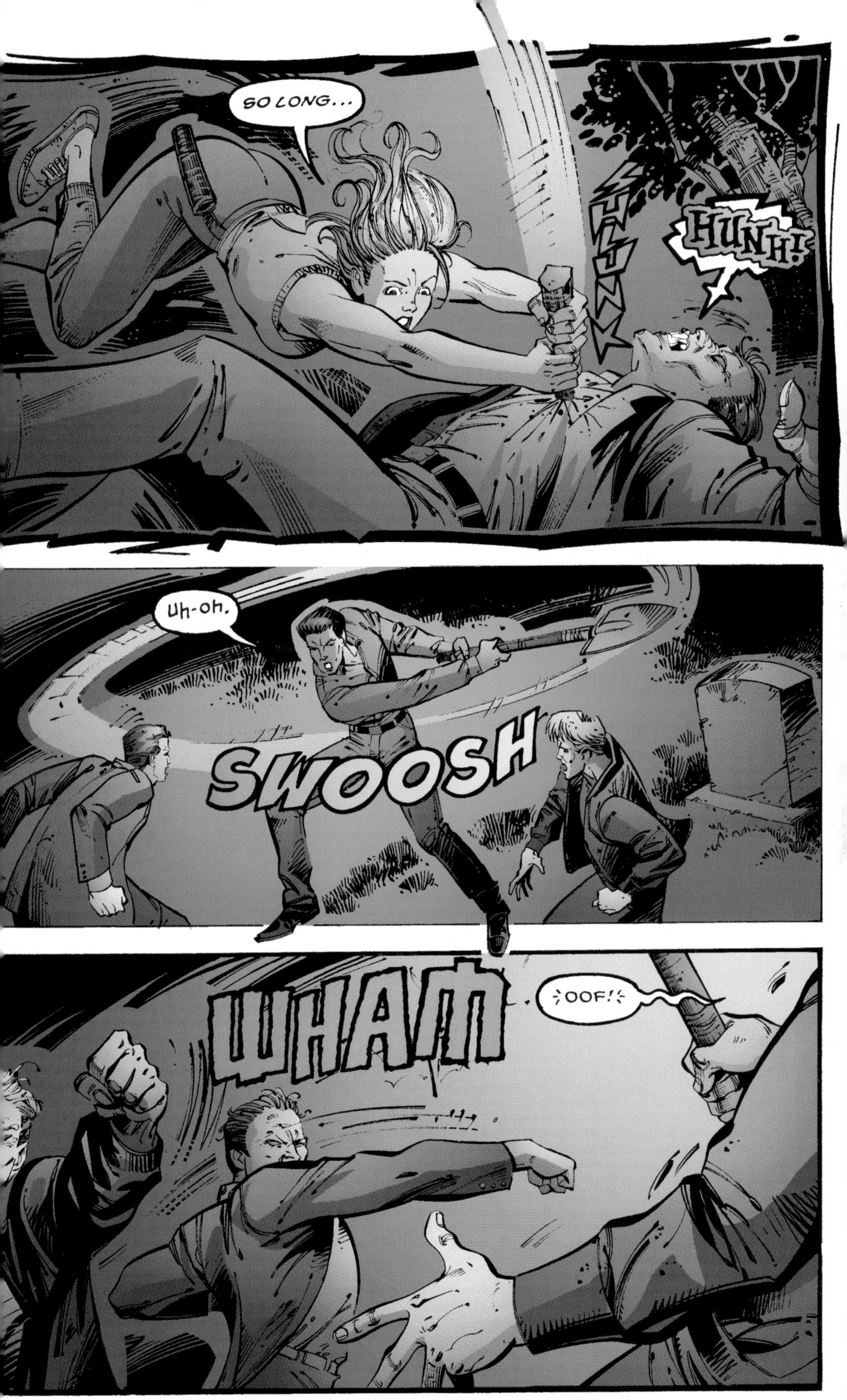
SO LONG...
THUNK
HUNH!
Uh-oh.
SWOOSH
WHAM
OOF!

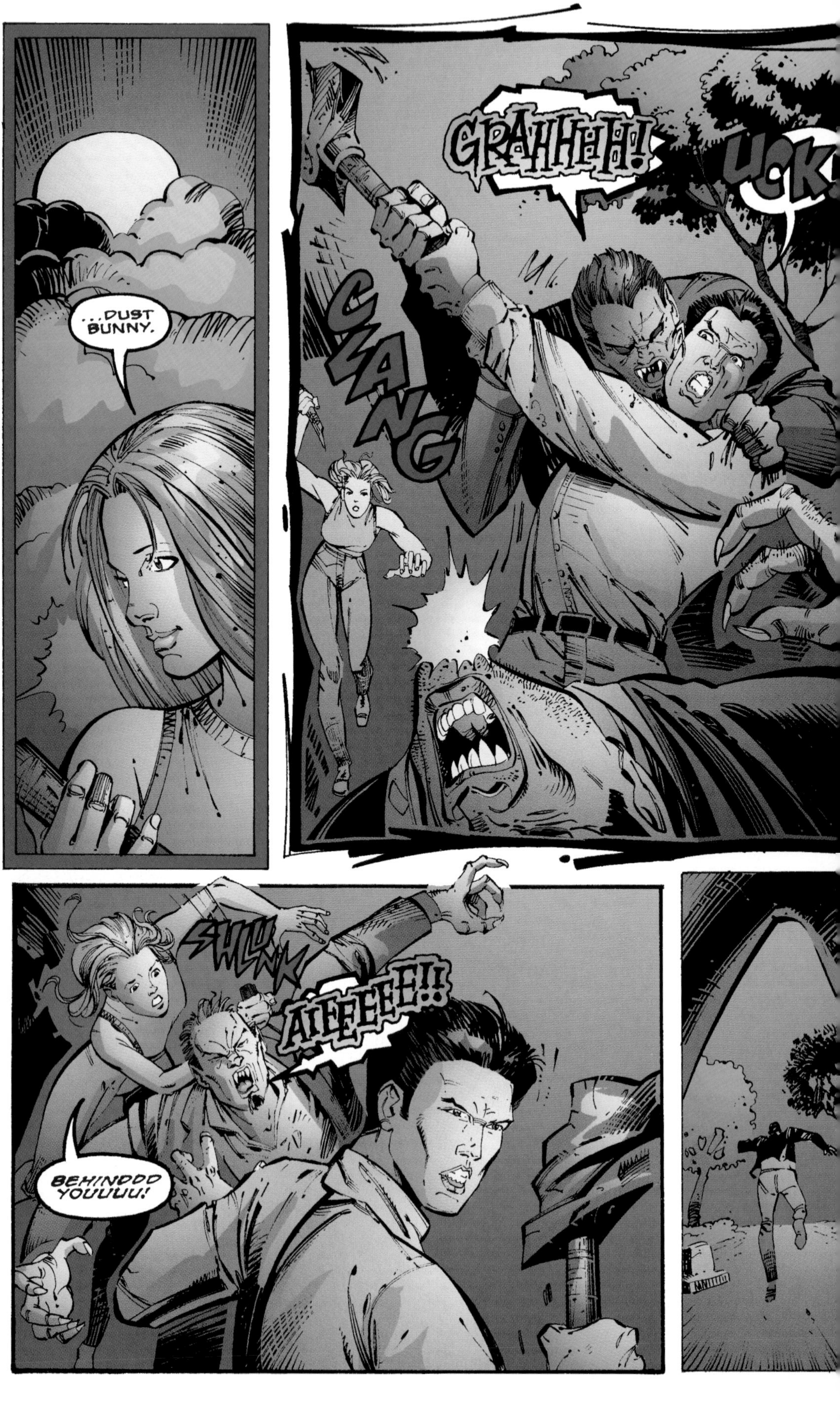

...DUST BUNNY.
GRAHHHH!
UCK!
CLANG
SHLUNK
AIEEEEE!!
BEHINDDD YOUUUU!

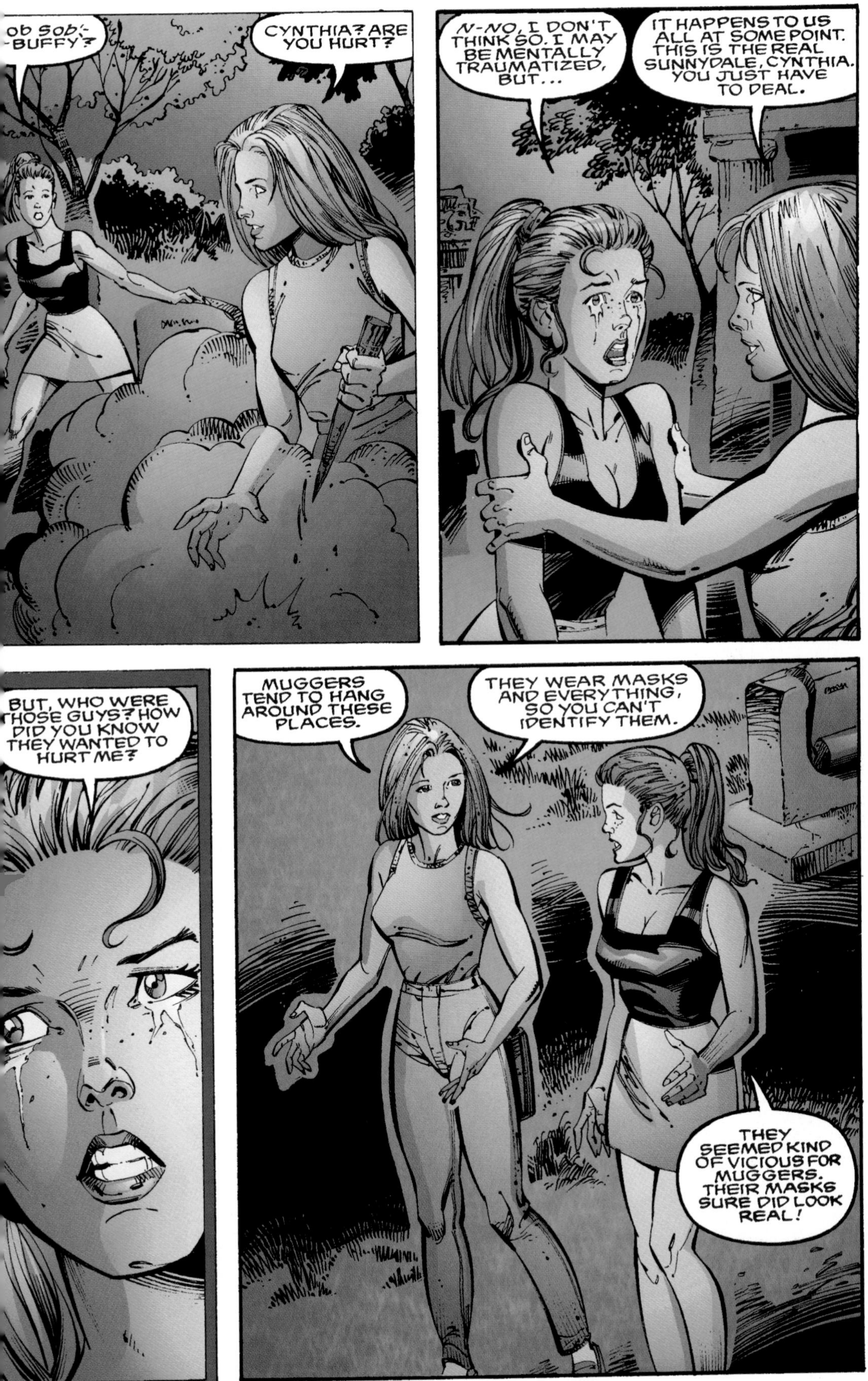
ob sob
-BUFFY?
CYNTHIA? ARE YOU HURT?
N-NO, I DON'T THINK SO. I MAY BE MENTALLY TRAUMATIZED, BUT...
IT HAPPENS TO US ALL AT SOME POINT. THIS IS THE REAL SUNNYDALE, CYNTHIA. YOU JUST HAVE TO DEAL.
BUT, WHO WERE THOSE GUYS? HOW DID YOU KNOW THEY WANTED TO HURT ME?
MUGGERS TEND TO HANG AROUND THESE PLACES.
THEY WEAR MASKS AND EVERYTHING, SO YOU CAN'T IDENTIFY THEM.
THEY SEEMED KIND OF VICIOUS FOR MUGGERS. THEIR MASKS SURE DID LOOK REAL!

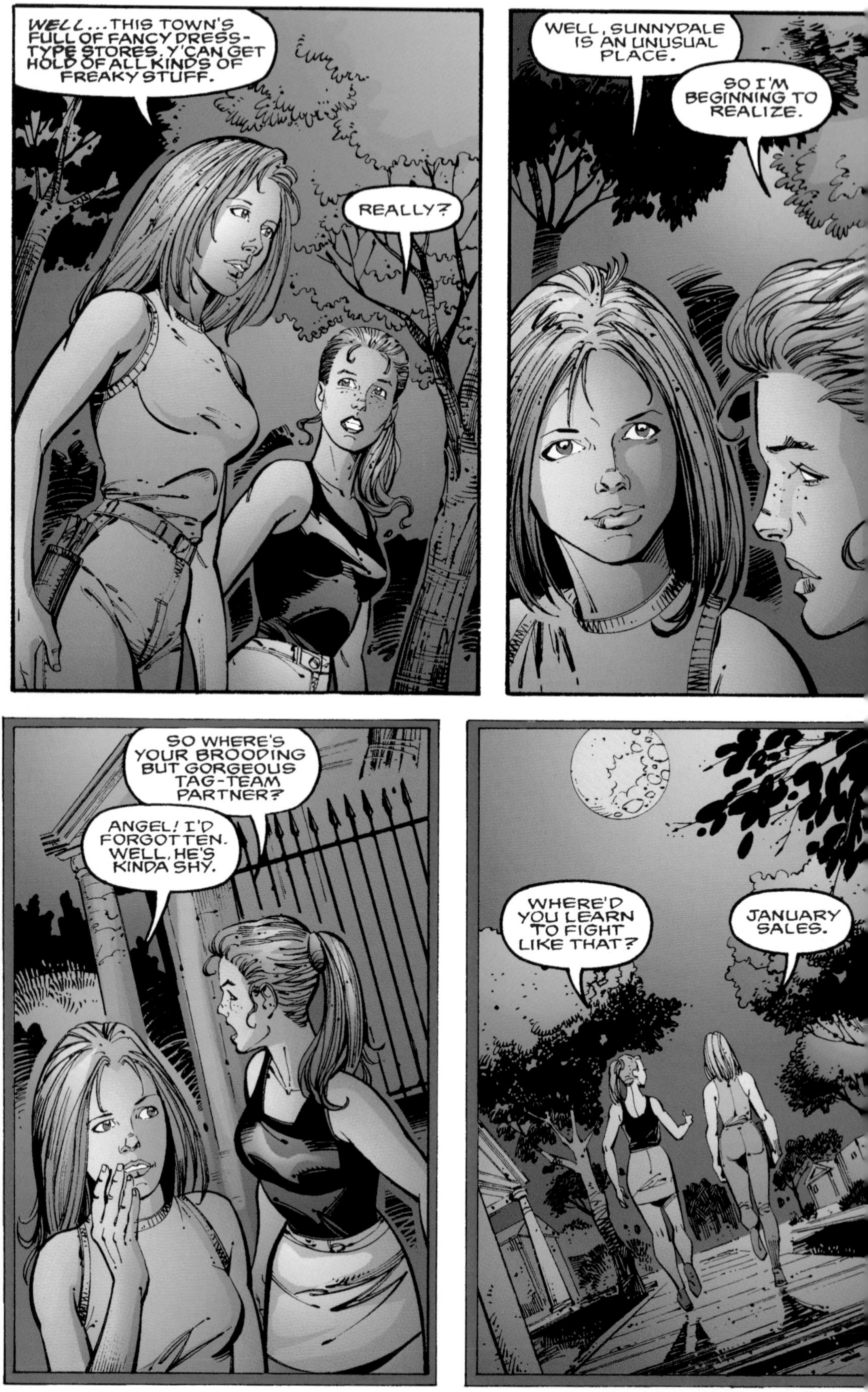
WELL... THIS TOWN'S FULL OF FANCY DRESS-TYPE STORES. Y'CAN GET HOLD OF ALL KINDS OF FREAKY STUFF.
REALLY?
WELL, SUNNYDALE IS AN UNUSUAL PLACE.
SO I'M BEGINNING TO REALIZE.
SO WHERE'S YOUR BROODING BUT GORGEOUS TAG-TEAM PARTNER?
ANGEL! I'D FORGOTTEN. WELL, HE'S KINDA SHY.
WHERE'D YOU LEARN TO FIGHT LIKE THAT?
JANUARY SALES.

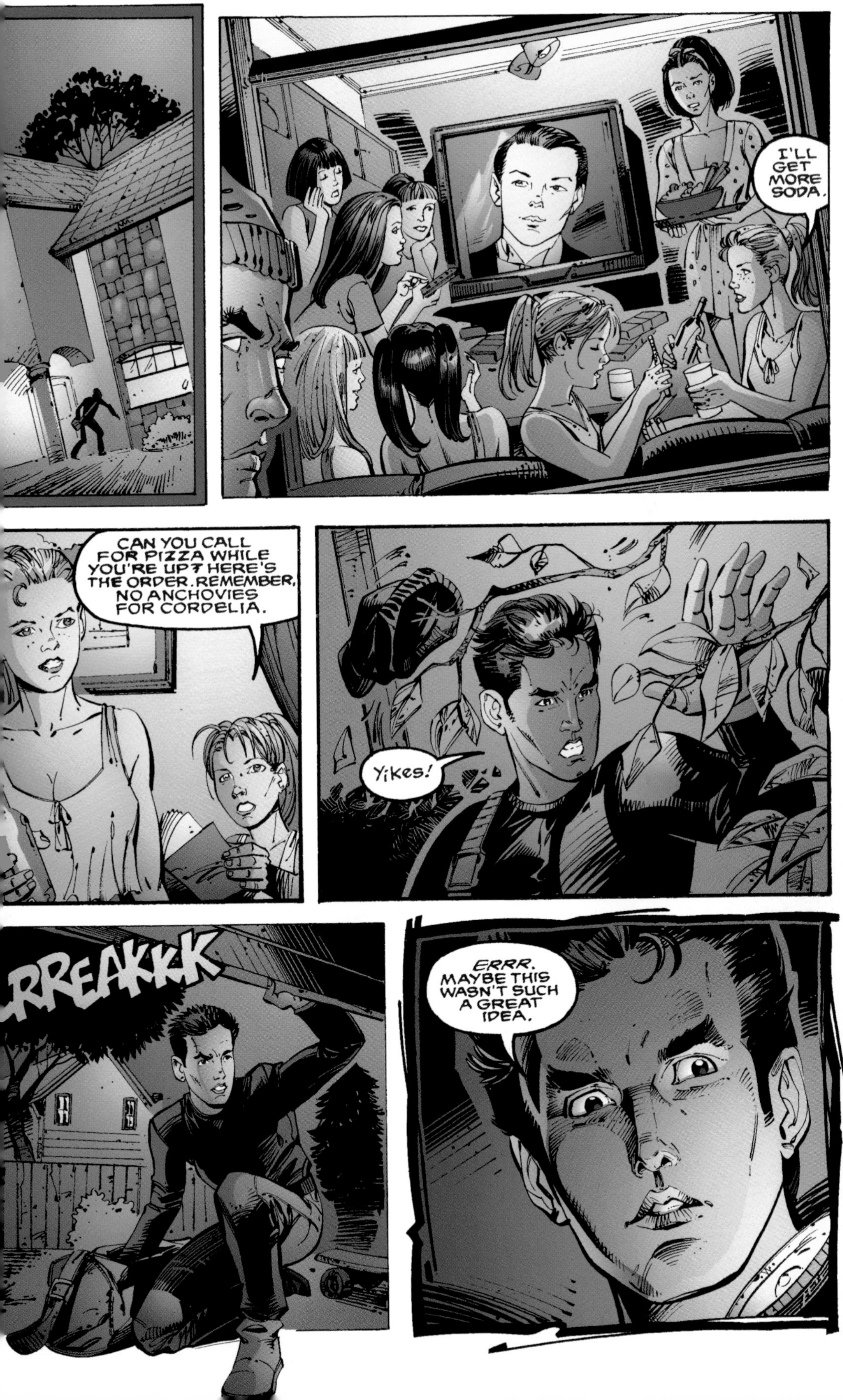
I'LL GET MORE SODA.
CAN YOU CALL FOR PIZZA WHILE YOU'RE UP? HERE'S THE ORDER. REMEMBER, NO ANCHOVIES FOR CORDELIA.
Yikes!
RREAKKK
ERRR. MAYBE THIS WASN'T SUCH A GREAT IDEA.

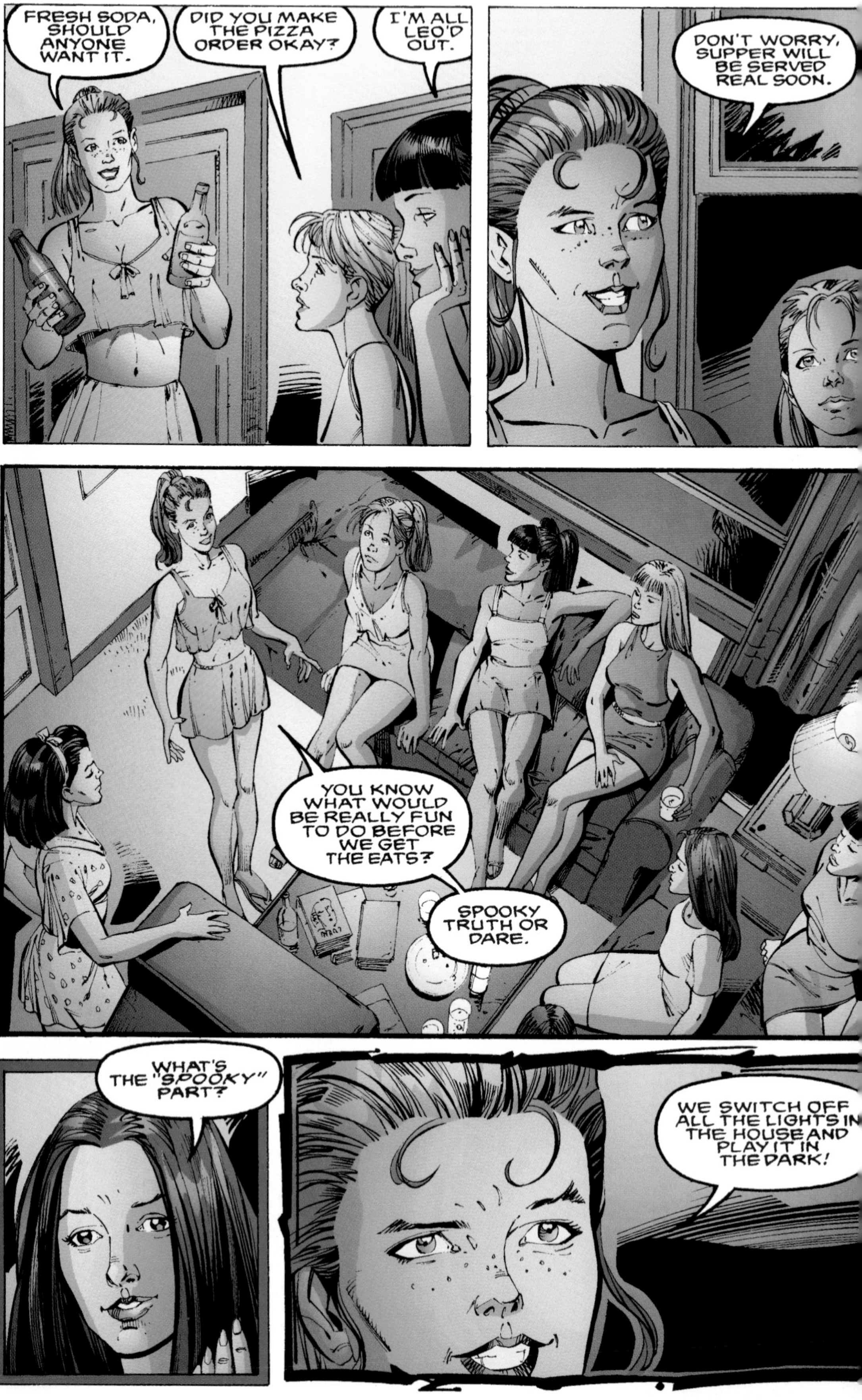
FRESH SODA, SHOULD ANYONE WANT IT.
DID YOU MAKE THE PIZZA ORDER OKAY?
I'M ALL LEO'D OUT.
DON'T WORRY, SUPPER WILL BE SERVED REAL SOON.
YOU KNOW WHAT WOULD BE REALLY FUN TO DO BEFORE WE GET THE EATS?
SPOOKY TRUTH OR DARE.
WHAT'S THE "SPOOKY" PART?
WE SWITCH OFF ALL THE LIGHTS IN THE HOUSE AND PLAY IT IN THE DARK!

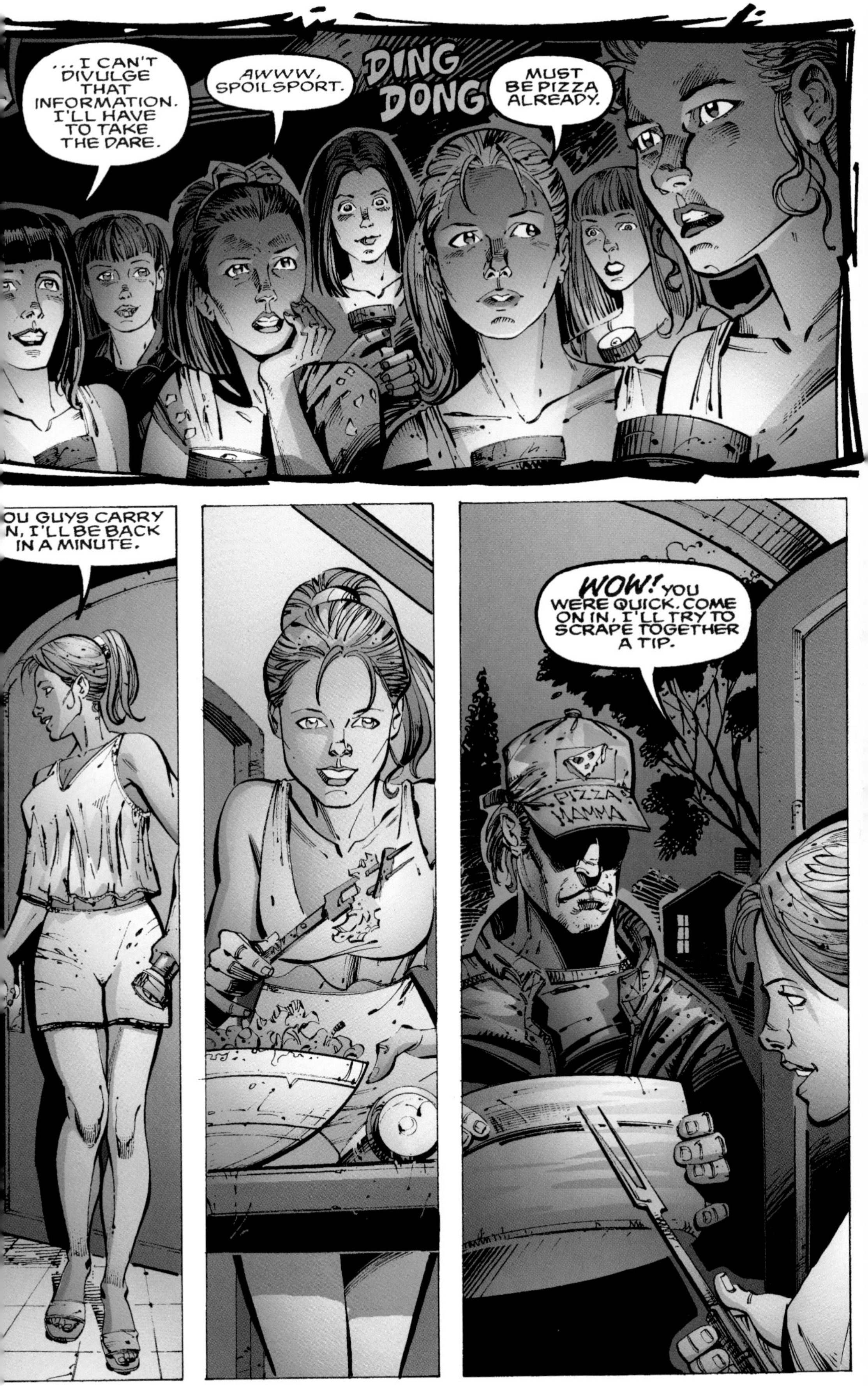

...I CAN'T DIVULGE THAT INFORMATION. I'LL HAVE TO TAKE THE DARE.
AWWW, SPOILSPORT.
DING DONG
MUST BE PIZZA ALREADY.
OU GUYS CARRY N, I'LL BE BACK IN A MINUTE.
WOW! YOU WERE QUICK. COME ON IN, I'LL TRY TO SCRAPE TOGETHER A TIP.
PIZZA MAMMA

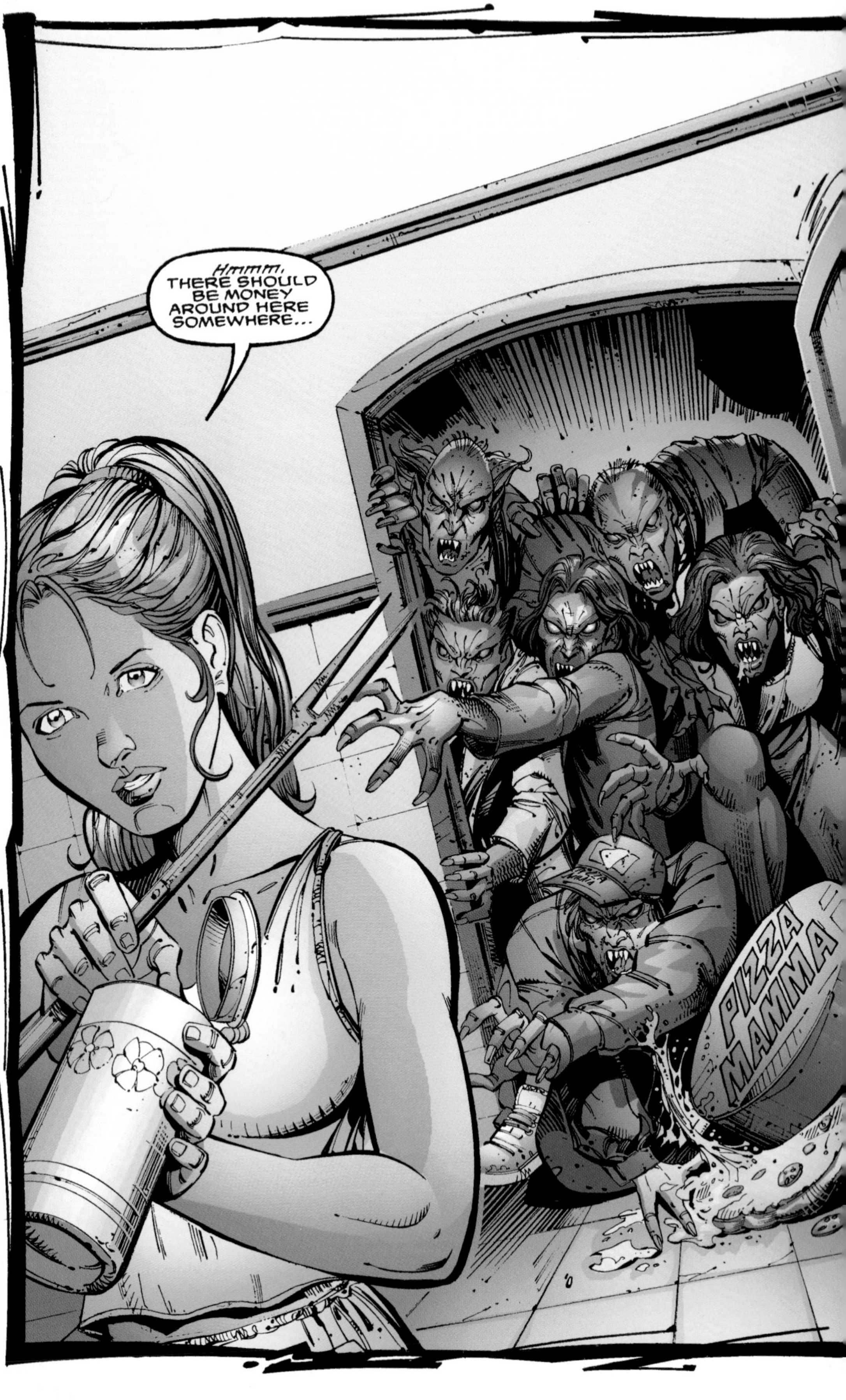

Hmmmm, THERE SHOULD BE MONEY AROUND HERE SOMEWHERE...
PIZZA MAMMA

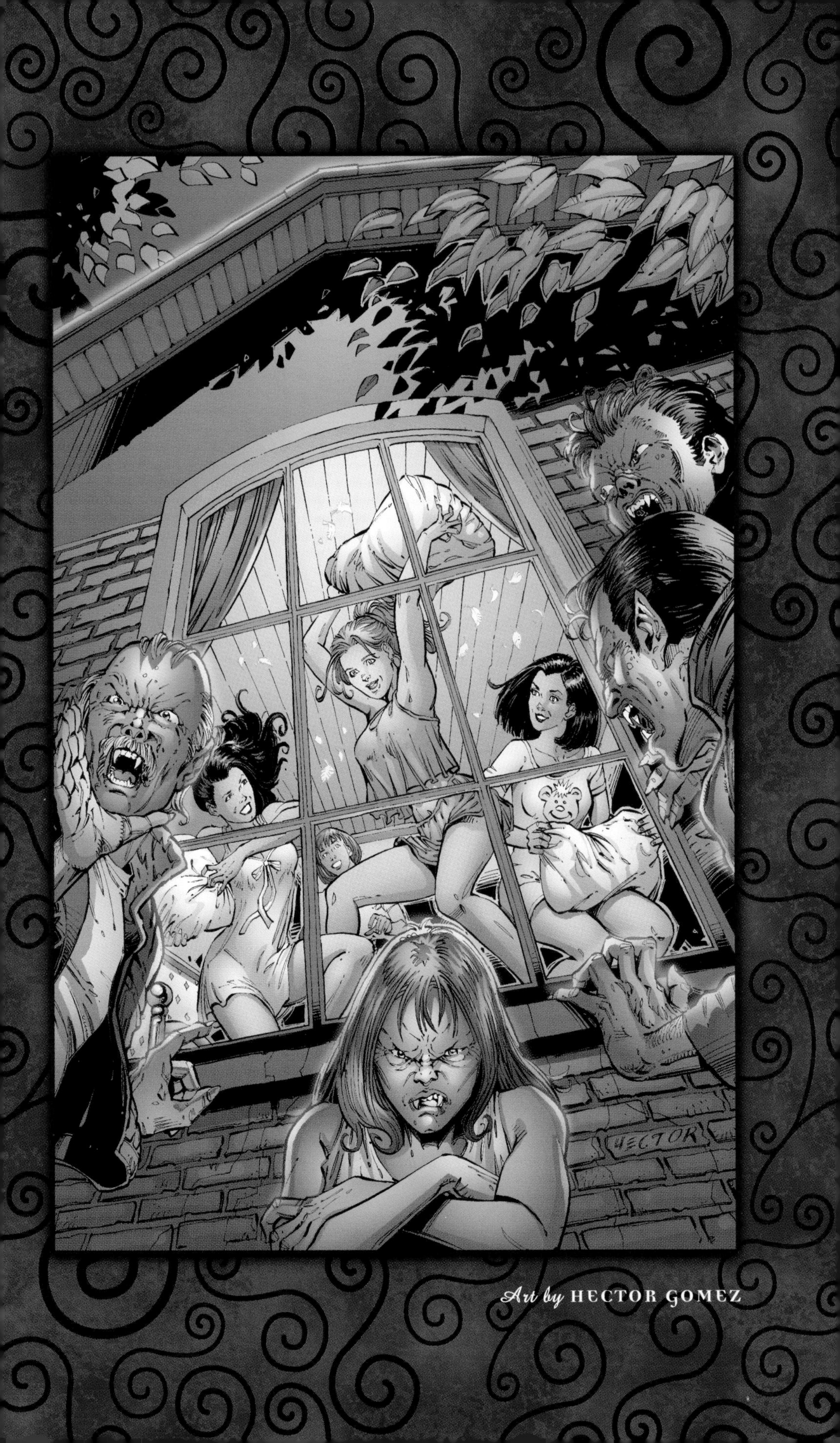
HECTOR

Art by HECTOR GOMEZ

New Kid
on the Block
chapter 2

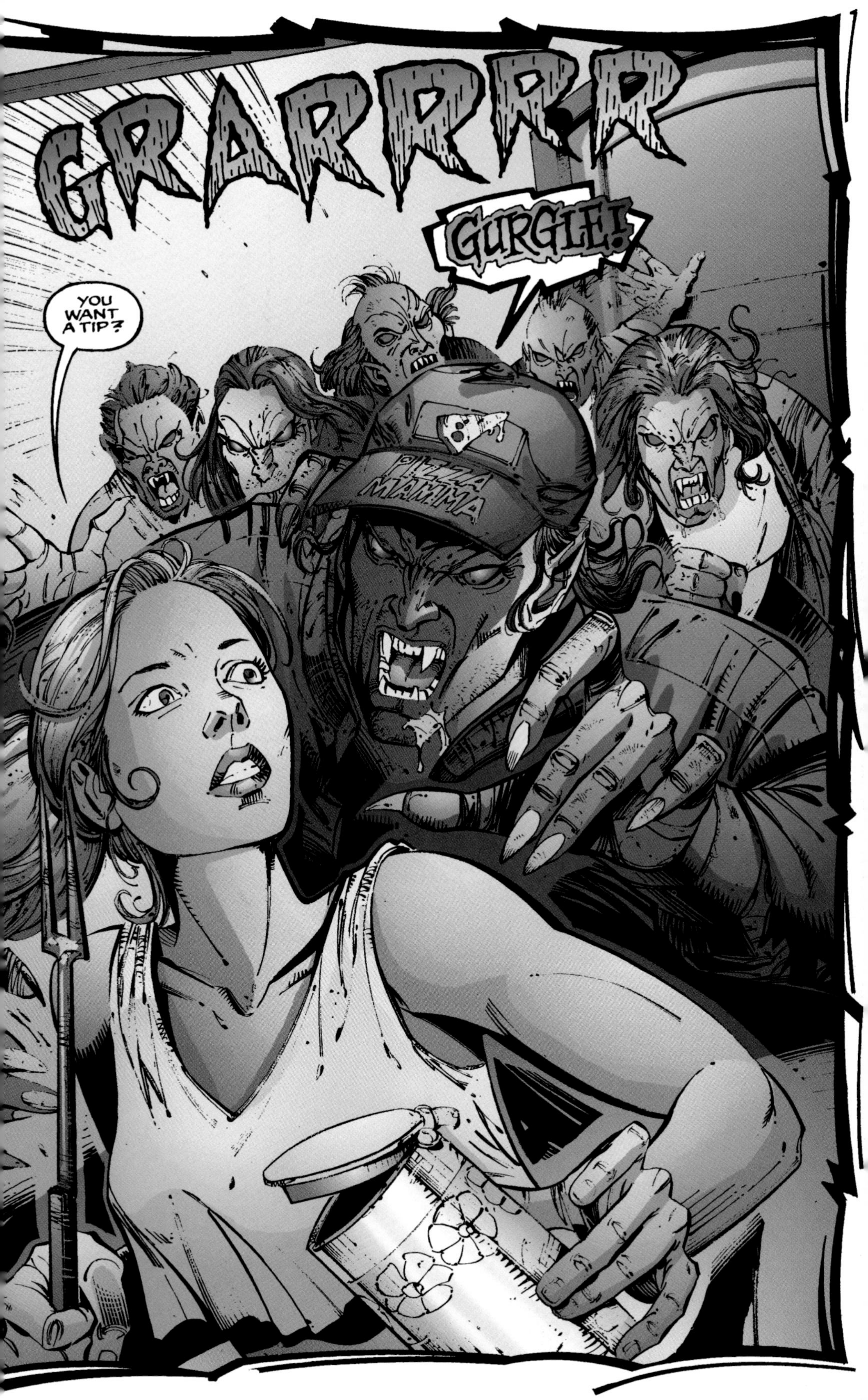
GRARRRR
GURGLE!
YOU WANT A TIP?
PIZZA MAMMA

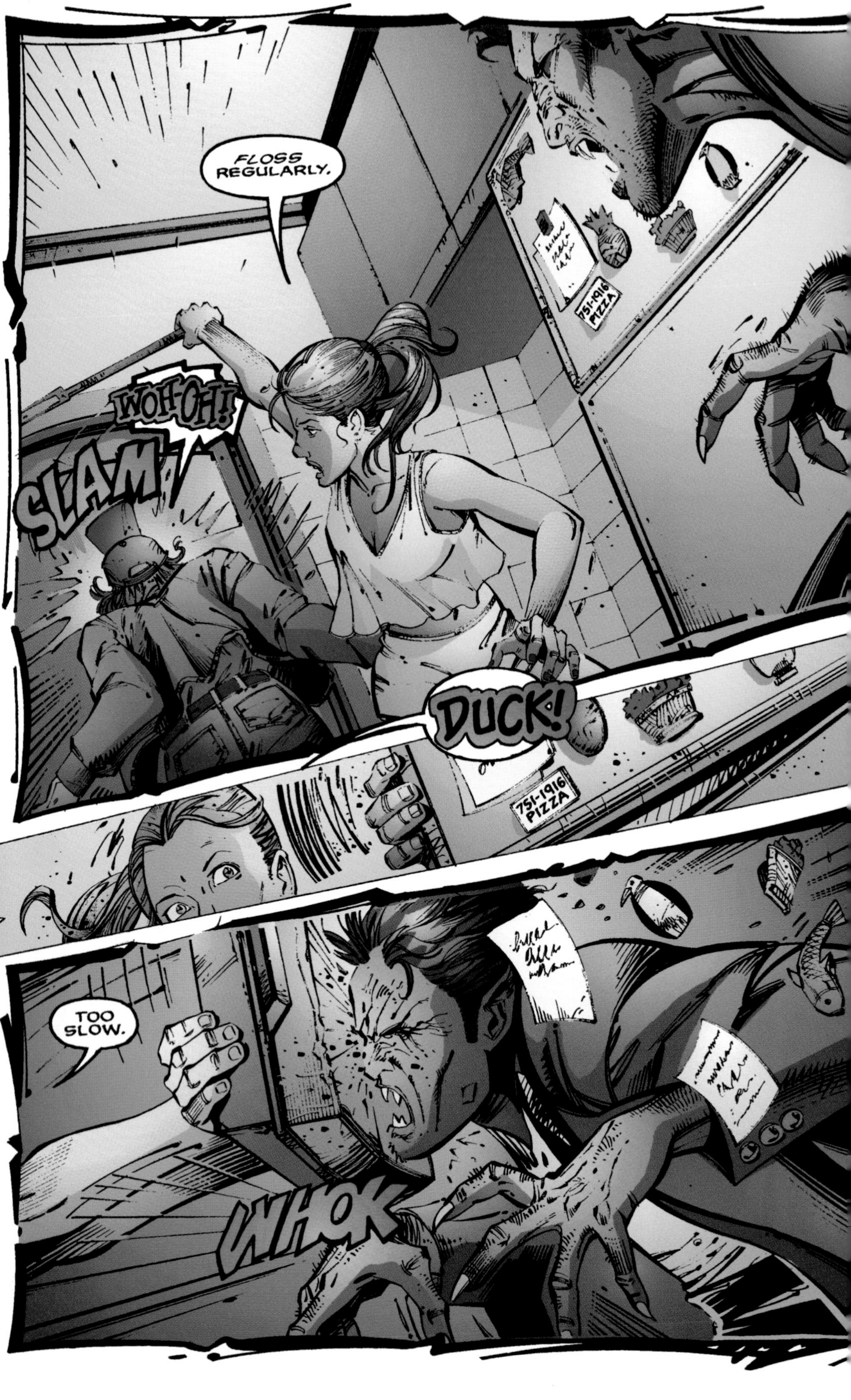
FLOSS REGULARLY.
WOH-OH!
SLAM
DUCK!
751-1916 PIZZA
751-1916 PIZZA
TOO SLOW.
WHOK

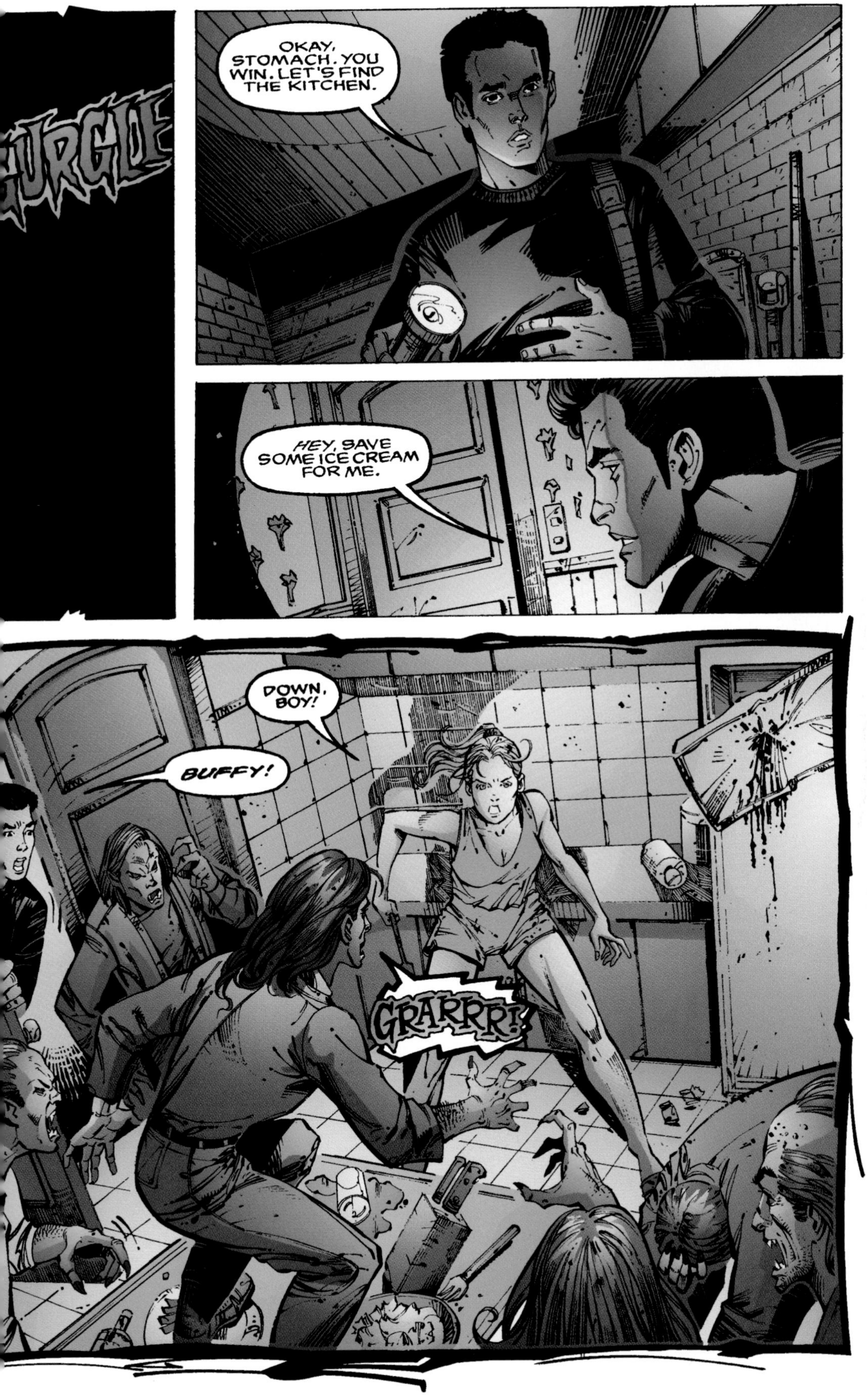
GURGLE
OKAY, STOMACH. YOU WIN. LET'S FIND THE KITCHEN.
HEY, SAVE SOME ICE CREAM FOR ME.
DOWN, BOY!
BUFFY!
GRARRR!

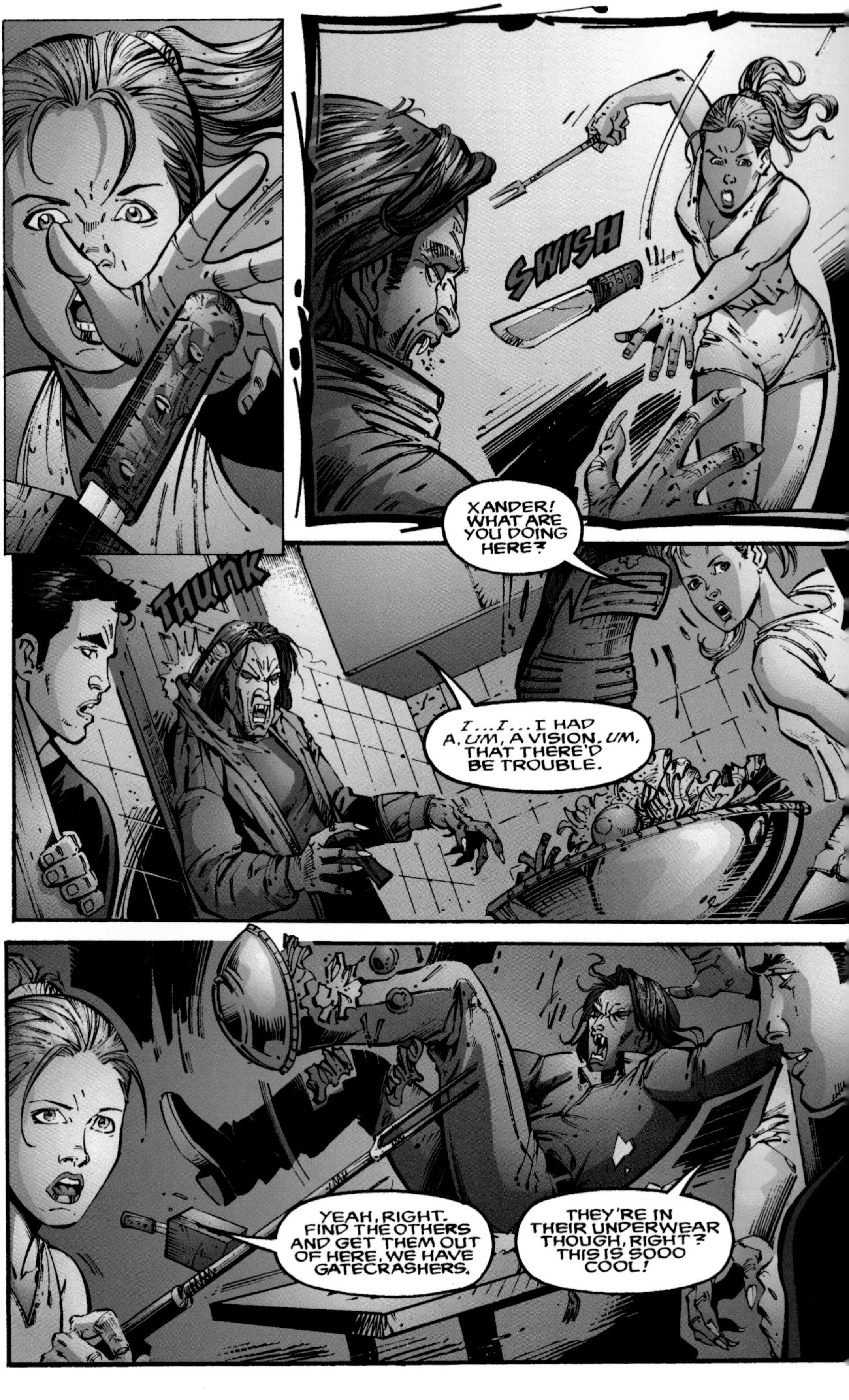
SWISH
XANDER! WHAT ARE YOU DOING HERE?
THUNK
I...I...I HAD A, UM, A VISION, UM, THAT THERE'D BE TROUBLE.
YEAH, RIGHT. FIND THE OTHERS AND GET THEM OUT OF HERE, WE HAVE GATECRASHERS.
THEY'RE IN THEIR UNDERWEAR THOUGH, RIGHT? THIS IS SOOO COOL!

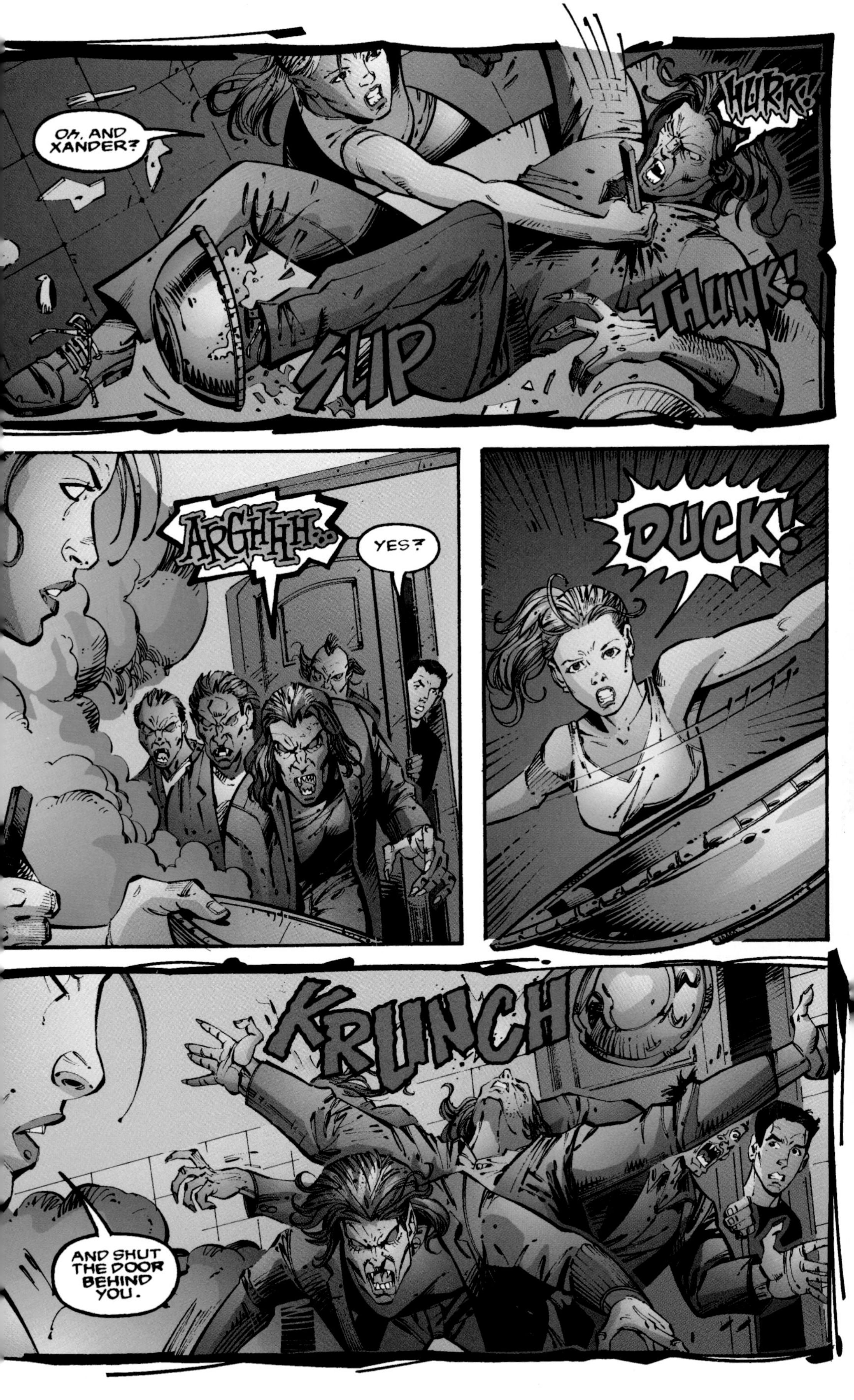
OH, AND XANDER?
HURK!
THUNK!
SLIP
ARGHHH..
YES?
DUCK!
KRUNCH
AND SHUT THE DOOR BEHIND YOU.

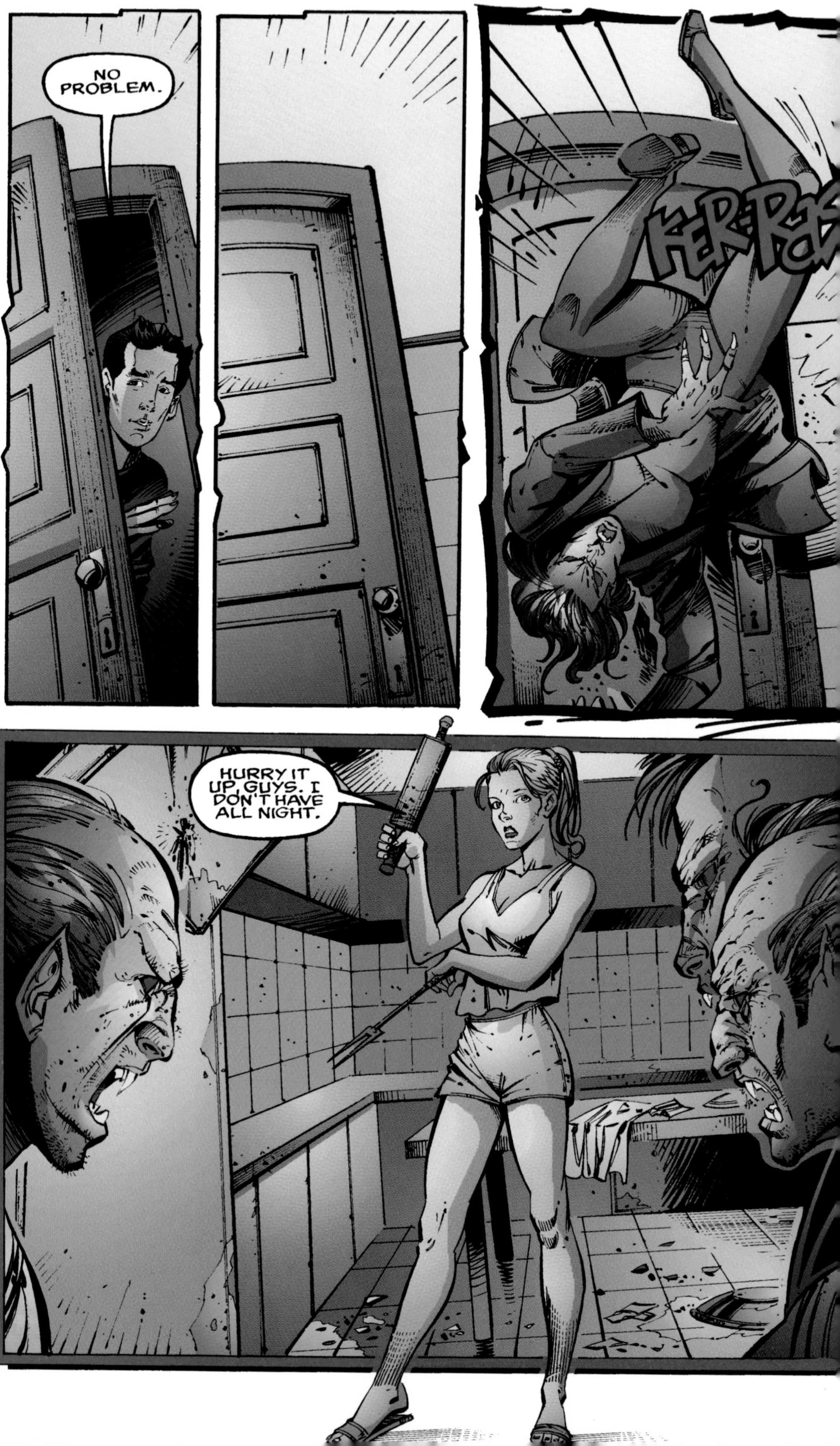
NO PROBLEM.
KER-RAS
HURRY IT UP, GUYS. I DON'T HAVE ALL NIGHT.

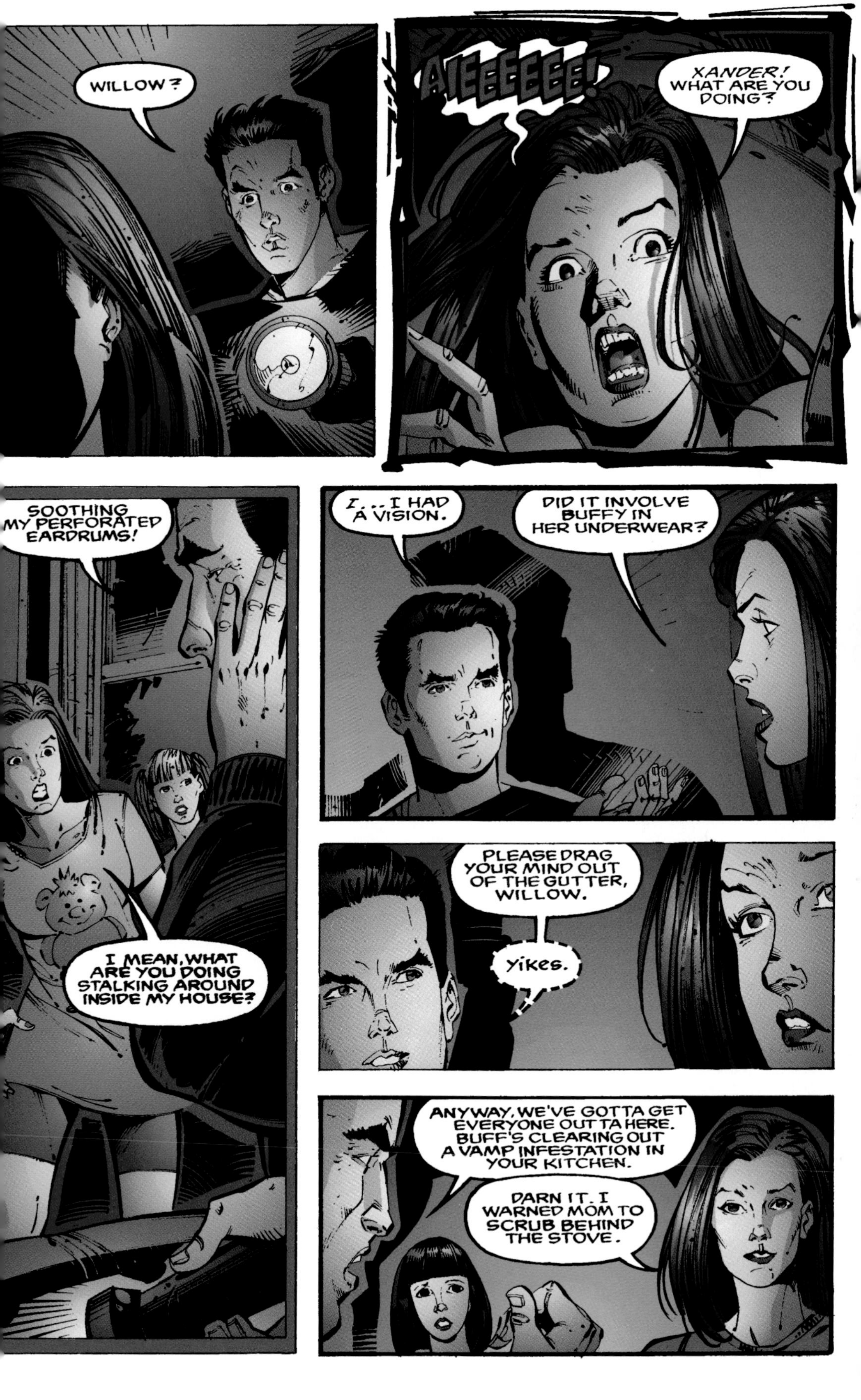
WILLOW?
AIEEEEEE!
XANDER! WHAT ARE YOU DOING?
SOOTHING MY PERFORATED EARDRUMS!
I MEAN, WHAT ARE YOU DOING STALKING AROUND INSIDE MY HOUSE?
I...I HAD A VISION.
DID IT INVOLVE BUFFY IN HER UNDERWEAR?
PLEASE DRAG YOUR MIND OUT OF THE GUTTER, WILLOW.
yikes.
ANYWAY, WE'VE GOTTA GET EVERYONE OUTTA HERE. BUFF'S CLEARING OUT A VAMP INFESTATION IN YOUR KITCHEN.
DARN IT. I WARNED MOM TO SCRUB BEHIND THE STOVE.

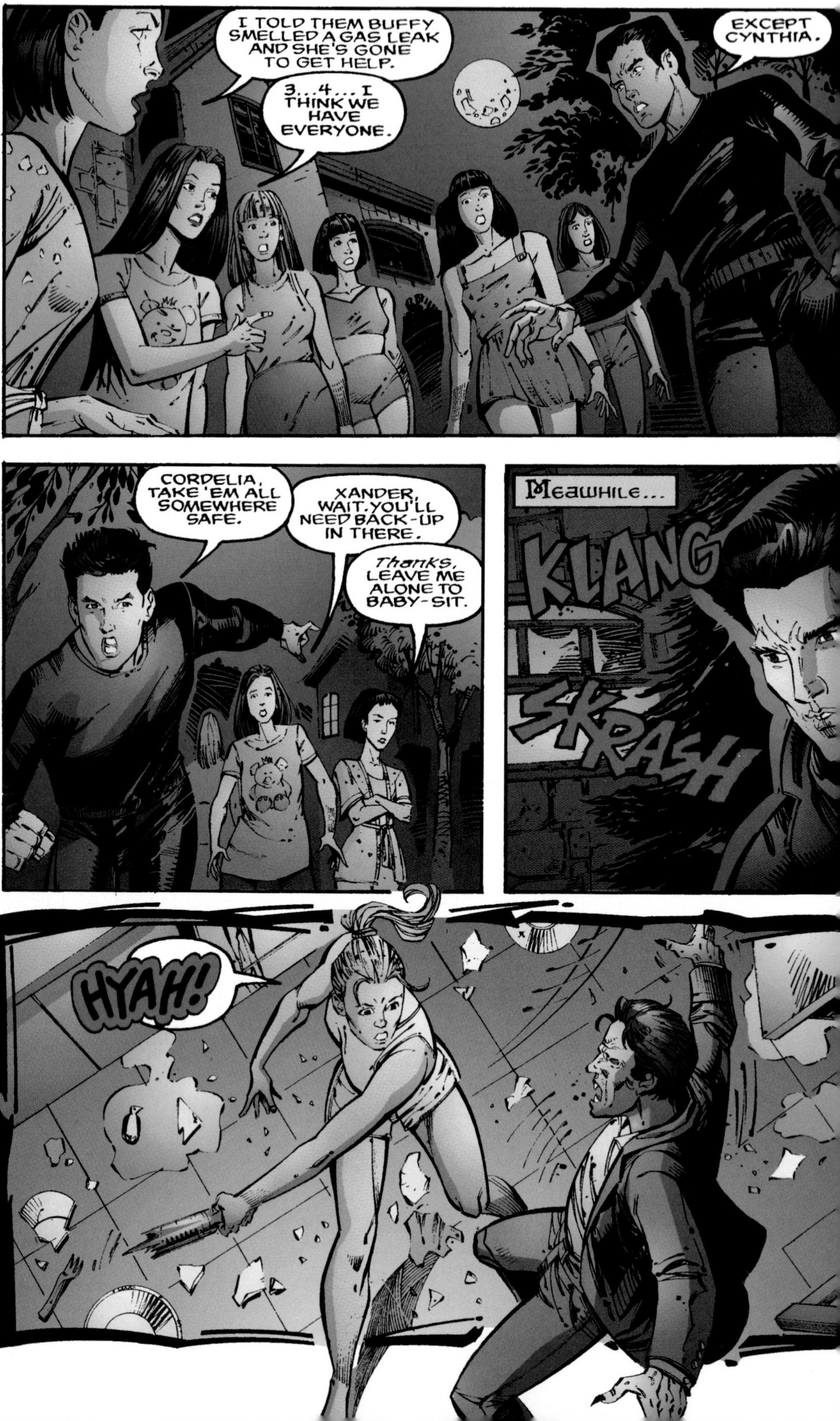
I TOLD THEM BUFFY SMELLED A GAS LEAK AND SHE'S GONE TO GET HELP.
3...4... I THINK WE HAVE EVERYONE.
EXCEPT CYNTHIA.
CORDELIA, TAKE 'EM ALL SOMEWHERE SAFE.
XANDER, WAIT. YOU'LL NEED BACK-UP IN THERE.
Thanks, LEAVE ME ALONE TO BABY-SIT.
MEANWHILE...
KLANG
SKRASH
HYAH!

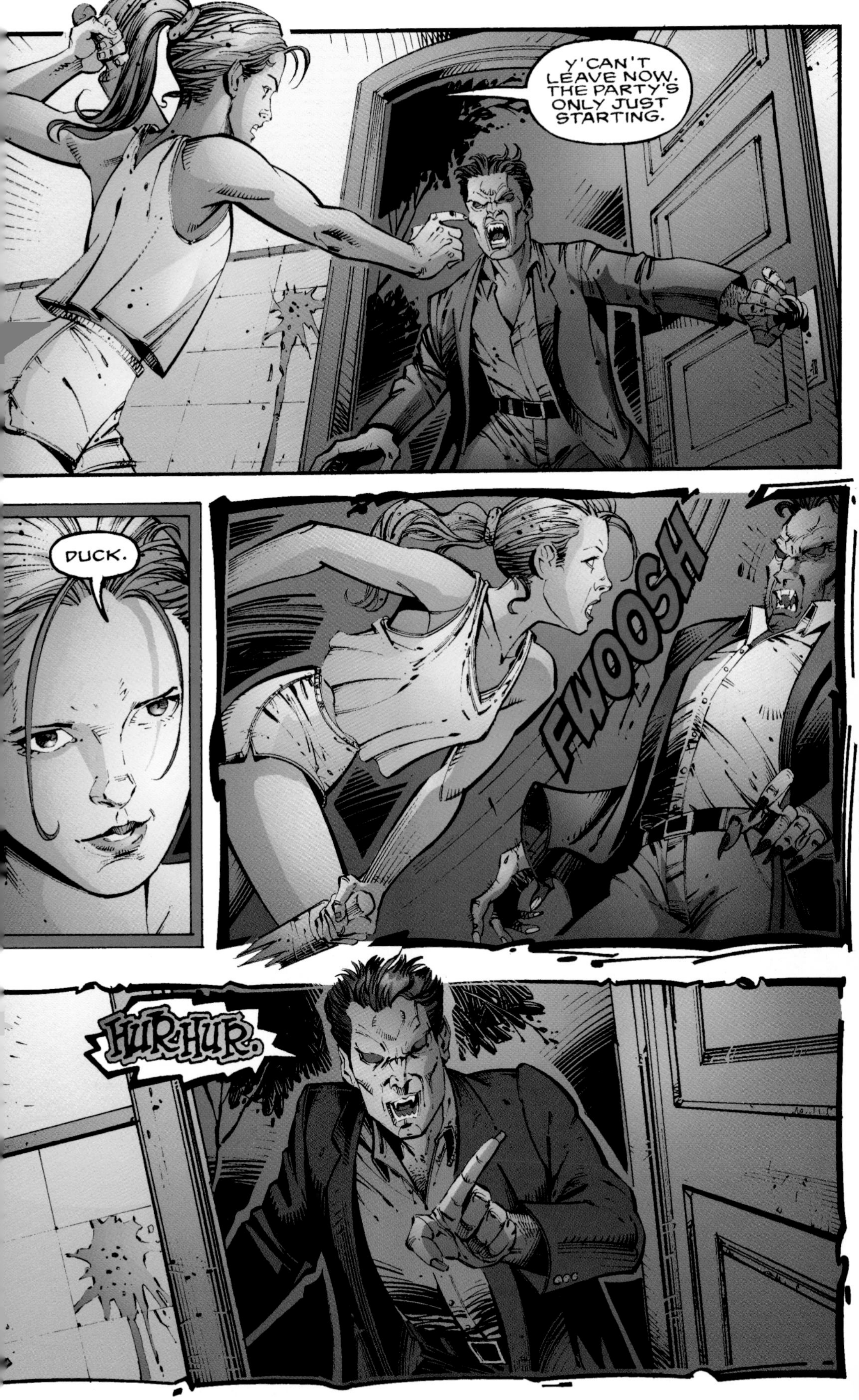
Y'CAN'T LEAVE NOW. THE PARTY'S ONLY JUST STARTING.
DUCK.
FWOOSH
HUR-HUR.

GLURK!

THUNK

ANGEL! WHERE'D YOU GO? WHAT HAPPENED?

I TRACKED DOWN THAT STRAY VAMP AND HE SPILLED THE BEANS. I'M WISE TO THE SCAM-- I'VE SEEN IT BEFORE.

SCAM?

THE GANG OF VAMPIRES YOU DUSTED WERE NEW TO THE AREA. THEY SIDLE IN AND PUT DOWN ROOTS WITH THE HELP OF YOUR NEW FRIEND, CYNTHIA.

SHE'S PART OF THE BITEY POSSE?

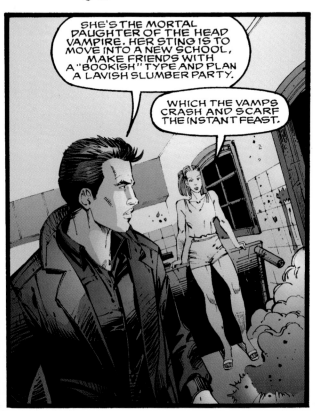

SHE'S THE MORTAL DAUGHTER OF THE HEAD VAMPIRE. HER STING IS TO MOVE INTO A NEW SCHOOL, MAKE FRIENDS WITH A "BOOKISH" TYPE AND PLAN A LAVISH SLUMBER PARTY.

WHICH THE VAMPS CRASH AND SCARF THE INSTANT FEAST.

THEN THEY EITHER WAIT AROUND OR MOVE ON TO A NEW TOWN.

NO BOSS VAMPIRE OUT OF THE BUNCH I TOASTED. SO WHERE IS HE AND HIS LOVING DAUGHTER--?

AIEEE

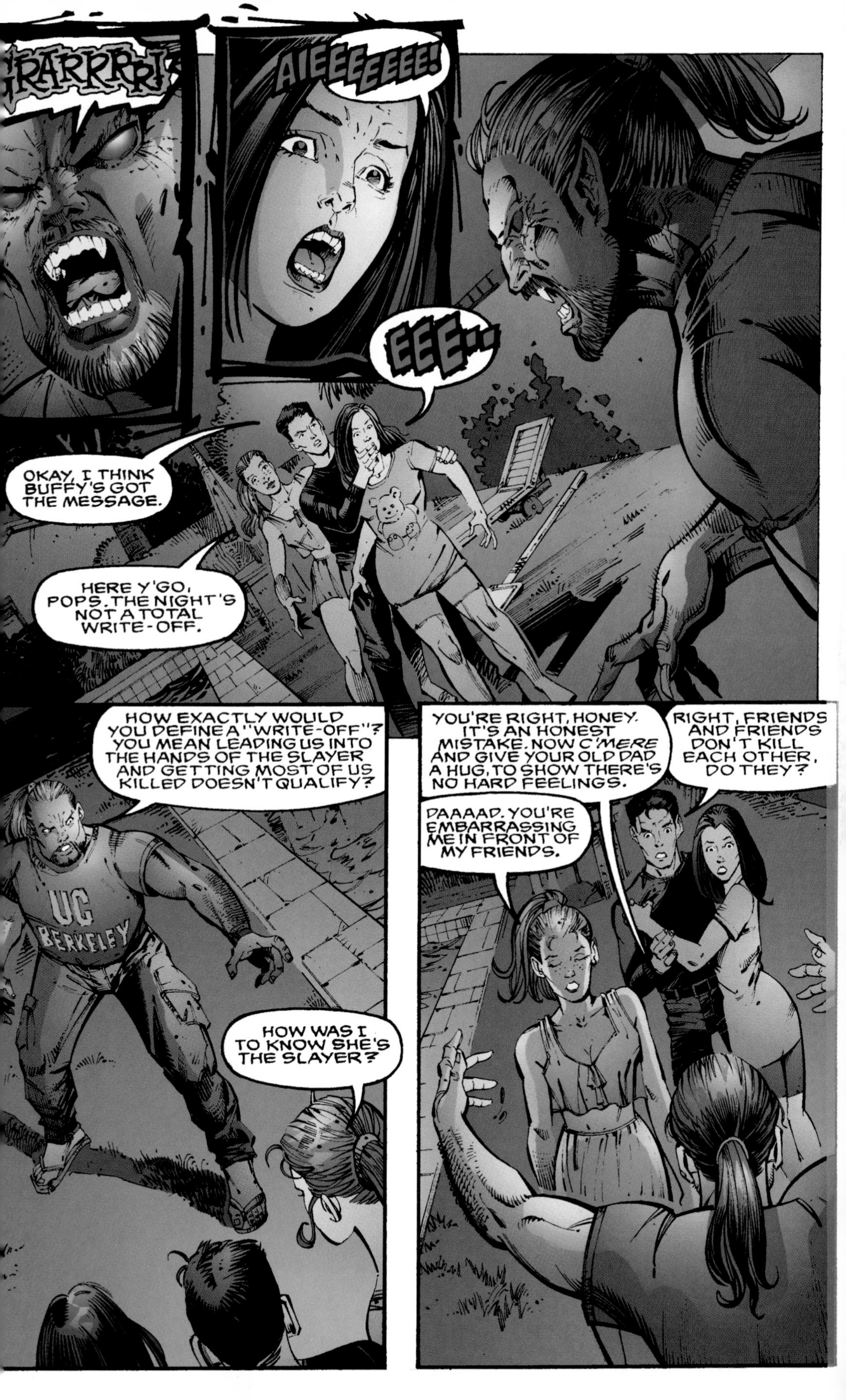
RARRRR!
AIEEEEEEEE!
EEE..
OKAY, I THINK BUFFY'S GOT THE MESSAGE.
HERE Y'GO, POPS. THE NIGHT'S NOT A TOTAL WRITE-OFF.
HOW EXACTLY WOULD YOU DEFINE A "WRITE-OFF"? YOU MEAN LEADING US INTO THE HANDS OF THE SLAYER AND GETTING MOST OF US KILLED DOESN'T QUALIFY?
HOW WAS I TO KNOW SHE'S THE SLAYER?
YOU'RE RIGHT, HONEY. IT'S AN HONEST MISTAKE. NOW C'MERE AND GIVE YOUR OLD DAD A HUG, TO SHOW THERE'S NO HARD FEELINGS.
RIGHT, FRIENDS AND FRIENDS DON'T KILL EACH OTHER, DO THEY?
DAAAAD. YOU'RE EMBARRASSING ME IN FRONT OF MY FRIENDS.

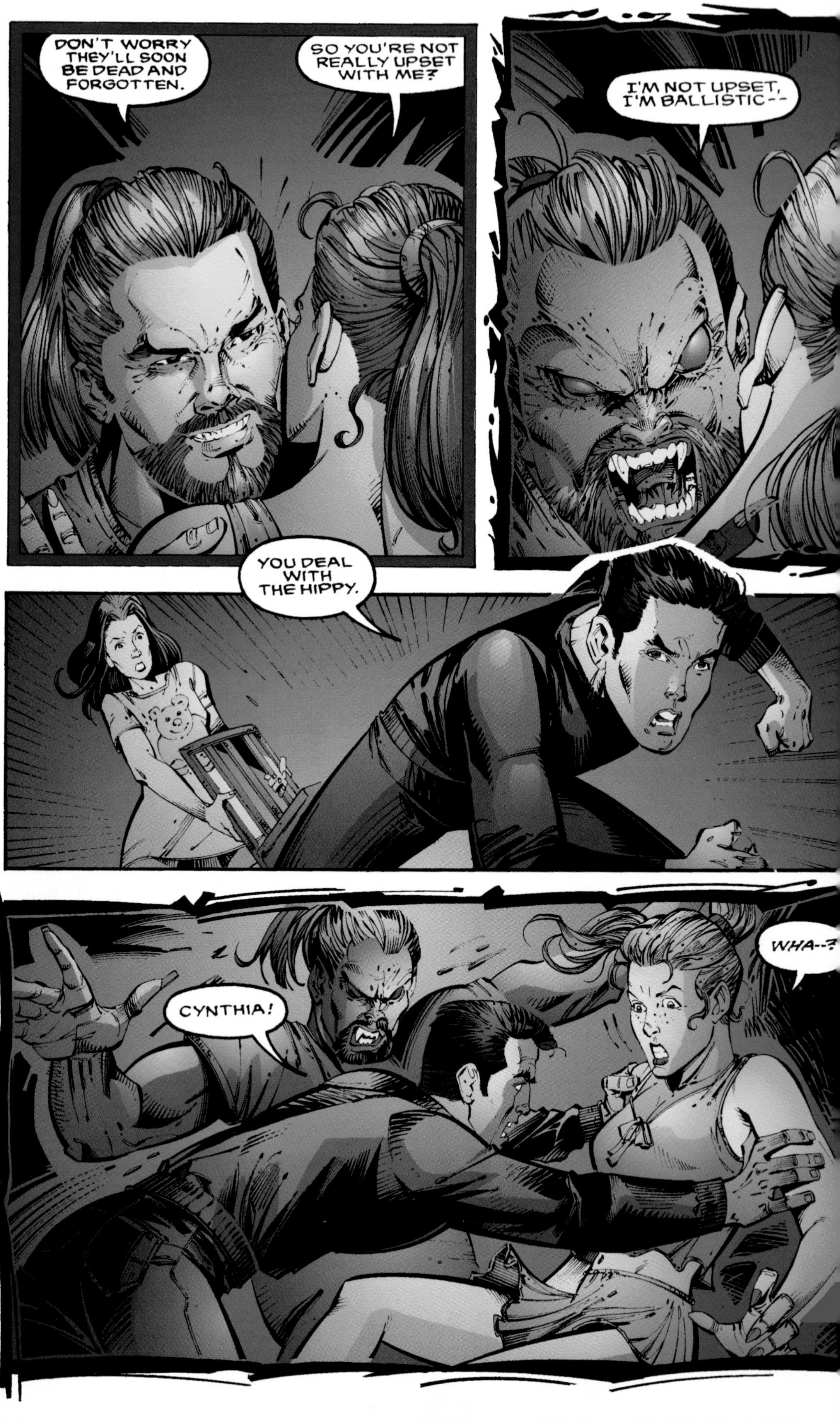
DON'T WORRY THEY'LL SOON BE DEAD AND FORGOTTEN.
SO YOU'RE NOT REALLY UPSET WITH ME?
I'M NOT UPSET, I'M BALLISTIC--
YOU DEAL WITH THE HIPPY.
CYNTHIA!
WHA--?

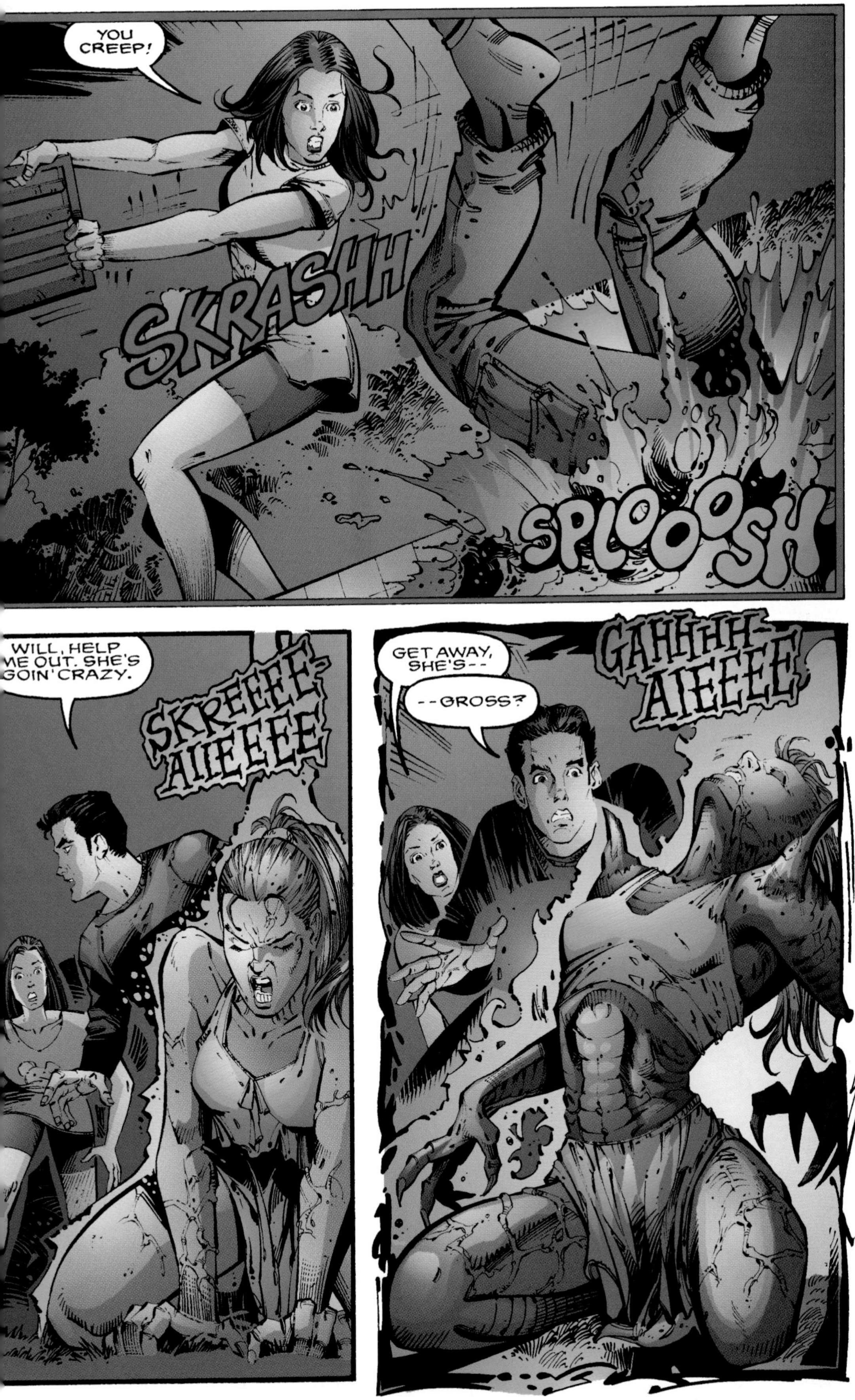
YOU CREEP!
SKRASHH
SPLOOOSH
WILL, HELP ME OUT. SHE'S GOIN' CRAZY.
SKREEEEE-AIIEEEE
GET AWAY, SHE'S--
--GROSS?
GAHHHH-AIEEEE

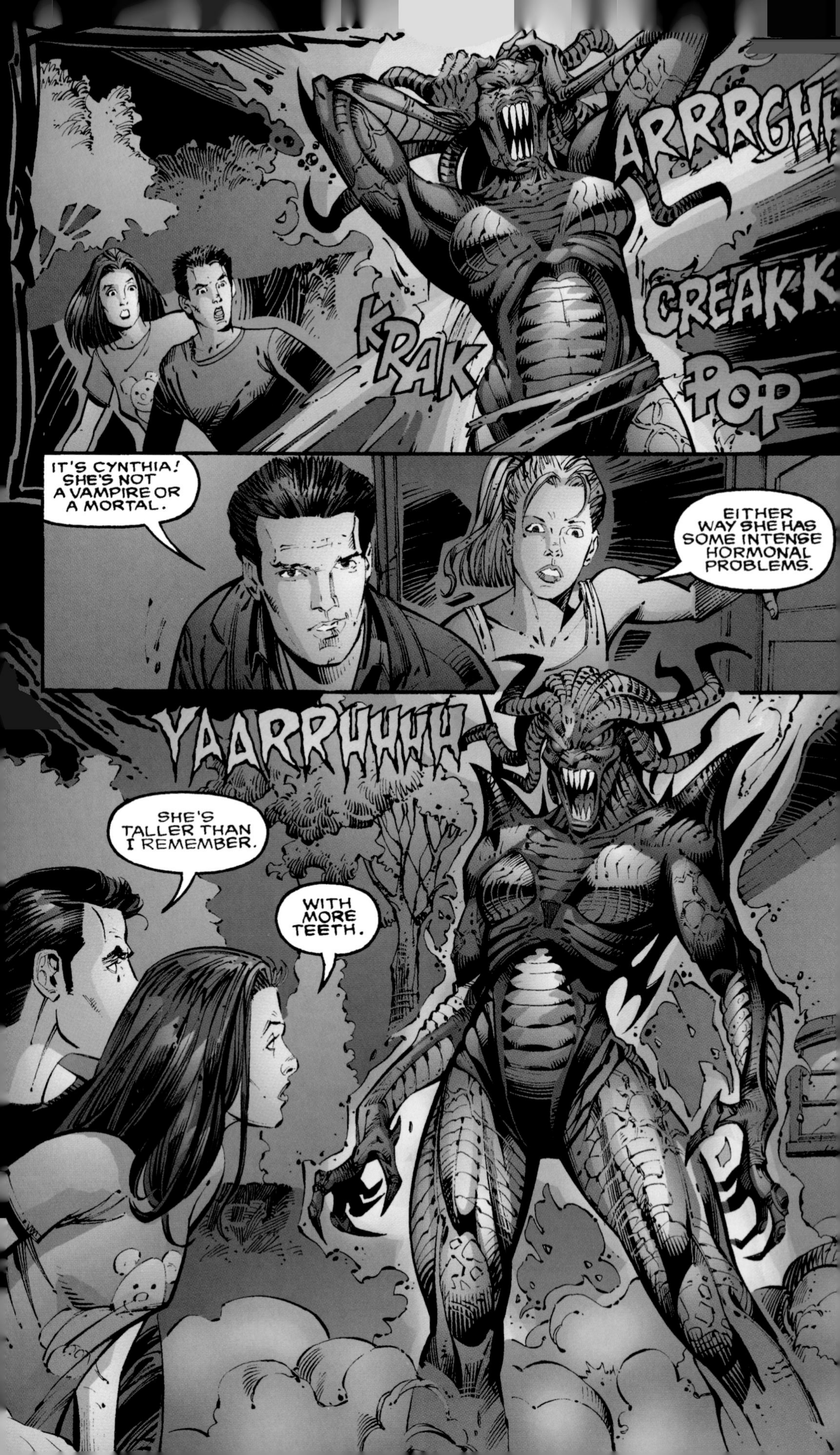
ARRRGH
CREAKK
KRAK
POP
IT'S CYNTHIA! SHE'S NOT A VAMPIRE OR A MORTAL.
EITHER WAY SHE HAS SOME INTENSE HORMONAL PROBLEMS.
YAARRHHHH
SHE'S TALLER THAN I REMEMBER.
WITH MORE TEETH.

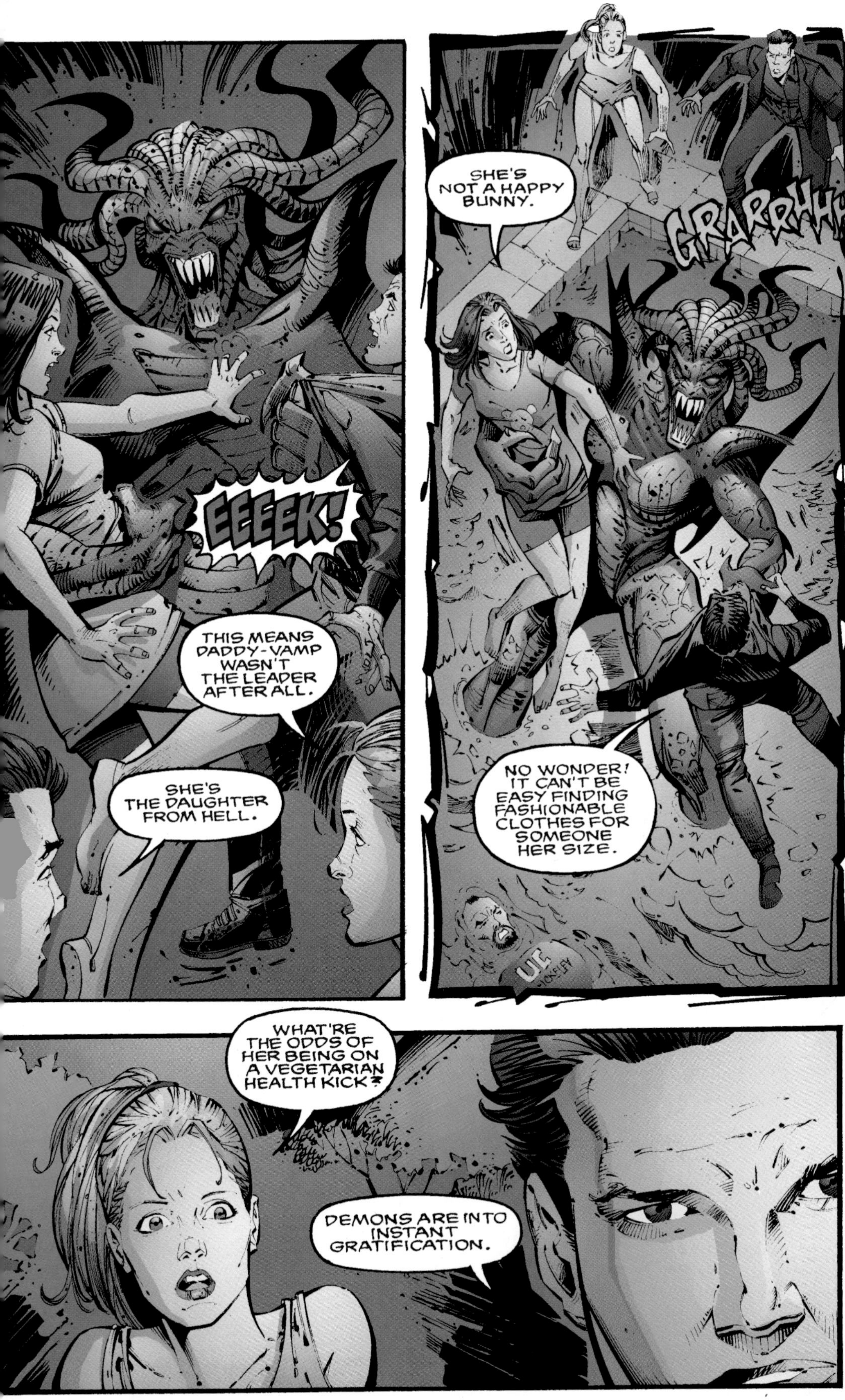
EEEEK!
THIS MEANS DADDY-VAMP WASN'T THE LEADER AFTER ALL.
SHE'S THE DAUGHTER FROM HELL.
SHE'S NOT A HAPPY BUNNY.
GRARRHHH
NO WONDER! IT CAN'T BE EASY FINDING FASHIONABLE CLOTHES FOR SOMEONE HER SIZE.
WHAT'RE THE ODDS OF HER BEING ON A VEGETARIAN HEALTH KICK?
DEMONS ARE INTO INSTANT GRATIFICATION.

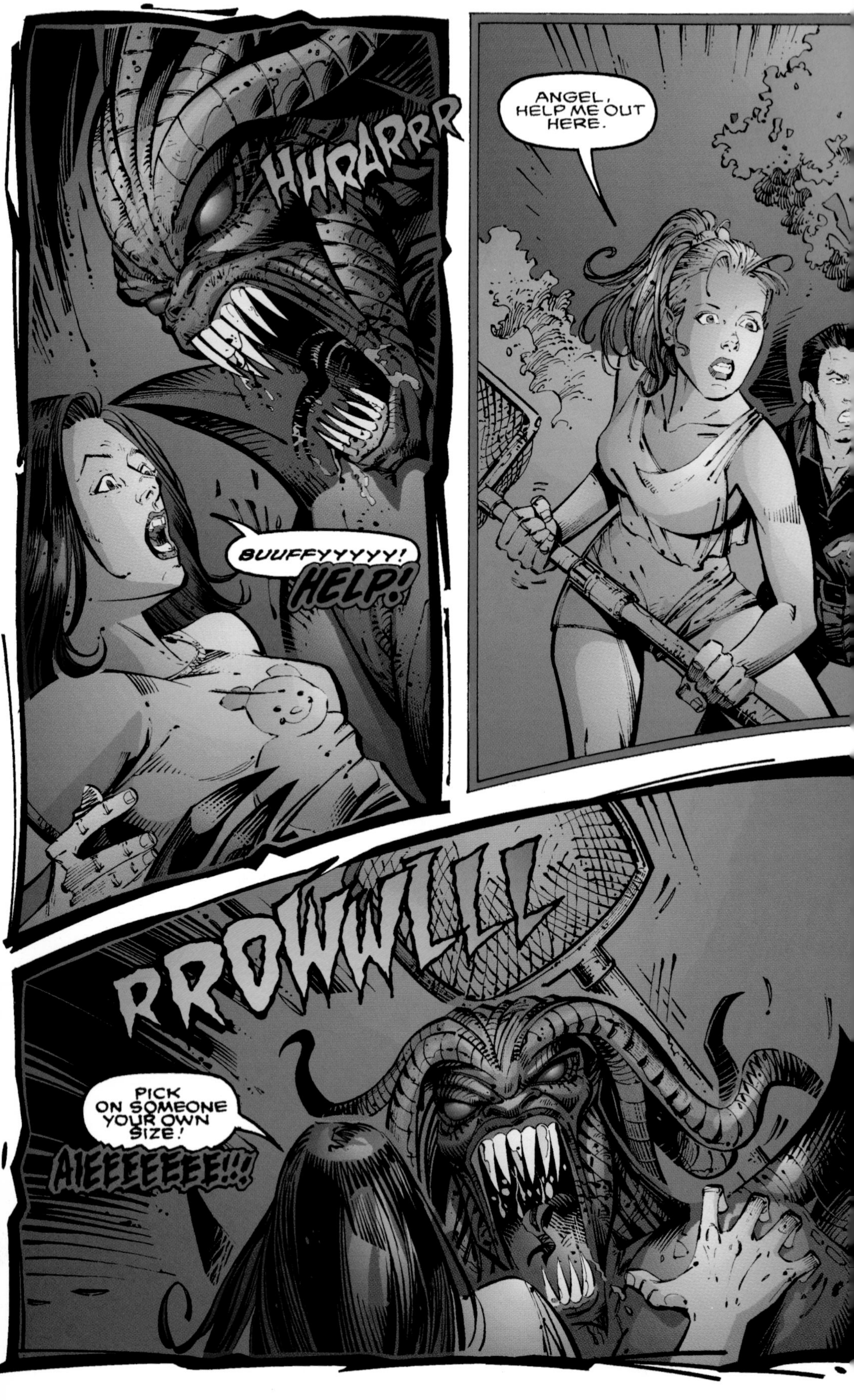
HHRARRR
BUUFFYYYYY!
HELP!
ANGEL, HELP ME OUT HERE.
RROWWLLL
PICK ON SOMEONE YOUR OWN SIZE!
AIEEEEEEE!!!

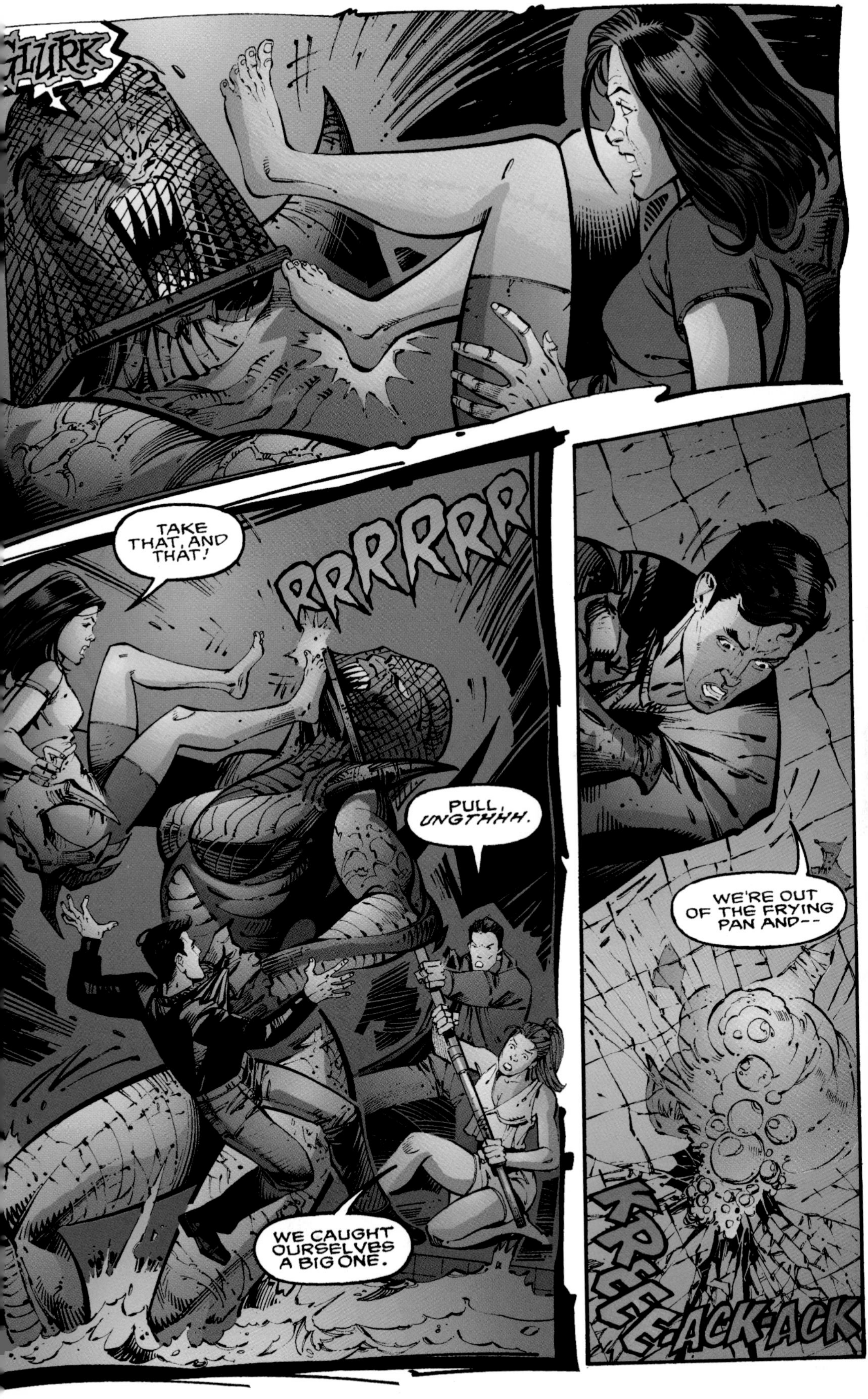
GLURK
TAKE THAT, AND THAT!
RRRRRR
PULL, UNGTHHH.
WE CAUGHT OURSELVES A BIG ONE.
WE'RE OUT OF THE FRYING PAN AND--
KREEE-ACK-ACK

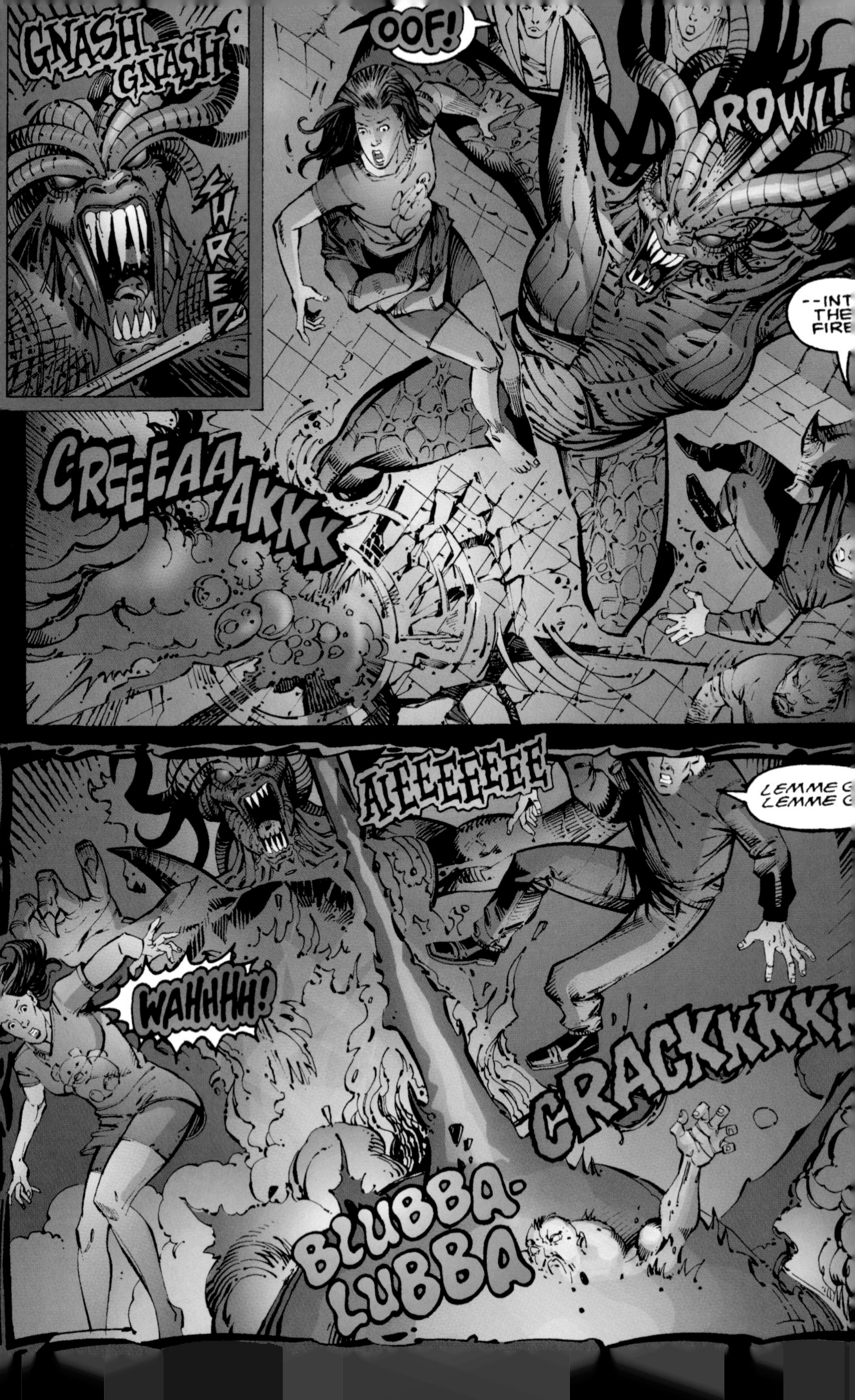
GNASH GNASH
SHRED
OOF!
ROWL
--INT THE FIRE
CREEEAAAKKKK
AIEEEEEEE
LEMME
LEMME
WAHHHH!
CRACKKKK
BLUBBA-LUBBA

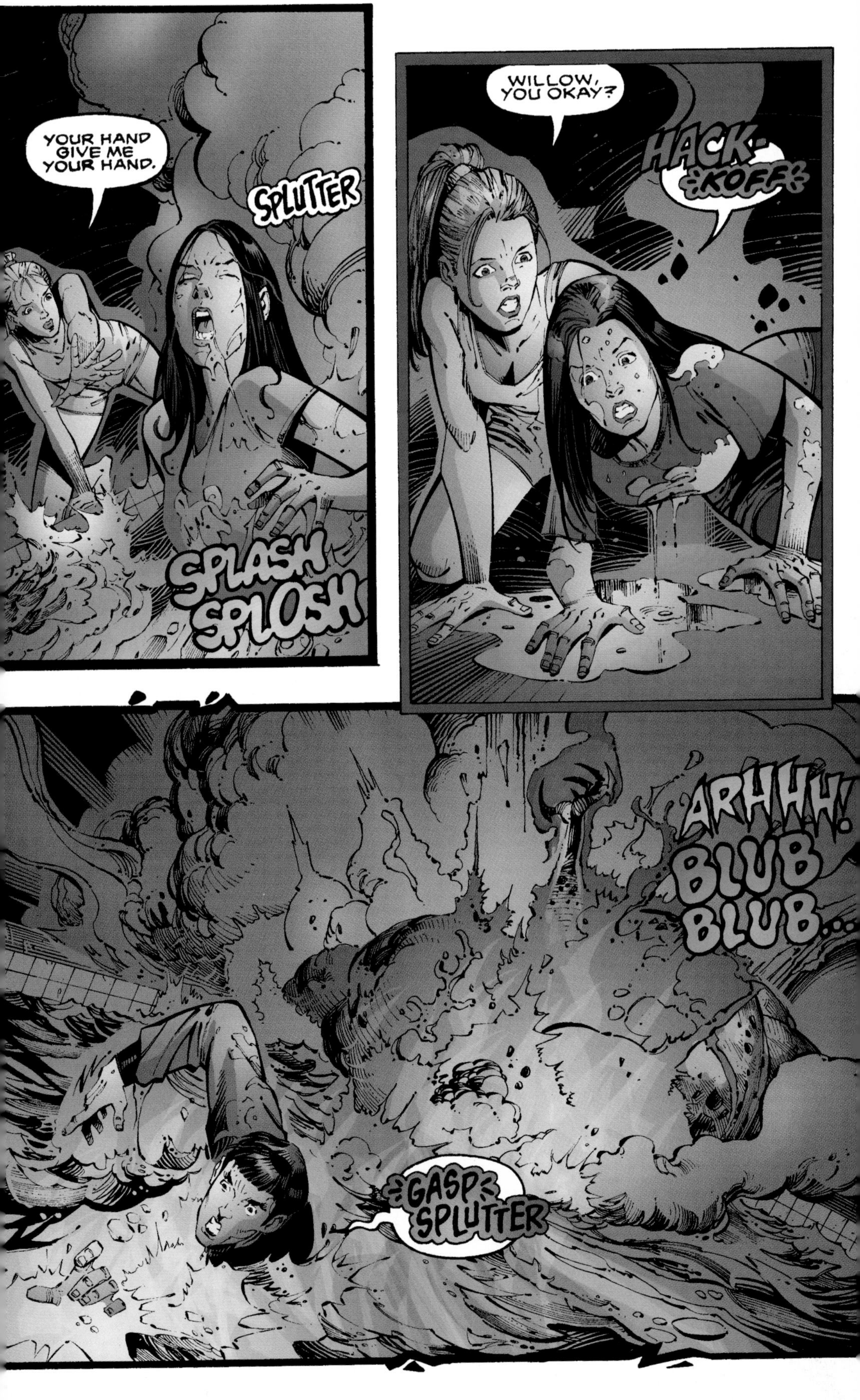
YOUR HAND GIVE ME YOUR HAND.
SPLUTTER
SPLASH SPLOSH
WILLOW, YOU OKAY?
HACK-KOFF
ARHHH! BLUB BLUB...
GASP SPLUTTER

HANG ON, XANDER. I'M COMING!
COUGH COUGH
XANDER?!
HHHHIIIISSSS
XANDER, ANGEL!
I'M GOIN' IN!
WAIT.
HSSHHHHHHH
THERE THEY ARE.

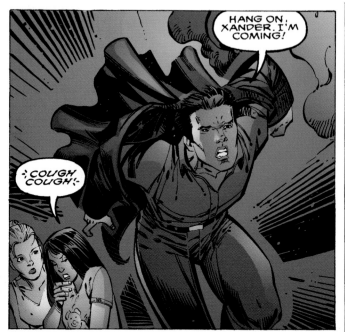

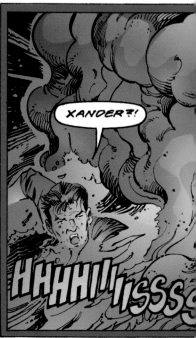

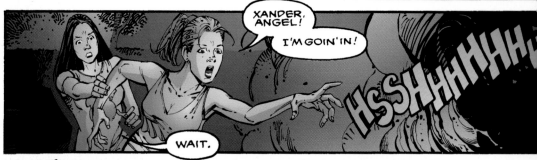

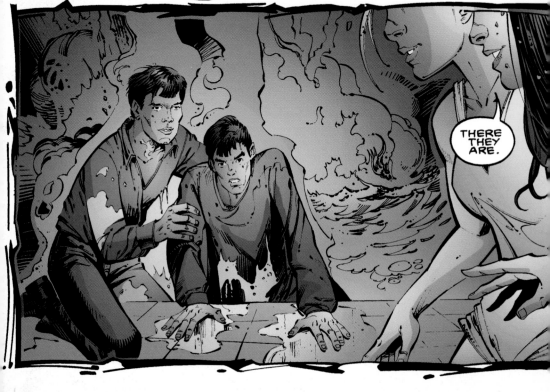

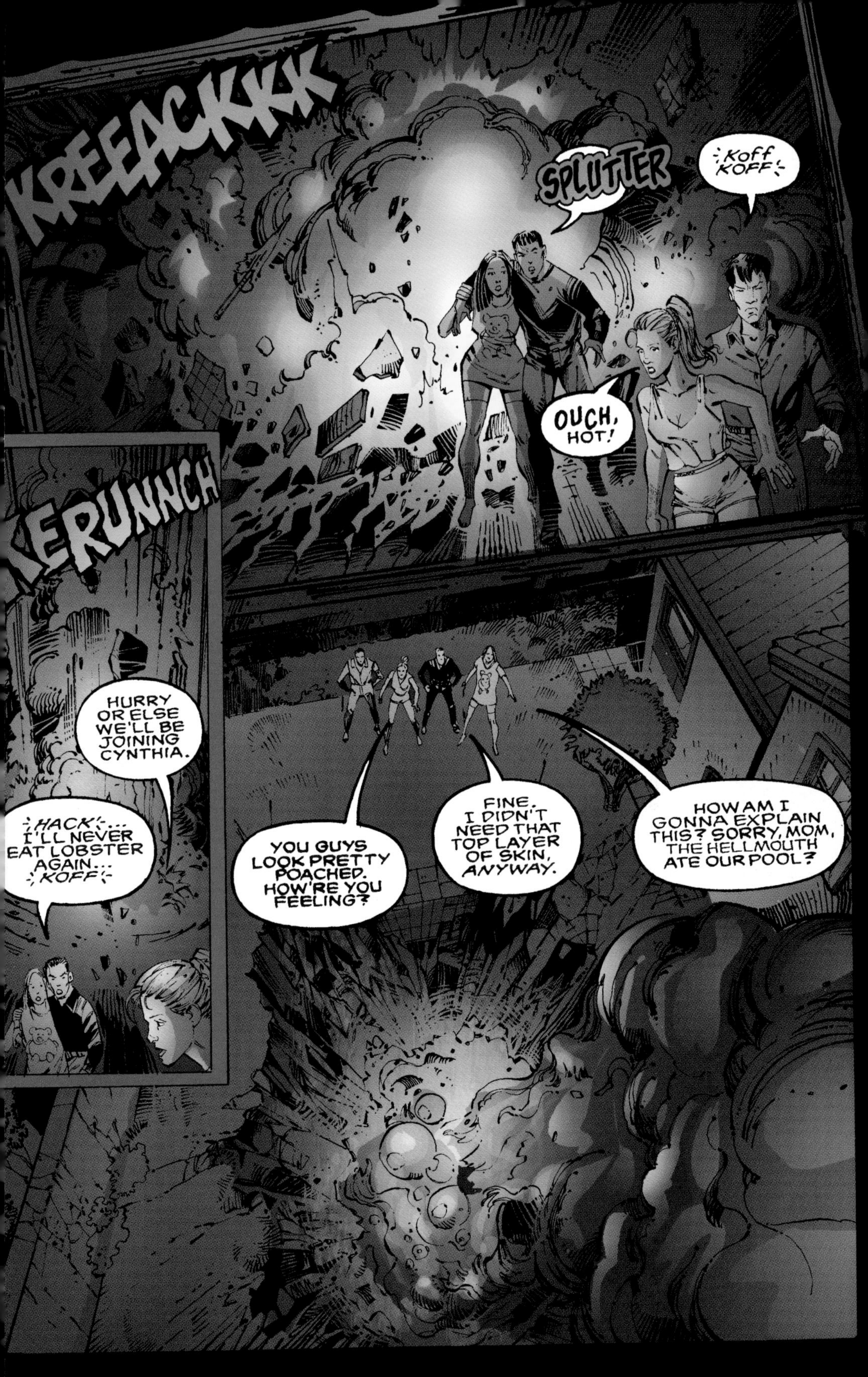
KREEACKKK
SPLUTTER
KOFF KOFF
OUCH, HOT!
KERUNNCH
HURRY OR ELSE WE'LL BE JOINING CYNTHIA.
HACK... I'LL NEVER EAT LOBSTER AGAIN... KOFF
YOU GUYS LOOK PRETTY POACHED. HOW'RE YOU FEELING?
FINE. I DIDN'T NEED THAT TOP LAYER OF SKIN, ANYWAY.
HOW AM I GONNA EXPLAIN THIS? SORRY, MOM, THE HELLMOUTH ATE OUR POOL?

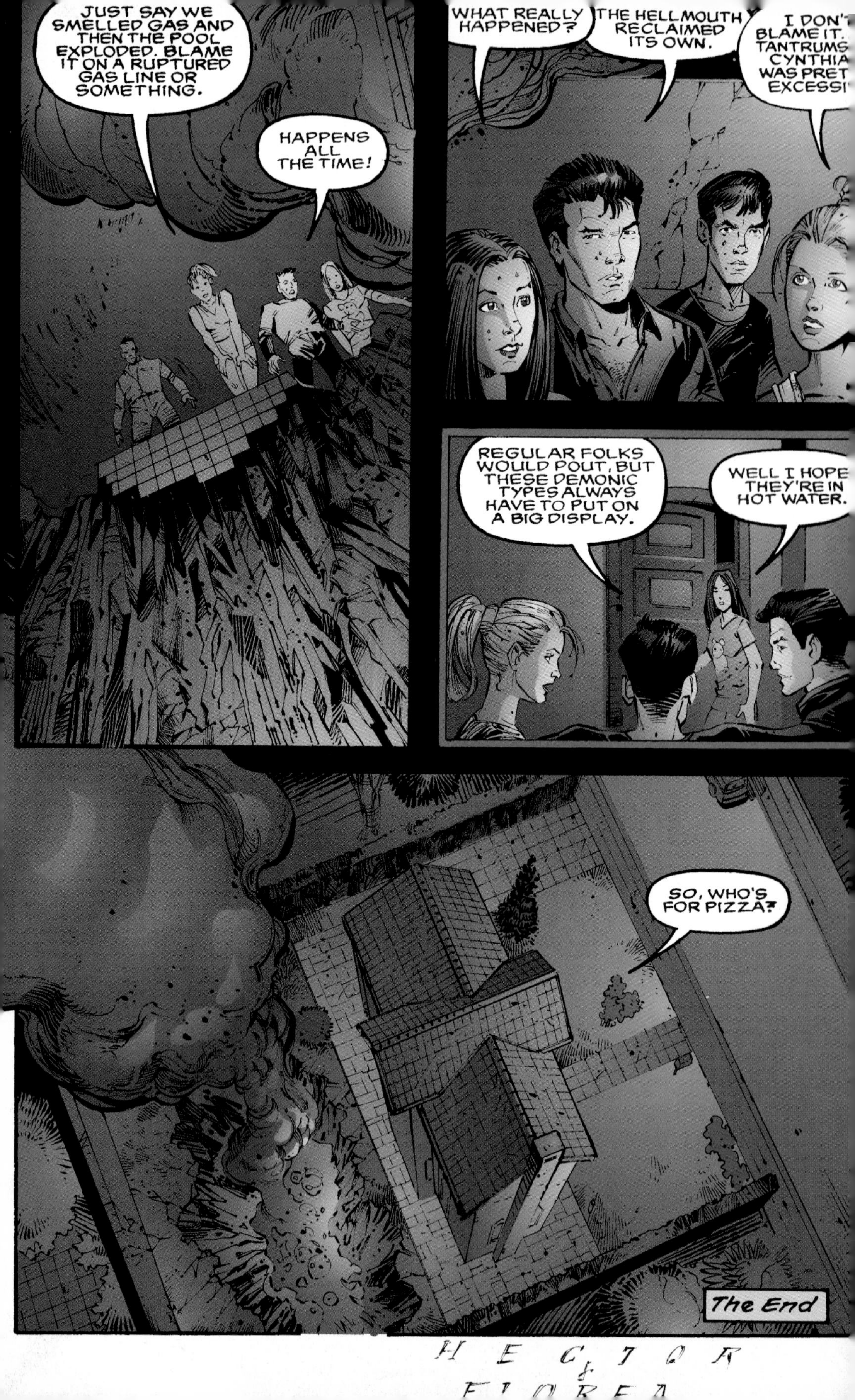
JUST SAY WE SMELLED GAS AND THEN THE POOL EXPLODED. BLAME IT ON A RUPTURED GAS LINE OR SOMETHING.
HAPPENS ALL THE TIME!
WHAT REALLY HAPPENED?
THE HELLMOUTH RECLAIMED ITS OWN.
I DON'T BLAME IT. TANTRUMS CYNTHIA WAS PRET EXCESSI
REGULAR FOLKS WOULD POUT, BUT THESE DEMONIC TYPES ALWAYS HAVE TO PUT ON A BIG DISPLAY.
WELL I HOPE THEY'RE IN HOT WATER.
SO, WHO'S FOR PIZZA?
The End
HECTOR & FLOREA

LOOK FOR THESE *BUFFY THE VAMPIRE SLAYER* TRADE PAPERBACKS FROM DARK HORSE COMICS

Buffy
THE
VAMPIRE SLAYER
the

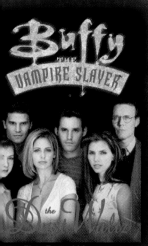

THE DUST WALTZ
Brereton • Gomez • Florea
80-page color paperback
ISBN: 1-56971-342-1 **$9.95**

Buffy
THE
VAMPIRE SLAYER
The
Remaining
Sunlight

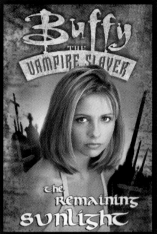

THE REMAINING SUNLIGHT
Watson • Bennett • Ketcham
80-page color paperback
ISBN: 1-56971-354-5 **$9.95**

Buffy
THE
VAMPIRE SLAYER
the ORIGIN

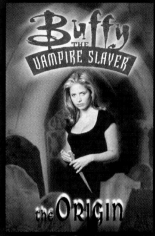

THE ORIGIN
Golden • Brereton • Bennett • Ketcham
80-page color paperback
ISBN: 1-56971-429-0 **$9.95**

AVAILABLE NOVEMBER 1999

Buffy
THE
VAMPIRE SLAYER
Uninvited Guests

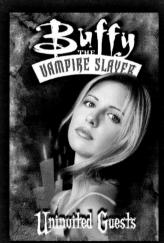

UNINVITED GUESTS
Watson • Gomez • Florea
104-page color paperback
ISBN: 1–56971–436–3 **$9.95**

AVAILABLE Spring 2000

Buffy
THE
VAMPIRE SLAYER
Supernatural Defense Kit

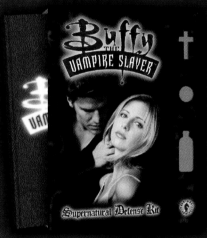

SUPERNATURAL DEFENSE KIT
Watson • Richards • Pimentel
30-page color hard cover
comes with golden colored cross,
"claddagh" ring, and vial of "holy water"
ISBN: 1-56971-486-X **$19.95**

Available from your local comics shop or bookstore!

TO FIND A COMICS SHOP IN YOUR AREA, CALL 1-888-266-4226
For more information or to order direct: • On the web: www.darkhorse.com
• E-mail: mailorder@darkhorse.com • Phone: 1-800-862-0052 or (503) 652-9701
Mon.-Sat. 9 a.m. to 5 p.m. Pacific Time

w.darkhorse.com
ww.buffy.com

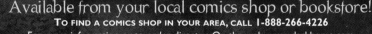

ALIENS™, AND *PREDATOR*™
TRADE PAPERBACKS AVAILABLE FROM DARK HORSE COMICS

ALIENS VS PREDATOR

ALIENS VS PREDATOR
Stradley • Norwood • Warner
176-page color paperback
ISBN: 1-56971-125-9 $19.95

DEADLIEST OF THE SPECIES
Claremont • Barreto • Guice
320-page color limited edition hardcover
ISBN: 1-56971-182-8 $99.95

WAR
Stradley • Saltares • Warner
200-page color paperback
ISBN: 1-56971-158-5 $19.95

ETERNAL
Edginton • Maleev
88-page color paperback
ISBN: 1-56971-409-6 $9.95

ALIENS

OUTBREAK
Verheiden • Nelson
176-page color paperback
ISBN: 1-56971-174-7 $17.95

NIGHTMARE ASYLUM
Verheiden • Beauvais
112-page color paperback
ISBN: 1-56971-217-4 $16.95

FEMALE WAR
Verheiden • Kieth
112-page color paperback
ISBN: 1-56971-190-9 $16.95

GENOCIDE
Arcudi • Willis • Story
112-page color paperback
ISBN: 1-56971-196-8 $16.95

HARVEST
Prosser • Jones
120-page color paperback
ISBN: 1-56971-198-4 $16.95

ROGUE
Edginton • Simpson
112-page color paperback
ISBN: 1-56971-267-0 $16.95

LABYRINTH
Woodring • Plunkett
136-page color paperback
ISBN: 1-56971-245-X $17.95

STRONGHOLD
Arcudi • Mahnke • Palmiotti
112-page color paperback
ISBN: 1-56971-262-X $16.95

TRIBES
Bissette • Dorman
72-page color hardcover
ISBN: 1-878574-28-0 $24.95

KIDNAPPED
Woodring • Green • Lopez
80-page color paperback
ISBA: 1-56971-372-3 $9.95

SUPERMAN VS ALIENS
Jurgens • Nowlan
152-page color paperback
ISBN: 1-56971-167-4 $14.95

BATMAN VS ALIENS
Marz • Wrightson
128-page color paperback
ISBN: 1-56971-305-7 $14.95

PREDATOR

CONCRETE JUNGLE
Verheiden • Warner • Randall
112-page color paperback
ISBN: 1-56971-165-8 $14.95

BIG GAME
Arcudi • Dorkin • Gil
112-page color paperback
ISBN: 1-56971-166-6 $14.95

COLD WAR
Verheiden • Randall • Mitchell
112-page color paperback
ISBN: 1-878574-79-5 $13.95

RACE WAR
Vachss • Stradley • Raskin • Pelle
144-page color paperback
ISBN: 1-56971-112-7 $17.95

HELL & HOT WATER
Schultz • Colan
88-page color paperback
ISBN: 1-56971-271-9 $9.95

KINDRED
Lamb • Tolson • O'Connell • Peters
112-page color paperback
ISBN: 1-56971-270-0 $14.95

TARZAN VS PREDATOR
Simonson • Weeks
104-page color paperback
ISBN: 1-56971-231-X $12.95

PREDATOR VS JUDGE DREDD
Wagner • Alcatena
80-page color paperback
ISBN: 1-56971-345-6 $9.95

Available from your local comics shop or bookstore!

To find a comics shop in your area, call 1-888-266-4226
For more information or to order direct:
•On the web: www.darkhorse.com •E-mail: mailorder@darkhorse.com
•Phone: 1-800-862-0052 or (503) 652-9701 Mon.-Sat. 9 A.M. to 5 P.M. Pacific Time